A spurt of dust jumped with a crack thirty yards to their left. It threw up a column of sand and stones that plopped against the armour of the tank.

'Christ!' said Thomson. 'That was meant for us!'

The second high explosive shell landed closer, and Evans ran to the lee of the tank.

'Get away from there, you mad bastard,' Midgeley shouted. 'What do you think they're aiming at?'

There was another whistle and the Matilda rocked under a direct hit. Red-hot splinters splattered through the thin sheet metal of the port fuel tank, spilling diesel into the hot engine compartment. Then a torch of twisting flame shot up into the air, followed by the sound of exploding ammunition.

'Sweet Jesus,' said Midgeley . . . 'that could have been us.'

David Williams

Tank

CORGI BOOKS
A DIVISION OF TRANSWORLD PUBLISHERS LTD

TANK

A CORGI BOOK 0 552 10454 X
First publication in Great Britain

PRINTING HISTORY
Corgi edition published 1977

Corgi Books are published by
Transworld Publishers Ltd,
Century House, 61–63 Uxbridge Road,
Ealing, London W5 5SA

Made and printed in Great Britain by
Cox & Wyman Ltd, London, Reading and Fakenham

Tank

Rastenburg. East Prussia. April 20th, 1942

SS Hauptsturmführer Weber glanced, out of the corner of his eye, down the precise, black great-coated line of the honour guard, made up from the Headquarters Company of SS Standarte Deutschland. The honour guard, consisting of two platoons, stood on either side of the regimental band, with its side drummers, brass and tinkling schellenbaum standard; horsehair plumes drifting from the ox horns below the swastika.

The honour guard was facing the range, their white cross-belts and shining silver buttons, glistening jackboots and parade-ground polish contrasting with the group of mud-stained, overalled panzer grenadiers clustered ahead of them by the range bunkers.

When the first shot reverberated across the heathland, the detonation of the twenty-pound trialen charge caused only a flutter of unease among the curlews and lapwings, by now conditioned to the background music of the Wehrmacht Heeres Waffenamt proving ground, here in East Prussia. The echoing explosion made no difference to the steadiness of the honour guard, however, who stood as stiff and unmoving as the curtain of dark fir trees behind them.

The effect of the direct hit caused a much greater stir among the watching staff officers and aides, their field glasses trained upon the battlefield litter three kilometres beyond; as they scanned the rusting hulls of T.34's, Renault Char B's and English Matilda Mark II Infantry tanks, that performed the role of sitting ducks in that particular shooting gallery.

The short, somehow unmilitary figure at the centre was also obviously impressed, standing as the focal point within the honour guard from the SS Standarte Deutschland. The rigid one-ended square ensured that Wehrmacht observers and even the Henschel and Porsche representatives, who were responsible for the demonstration, should not presume too far, since it was, after all the Führer's birthday.

Weber heard the murmur of surprise, mixed with pleasure, that arose from this group, as a momentary scarlet glow flickered on the frontal armour of a distant Matilda just below the driver's visor. This indicated that the twenty-pound panzergranate, armour-piercing shot had sliced through the one and three-quarter inch shield of frontal armour below the turret. As the shot struck home, the Matilda seemed to shake weakly and for a moment plumes of grey-white smoke spiralled from the edge of the turret race. Then with a roar the turret, its two-pound armament rakishly angled, lifted, like a champagne cork in slow motion out of the hull, above a fountain of blood-red flames.

From where he stood, his sword resting lightly on his shoulder, the SS Hauptsturmführer could observe the gathering of olive and black great-coated staff officers, as well as the impact of the distant shot which swung the Matilda left, its suspension rippling with the interior explosion, as it settled, a blazing hulk, into the sand of the heath.

There were two unusual uniforms in the group; Major Krause and his companion Colonel Muller were the only two officers wearing the drab khaki of the Deutsche Afrika Korps, although they were not alone in wearing the pink lapel piping of armoured troops.

Krause turned his lean, thin-lipped face, that seemed forever hungry, to the puffy, phlegmatic Colonel Muller, as the author of this piece of destruction growled forward on its battle-tracks, now searching for a demonstration target among the Russian T.34's.

Squat, square and monstrous, the heavy tank that the Führer had personally brought to birth, traversed its eighty-eight millimetre gun menacingly across the heath.

Weber caught a comment from one of the olive great-coated staff officers:

'A knightly weapon; just the kind of weapon we need to destroy the Russian bear.'

Weber regarded the square, mobile pill-box with its low profile and truly massive armament, as the Tiger tank, officially described as the VK 4501 (H), continued to traverse its twelve-foot 88mm gun enquiringly; its 62 tons of precision equipment and Maybach engines encased in a gigantic carapace of steel, two to four inches thick.

'We have given you the best tank in the world, my Führer,' the Porsche president said as a simple statement of fact.

Krause looked again at the glistening, silver monster that had not yet received its spray of primer, so urgently had it been demanded. He looked at it hungrily; for he desired to possess it more than the body of his mistress Lotti Nehring, or even the gold and silver shoulder knots of a general. Even with an underestablished regiment of forty of these panzers they could smash through the British, Krause thought bitterly, the corners of his narrow lips turned down in resentment. It made him look more bloodless than ever, for he was already sallow with the jaundice that was endemic in Africa.

Krause had often tried to analyse why he had been passed over so obviously in the promotion lists and despatched to Cyrenaica, which OKH considered strategically unimportant as against the mighty offensive driving across the heart of Russia. So far as Berlin was concerned, North Africa was a side-show; a holding operation, designed to put some muscle into the flabby Italian underbelly of the Axis. When it came to a war of words, Mussolini would usually be the victor, but faced with the harsh realities of Greece and Africa, he was the worst kind of military adventurer, a failure.

Only the Italian M.40 self-propelled gun had proved to be in any way effective against the British Valentines and Matildas; otherwise their light and medium tanks were iron coffins armed with pea-shooters. It was the same in the air, the Italian 'Cigogna' and SM 79 bombers were too slow and underarmed. Krause still limped from a shrapnel wound in his right calf due to the Regia Aeronautica's failure to recognize the German front line.

Krause was aware that the British army had amply demonstrated its shortcomings on the broad plains of northern France; the only military successes being the twenty-five pounder gun and the heavy armour of the Matilda and

Valentine tanks. Otherwise English leadership and rigid command structure had demonstrated all the lack of tactical imagination and inflexibility of the trench war. It was almost, thought Krause, as though they preferred to die, rather than to win. This set them apart from the Italians, who, generally speaking, wished to do neither.

The Tiger, Panzer Mark IV, finally selected another target among the rusting hulls; a T.34 with sloping frontal armour. Both the Matilda and the T.34 had come as an unpleasant surprise to the technical panzer staff; and it was their superior armour that had initiated the development of the giant lumbering to a halt in front of them, preparatory to firing.

This time, the shot landed against the face of the T.34's round turrent, penetrating it as easily as a surgeon's scalpel probes flesh, so that the turret rolled back against its race, like the lid of a tin can, while black smoke wisped along the starting seams of the tank's seventy-five millimetre steel plates.

Colonel Muller turned to his aide:

'Well? and what do you think of that?'

'She uses a lot of petrol, five litres to the kilo.'

'Most tanks are heavy on petrol; the cannon that one's got is the same as the Flak eighty-eight.'

'That's where the real beauty lies.'

The eighty-eight millimetre anti-aircraft gun had first been used against armour with success by the Condor Legion in Spain. Rommel had ensured its continued use in that role, as a tank destroyer in France, and, more recently in the battles round Halfaya Pass. There was nothing to beat the eighty-eight in the desert, and before the Mark III and IV panzers had been upgunned, they only had the equivalent fire power of the inadequate two-pound shell, still used by British armour. It was typical of British inefficiency, Krause thought, that they designed a tank gun which could only fire armour-piercing shot and not high explosive. The German panzers always had this alternative.

'A mobile, steel pill-box armed with an eighty-eight,' Krause said. 'The best of both worlds.' He glanced with a look of silent intolerance at the rotund, complacent face of his superior. Secretly he thought that Colonel Muller was just the sort of officer who would be posted to Africa, rather than France or the Balkans, since he still had enough edge to be given a military rating.

'Ah,' said Muller, and smiled sarcastically, 'but that's just what we don't have; we can't lay our hands on them.'

The group of staff officers had closed in round Hitler, for the demonstration, which had been a complete success, was now virtually over. Weber knew that in a moment he would have to gather the honour guard together for march past. He recognized a few familiar faces in the crowd of observers; most of them were generals from OKH and the Russian Army Groups, or the OKW staff including representatives from the Armaments Office, Army Ordnance, Special Equipment Acceptance Group, and Contracts and Price Control.

Weber guessed that this fine new weapon was destined for the Russian front and the 1942 autumn offensive. In the weeks ahead the new heavy tanks would be pouring out from the Rheinmetall and Krupp factories. The SS Hauptsturmführer focused his attention on the saluting base to which the Führer was now walking, since his arrival there would be the signal for the march past to begin.

As he waited, the staff officers moved to the back of the saluting base and the regimental band struck up the opening bars of 'Prussens Gloria'. Simultaneously Weber stepped forward to take up position beside the standard bearer, with SS Obersturmführer Necker on the far side.

All three of them continued to goose-step forward, wheeling in front of the dais, followed by the two platoons of the Deutschland Standarte moving as one man with the curious skimming-the-earth motion of the goose step. The black parade helmets jerked left as they passed the saluting base, the red swastika colour leading. From time to time Hitler raised his right arm.

When the honour guard had passed, Hitler, and his entourage turned away towards the waiting Mercedes. The Führer paused en route beside the two Afrika Korps officers. Krause wished that he could have handled the questions he felt were coming. Muller stood stolidly beside him like a lump of 'landbrot', ready to accept anything that came his way, good or bad.

'You are returning to Africa, Colonel?'

'Yes, my Führer.'

A flash bulb popped as a Propaganda Company man recorded the scene. Krause now realized why Hitler had stopped beside them.

'It must be almost a year since Geschwader 27 was posted to your theatre. Please send my good wishes to Joachim Marseille. I gave him his Ritterkreuz for his three hundredth kill at Berchtesgarden in February. I hope it won't be long before I can add the diamonds.'

'Yes, my Führer,' said Muller with the kind of wooden response a cadet might give to a senior NCO, if he was on report.

Suddenly Krause's heart beat faster, as he felt himself transfixed by those curious, misty blue eyes that generated such certainty; and yet he knew that Hitler was waiting for some real response; some political point was about to be made.

'And what does the Afrika Korps think of the new Tiger?'

Krause heard himself say:

'With a battalion of those and the new storm gun, we could be at Alexandria inside a week.'

'That is good news indeed, Herr Major. Others say the same about Stalingrad. But what would you do then? What about Supply? Commando Supremo must be left to paddle in their Italian Lake. Still, I suppose it might be arranged, but Erwin Rommel is the prophet of movement and those Tigers might get bogged down in the desert, at twelve kilometres an hour; I doubt whether even the "Desert Fox" could part the waters of the Red Sea for them.'

An SS Brigadeführer coughed to conceal a snigger. Rommel, a political moderate, was not overpopular in certain quarters.

Hitler started to move on.

'We should wish to have our request seriously considered,' Krause said.

'No-one can quarrel with that; it's a matter between you and procurement. I've no doubt I shall see you at the birthday party they're giving me at "The Wolf's Lair".'

Then Hitler and his entourage moved away, as Krause considered whether he had spoken too boldly, after a moment deciding otherwise. It had been the brief from Rommel himself before they had flown out from the forward area beyond Mechili. Muller had been too scared to open his mouth and would have let the opportunity slip.

Hitler's personal bodyguard separated out the Wehrmacht and Supply Ministry observers and shepherded him to his Mercedes, now ringed by SS Liebstandarte motorcycle troops on BMWs.

Krause turned to Muller:

'What did that mean, Colonel?'

Muller was disposed to overlook his subordinate's unauthorized initiative.

'He did not say "no", he did not say "yes". That means there must be possibilities.'

Krause stroked his chin and thought of the intelligence reports warning of a new American medium tank on its way to Suez; the M3 Grant.

'We must try,' he said at last. 'After all, the storm guns have been promised.'

Muller said, without enthusiasm:

'Yes, we must try. I hope that between us we will be able to raise enough contacts to help us achieve our end.'

Muller, at any rate, had impeccable Wehrmacht connections, and was generally liked; perhaps because he had served in Flanders and on the Eastern front in 1916. Krause was far too young to be able to compete with that.

But then, he did have other friends who might be just as useful, not least of them Lotti Nehring.

Brigade Headquarters Gazala Line

Corporal Midgeley, RTR, suppressed a yawn, not because he was bored – this trip to Brigade broke the monotonous tension of the front line – but because he had stood guard from one o'clock that morning until dawn, outside the Leaguer of Matilda Infantry tanks, when the desert lay cold and dead. He spent the night watching for a distant blaze of flares and verey lights which would announce the presence of an Afrika Korps formation.

With an effort he recalled himself to listen and wait as the officers settled themselves in the bright morning sunlight and the ever-present glare.

Military briefings were all very fine in theory, Midgeley thought, dressed in khaki slacks, shirt and black beret that were as clean as they could be after a week of constant movement across the desert. He did not like feeling dirty, but there was nothing he could do about it. It ran as a constant undercurrent, even against his aching desire for sleep.

He had, of course, no right to be at Brigade, since it was the CO who had sent Captain Phillips to the briefing. He was, however, Captain Phillips' driver for the morning, and so his presence was tolerated simply because as a corporal he was expected to know nothing and understand less. The big map board stood on an easel a few yards away, a sheet of talc stretched over it, on which a string of red chinagraph boxes had been drawn. The map covered the coast of Cyrenaica from Tobruk to Benghazi. The red boxes ran, like an unlinked chain, forty miles to the west of Tobruk, south from Gazala to Rotunda Mteifel and seventy miles on to Bir Hacheim. In front of the boxes were broad red bands representing minefields. Taken as a whole, the crude drawing gave a subtle impression of a thick and substantial barrier. Behind this apparently solid line were more red lines running back to the railhead at Matruh and Egypt to mark the three principal supply lines, with scribbled figures added, to show distances, and the petrol requirement needed to lift one ton of stores westwards for the replenishment of the forward areas.

Midgeley, who looked old for his twenty-three years, stood at the back of the semi-circle of officers, who sat in canvas chairs, his hands automatically clasped behind his back in the 'at ease' position. Captain Phillips was among the audience. The squadron commander had ordered him to come with him to Brigade on the pretext that he should pick up some new clutch plates and other spares for the Matildas from Ordnance. But there was another reason; Phillips, who had been a journalist before the war, liked his company; there was a latent friendship between them that overran the official class barriers.

The brigade major, Brady, who was conducting the briefing, looked tired and drawn, and his face had a jaundiced pallor that announced he had been in the desert for some time. His uniform was crumpled and untidy. He had thin gold-framed spectacles, and a delivery that reminded Midgeley of an elderly classics master at his grammar school, lecturing the scholarship class on the strategy of the Punic Wars. Yet there was a tension, an urgency, here in the flat, open desert, as though everyone there knew only too well that it was not an academic game, and were desperately trying to make it different.

The brigade major said:

'The brigadier is still at Div, gentlemen. However, I have to tell you that the intention of the Gazala Line is to bring the Afrika Korps to battle and deny access to Tobruk.'

He paused. There was no-one there who did not realize the importance of Tobruk in this fluid war, where so much depended on supply. Tobruk was the only port worth the name after Benghazi to the west. To retain it was of double importance, first, to maintain the Eighth Army Supply, and secondly, to prevent the Germans from using it, and the adjacent airfields.

'Information. Enemy. Intelligence reports tell us that the

DAK supported by Italian armoured and infantry divisions, including the "Ariete", are about to mount a major offensive. Own troops. Eighth Army are in prepared positions of all-round defence, along this line. The main formations are in the north, First South African Division, Fifty Div. with the Free French to the south at Bir Hacheim; these are in self-supporting Brigade boxes. They are backed by an armoured reserve of First and Seventh Armoured. As you can see the entire line is protected by minefields.

'Method. Infantry formations with Artillery and Anti-tank gun support will hold attacks with their weapons and the bayonet. Armour, as I have said, will be held in mobile reserve.

'Administration. There will be the usual supply columns to Brigades from Tobruk, Belhamed and Jarabub. Replenishment as usual.

'Intercommunication. Wireless silence will be preserved and priority signals traffic cleared by line. Armoured regiments will use wireless only when engaged.'

That, thought Midgeley, is the bare bones of the briefing. It did not offer much reason for complacency. As usual, there was more not said, than said. There was no firm information as to the movements of the enemy. The supply dumps that Brady had referred to were as much a liability as an asset in defence, since they would have to be denied to the Afrika Korps, whose policy, of necessity, was one of living off the land. The fact that wireless silence was ordered was due to the efficient monitoring of the German Wireless Interception Service, and it was rumoured that Rommel had given orders that a résumé of all Eighth Army wireless traffic, picked up by that source, should be passed on to him every day.

'For once, in this theatre,' Brady went on, 'it looks as though it will be all up to the infantry, they must hold the line with the armour backing them up.'

That in itself would be cold consolation. Infantry against panzers was never a welcome prospect, when the infantry had to clear support from Brigade, and the only anti-tank weapons available were the six-pounder portees carried on a high profile Austin truck. Their solid shot could only penetrate the German armour at a range of five hundred yards, which was much too close for comfort.

'On this show, the infantry is to be queen of the battlefield once more, and the proposal is that we shall decide the issue with the bayonet.'

Midgeley rocked on his toes, feeling pleased that he was not in the infantry.

The logic of armour had always appealed to him, and this was why he had joined the Royal Tank Regiment in 1938, at the time of Munich. He had chosen the Royal Tank Regiment deliberately, since he did not want to learn how to ride.

Now Brady began to elaborate on the outline and Midgeley screwed up his eyes against the sun, to re-examine the map on the easel. Brady was now referring to the loosely linked group of boxes as a line, but Midgeley noted that a minefield thirteen miles long filled in the gap between 150 Brigade and the Free French at Bir Hacheim. In Midgeley's experience this seemed an open invitation to disaster, a conveniently fitted pair of blinkers, more reassuring than realistic. It was the kind of obvious invitation that Rommel might well accept, since he never made use of fixed positions himself, but exploited the tactical situation once he had engaged his opponent.

Brady continued to talk and Midgeley lost interest. The Brigade Headquarters was situated on a reverse slope and consisted of a widely-ranged group of windswept Matador ACVs and three-tonners. Looking eastwards, beyond the squat armour of the ACVs, Midgeley could see a litter of fifty burnt-out Italian lorries resting on their axles, like a derelict queue of wounded waiting for treatment that never arrived.

He felt almost relaxed in the centre of the scattered vehicles that formed a rough leaguer, perhaps half a mile across, after the battlefield stress of the last few days. On the way back, he suspected that Phillips would make a detour to the sea for a swim. After all, according to the map, there were several belts of mines between them and Rommel.

However the principal question of where the Germans were remained unanswered. In the desert, nothing was ever really certain; in a couple of minutes a column of Panzer

Mark IV Specials could suddenly appear over the western horizon in a cloud of dust. And yet, there was the map, covered in red chinagraph, showing British, South African and Indian dispositions, with no indication as to where the main German force might be.

Suddenly Brady came to a stop. There was a rustling of maps and a snapping to of notebooks from the cavalry, infantry and forward support arms as colonels glanced at their watches and shifted uneasily, anxious to get back to their units.

The sun was getting low in the sky; it was late afternoon. Junior officers queued to collect the inevitable file of papers that included Brigade daily orders, zones of artillery fire, cipher, air to ground liaison and wireless frequencies, besides individual battalion tasks and responsibilities, along with map references of POL and supply dumps. Phillips stood up and beckoned to Midgeley:

'Sir?'

'Find out about Recovery, will you?'

Midgeley wandered over towards the 'B' Echelon liaison vehicles that were grouped together near the rear link wireless truck. A REME sergeant in off-white tank overalls, his black beret deliberately shrunk, was standing in the shade beside a workshop vehicle. The sergeant said:

'The pow-wow nearly over?'

'That's right, Sergeant.'

'Want a Stella, chum? It'll cost you ten ackers.'

Half a dozen bottles of Egyptian beer stood on a trestle table alongside an oxy-acetylene cutter.

'Thank you, Sergeant.'

'On the scrounge? What you after?'

'Any idea where Recovery's out on the swan?'

'You should try Div for that.'

Midgeley put down some loose change and the sergeant uncapped a bottle of Stella. Midgeley swallowed a mouthful of warm beer. He did not care for drinking very much.

'They prefer it from the horse's mouth in my mob.'

'Well then, Recovery's over the hill a couple of miles.'

The sergeant paused, slowly rattling the coins in his hand.

'Anything special?'

'An RASC company, Scammels, the odd Diamond T Yankee job. What's the matter? Thinking of pulling out?'

'We just don't like bashing our Matildas too hard.'

The sergeant smiled:

'Nice of you to think like that.'

Phillips was waiting by the jeep when Midgeley got back; he was wearing dark glasses, not out of affectation but because he found the glare unbearable.

'Did you get the griff, Corporal?'

'Yes sir, there's a recovery company round the corner.'

'The colonel will be glad to hear it.'

Midgeley climbed in and the driver moved off north-east across the open desert towards the 'Axis By-pass' that ringed Tobruk. Midgeley was right; they were heading up to the sea. The jeep bumped jerkily over the rock and sand. In a few miles they would cross the Trigh Capuzzo, then down the Solaro escarpment to the Via Balbia, the macadam road that led back to Egypt. Then finally the sea.

'Any comment, Corporal?'

'Only that it sounded like a tactical exercise without troops. Without enemy troops that is.'

Phillips said:

'I ask you, infantry boxes. Lambs to the slaughter.'

'That lets us out of it for the moment then.'

'Except that a Matilda is an infantry support tank.'

There had been a time when the Matilda could stand up to anything the Germans could put up against it, except an 88mm gun or the 5cm PAK. Now, the panzers had been modified; their armour had been strengthened, with additional plates on the hull face; furthermore the Mark IV now mounted a 75mm gun that had twice the muzzle velocity of the earlier models. This meant that it could penetrate the Matilda armour at twice the range.

Midgeley said:

'Maybe, the Germans have a few surprises in store.'

'Perhaps we have too.'

'You mean the American Grants?'

A few dozen of these new medium tanks were rumoured to be in the line. They had good armour and a 75mm gun, but a high profile that would make an easy target.

'That's right. There are three factors in the desert, logistics, technology and morale. They're all interdependent. On balance I think we have lousy technology.'

'I'd say we have lousy morale; most of the battles I've fought in, seemed to have been conducted with civil service rules; not only does the left hand not know what the right hand is doing, but we have to indent for artillery as though we were filling an income tax return.'

Phillips laughed. By now they were winding down the Solaro escarpment as the jeep followed a track that would take them down to the sea. Up there to the north was Malta, a stiletto in the side of the axis from which the Italian convoys to North Africa were smashed. Midgeley said:

'But I think we should get ten out of ten for logistics.'

'Something else,' said Phillips, 'there's talk of a new German Assault Gun, a Mark II panzer modification with a PAK 36 gun. Nasty bit of work.'

The water lapped clear and blue at the edge of the rocks. It was funny to think, thought Midgeley, that here with the enemy five miles away you could go for a swim, but back in England the whole coastline was covered in mines and barbed wire. Out there to the north, there were navies on the move, but this stretch of sun-baked rock was not important for the moment.

The water felt good, although Midgeley knew that later he would be sticky with salt and would regret it. He swam out fifty yards and almost forgot the war. Tomorrow could wait. Tomorrow, he would be up in the line ready to be shot at.

South of Aslagh Ridge

TWENTY-FOUR hours later the highlights of the shimmering Mediterranean had become a memory in Midgeley's mind against the oppressive closeness of the desert. Now the Matilda 'K' King was crossing a flat sea of sand broken with limestone boulders, with the faintest smudge to the north-west hinting at the foothills of the Jebel el Akdar. In the intervening period Midgeley had lost the assurance of survival he had had while visiting Brigade, when fear of the future had been lost in the luxury of comparative safety now. This feeling had been replaced by an almost unbearable tension the closer he had come to the forward positions, and was only made tolerable by a stoical fatalism. But since he was face to face with an invisible enemy, Midgeley found the best antidote to terror was to concentrate on his role as gunner, so that he was not interested in the distant landscape but his immediate surroundings. Therefore his forehead was pressed into the glass periscope block pad, the limits that presently defined his little world. Thomson, the Glaswegian loader and wireless operator, was at his elbow, separated by the recoil cage and the breech block of the puny two-pounder gun.

Immediately behind him in the turret, he sensed the legs and desert sand boots of Anderson, the commissioned tank commander. Anderson braced himself against the motion of the lurching tank by wedging his body against the hatch. Forward, in the driving compartment, he could see 'Gnasher' Evans, formerly the proprietor of a small garage in Newport, Monmouthshire, his hairy hands stolidly clutching the two steering levers.

Stuck in the handbook holder on his right was a dog-eared copy of Sexton Blake, Evans' favourite reading material, next to the more explicit Egyptian pornography available from Cairo and Alex.

Midgeley, however, was concentrating all his attention on the view ahead, waiting for whatever instructions would be piped down to him by Anderson on the intercom. Experience had taught him to allow for the juddering of the tank so that he had a continuous, though occasionally interrupted, view of the surrounding desert. If he traversed left or right he could see the other tanks in the troop, their profiles curiously reminiscent of paddling ducks, throwing up spumes of dust, as they ploughed across the desert at twelve miles an hour.

For a moment Midgeley considered the day which was already beginning to merge into all the others: the smell of oil, the tight fear in the pit of his stomach, the heat that would reach a climax of one hundred and twenty degrees at noon, the sand fleas and a clinging stale condensation of sweat and other body odours which clung to the metal walls of the tank. All these sensations were spasmodic and dominating in turn against the underlying motion, as the tank bucketed interminably on, like a trawler wallowing through a heavy sea.

Worst of all, in some ways, was the predictability of the other tank crew: one moment he hated them, and the next he needed them desperately, even Anderson. To survive they had to work together, to rely on each others' judgement, and yet there was Evans with his farts and dirty jokes, and Anderson with his divine, commissioned right of superiority. It was a relief that he could tolerate Thomson. His threshold of irritation always dropped when they were advancing to contact the enemy.

Suddenly Midgeley's head slammed into the metal of the turret roof, and through a tide of flashing pain, he instinctively clawed back towards the upper turret side hatch, thinking, 'Christ, we're dead.' Cordite smoke would fill the turret, red-hot shot splinters would penetrate the racks of two-pound shell cases and the Matilda would explode as certainly as a Roman candle. The tank was swivelling to the left, as Evans worked the gears and shouted:

'We've blown a track; it's a bloody mine.'

'K' King had, in fact, detonated a Panzerschnell mine, its

six kilos of picric acid sufficient to sever the links in the track plates behind the port jockey roller, so that the tank had slewed, after running off its track.

Anderson shouted to Evans to stop and for them all to get out.

Midgeley dazedly slipped the hatch bolts and pulled himself quickly out and over the turret side and then clambered down the skirt, still shaking with pain and blinded by the glare of the desert.

The other Matildas had left them behind and were now a hundred yards ahead. Thomson climbed out and said:

'Jesus, Midge, I don't half feel sick.'

Anderson was still perched in the turret, scanning the western horizon with his glasses, and setting an example.

Midgeley said:

'Don't worry, Jock; if we sit here long enough, 'A' Echelon will come forward and give you a Rennie's stomach pill.' He rubbed his head gingerly.

The desert was silent now, after the grinding roar of the Matilda II's ninety-five horsepower Leyland engines. Evans at last struggled, swearing, out of the driver's port.

'Why the hell couldn't you give me a hand?' he demanded.

The corporal and Thomson ignored him. What did he want, Midgeley thought, he was out of the bloody tank.

'Shall I brew up?' Thomson asked.

'You better ask the skipper.'

Anderson swung his legs over the side of the turret and slithered down, the calculation of the movement carrying with it a touch of arrogance. Nonetheless he was shaken, his face was white and emphasized his little red moustache and worried eyes.

'We better get that track fixed.' The damaged track lay like a dead snake behind the Matilda. It was not a difficult job, for the Matilda carried spare track links on the hull walls.

A spurt of dust jumped with a crack thirty yards to their left, throwing up a column of sand and stones, a few of which plopped against the armour of 'K' King. Thomson's teeth were chattering and then he said:

'That was meant for us.'

The second high explosive shell landed much closer and Evans ran to the lee of the tank.

'Get away from there, you mad bastard,' Midgeley shouted. 'What do you think they're aiming at?'

There was another whistle and the Matilda rocked under the impact of a direct hit. Evans had stopped as he heard Midgeley and directed his fifteen stone away from the tank, sprawling heavily against a ring of boulders. This time the shot, having penetrated the armour, splattered red-hot splinters through the thin sheet metal of the port fuel oil tank, spilling diesel into the hot engine compartment. A torch of twisting flame erupted from the rear inlet grill, and this was followed by the sound of exploding ammunition.

Midgeley watched fascinated as the tank shook and juddered to the chain of explosions, while another pillar of multicoloured fire spilled out from the turret hatch. He was so hypnotized by the spectacle that, for the moment, he did not see what was happening to the rest of the squadron. When he did, he gasped. Forward, seven tanks were stationary and ablaze, their guns depressed or eccentrically elevated. He could hear the screams from one of them. The other two Matildas had paused uncertainly, one of them starting to reverse to the cover of a burning tank.

'Sweet Jesus,' said Midgeley, 'that could have been us.'

It was not the first time that he had witnessed such a scene, or watched his own tank disintegrate into a smoke-blackened wreck, but he would never get used to it, nor the fact that the line between life and death, survival and destruction was so apparently narrow.

'Where are the gunners?' Anderson asked helplessly, his little moustache twitching. Midgeley could sense that he was on the edge of tears. It was his first command and it was not supposed to be like this at OCTU.

'We better clear out, Sir,' said Midgeley. 'Unless we want to be picked up by whatever's doing that. At least there's no point in asking for a tow. Recovery will be busy enough tonight.'

However hard he searched with his glasses, Midgeley was unable to locate the source of the savage defeat which had been inflicted on them. Only once he glimpsed the squat profile of a German eight-wheeled armoured car traversing the battlefield, but nothing more. There was no other movement from the west. The sun shone down brilliantly and harshly, casting short shadows. At last Anderson said:

'Well, thank God none of us is hurt.'

For once, Midgeley could only agree with him.

Procurement. Potzdamerplatz Berlin

SPRING seemed to have come unusually late to Berlin on that particular day. The wind blowing from the north-east brought with it the uncertainty of the Russian front, which, in spite of the lingering optimism, already sounded a note of caution. The fighting around Kharkov had been harder and grimmer than anyone could have thought.

The mood of restlessness seemed to be reflected in the clouds scudding beyond the high roofs of the military administration blocks through which Colonel Muller and Major Krause were walking. The thought remained unspoken that the 'Blitzkrieg' tactics of earlier campaigns were no longer working with the speed and élan that had conquered Europe in something less than forty days.

Muller and Krause were there, of course, to conclude their mission. After ten days in Berlin Krause felt that they were getting nowhere, and that Muller's nervous telephone calls to senior colonels, with whom he had once served, were about as productive as an attempt to sell ice-boxes to the Eskimos. Nonetheless, although he brooded constantly over his own alternatives for obtaining the release of forty Tiger tanks to the Afrika Korps, he had to put up with Colonel Muller's laborious lobbying. He knew that he could not put forward other proposals, until all else had been explored. Now Muller had produced what he obviously thought was a trump card, a meeting with Von Rodalbe, Generalmajor, who acted as an intermediary between the Ministry of Supply and the Army.

The big office, in which the meeting was to be held, was deliberately old-fashioned, as though its asceticism was intended to snub the more vulgar excesses of the Third Reich.

The conference table itself barely allowed much room for the group of five men to discuss the matter in hand. The nineteenth-century quasi-baroque plasterwork covering the ceiling was dusty and unpainted; the wooden floor was uncarpeted but highly polished.

The Generalmajor was a dried and wizened veteran from Hanover. He held his position at the insistence of the Wehrmacht because of his well-established integrity, and he was directly responsible to the Inspectorgeneral of armoured troops. He did not allow the huge fortunes that could be made from Army contracts to influence his judgement.

The meeting did not begin on a particularly happy note.

'Your General Rommel is like a film star,' Von Rodalbe pronounced, with a tight-lipped smile, 'he likes an audience, but you will not find many among his fan club round here. You would be much more welcome at the Ministry of Information, or perhaps the Konstantin film studios.'

Von Rodalbe's staff remained silent. One was a colonel in the Engineers, just below retirement age, the other a captain in his early thirties, who wore the Ritterkreuz and the special badge for single-handed destruction of a tank, on the empty sleeve of his tunic. His good hand, resting on the blotting-pad, shook constantly, and his face twitched. Von Rodalbe turned to Colonel Muller, ignoring Krause, with the air of a schoolmaster discussing which of the class shall be awarded the prize for the best Latin prose composition. He took no notice of Krause's diplomatic smile. The major could assume a certain charm when it suited him, which was why Rommel had entrusted him with the joint responsibility for this lobbying mission. Krause said:

'We are here on the advice of the Supreme Commander.' He added, on catching the shadow of disapproval cross Von Rodalbe's face, 'That must be said.'

Von Rodalbe made a little brush-away motion, as if to say, 'I've been in the army a long time; there have been many Supreme Commanders, but not many like this one, thank God.' Then his wizened face opened up slightly.

'It is a matter of interpretation. The priorities are quite clearly laid down in OKH policy directives. We are fighting a war in the east, and that is where the main effort must lie. North Africa is a public relations exercise, a holding action. After all, what are we talking about? A couple of

Wehrmacht divisions and some Italians, who are presently running rings round the amateur British. There is no need to commit new armour.'

'It will make the outcome decisive. All the more reason why we should have adequate supply, which has, in any case been agreed.'

Krause realized at once that he had made a tactical mistake in raising the question of supply generally. It was a constant nightmare for the Afrika Korps, who were now reduced to relying on air lift for essential supplies.

'Then, Major, you should address yourself to Field Marshal Kesselring and Commando Supremo in Rome on that score; we supply you with your quotas according to the logistics schedule, as far as the Italian frontier. It is the self-appointed task of our Italian allies to get them to you. I am afraid it may be difficult, but it is a political question.'

Krause suppressed a sigh, all too aware of the problem. The Afrika Korps was Cinderella so far as OKH was concerned, and likely to stay that way. The Italians were prickly about the involvement of the Afrika Korps in the Libyan rescue operation, they insisted that supply generally be controlled by themselves, and as usual, there were not so obvious reasons for this, besides amour propre. The Rumanian petrol that regularly reached the Brenner Pass was often subsequently lost in a plethora of corruption and inefficiency, under a system of priorities that the Italians loaded heavily in their own favour. Such as Supermarina delivered to Derna or Benghazi had to run the gauntlet of the RAF and Royal Navy. But he reminded himself that he was not there to talk about petrol.

'We do know the problems, Herr Generalmajor, and we appreciate the support that we are getting. That's why we want to ship the armour from Piraeus. That way we would keep control.'

The younger staff officer, who was called Von Bülow, stirred. Krause noted that he wore green panzer flashes; obviously he was an adviser on armour.

'A company of Tigers? You don't want much.'

'Then Sturmgeschützes and the new Nebelwerfers have been promised.'

'But you have assault guns,' Von Rodalbe cut in icily. 'Marder III's and the Lorraine Schlepper.'

'You know as well as I do, Generalmajor, that these are second-line weapons. They are basically the old panzer Mark II Czech chassis, modified to mount a captured Russian 7.5cm.'

'They have a capability of destroying any British armour you are facing.'

'You must have seen the Abwehr reports.'

'The American medium tank, you mean, well, it's not there yet, is it? Even if it's true.'

'That's not the point, if I may say so, the Mark IV panzers are now being rebuilt as an assault gun with an 88mm.'

'That is correct.'

'We need them. Erwin Rommel is convinced that with the right resources, we shall be at the Suez Canal by Christmas, in Iraq by the spring and join up with Sixth Army by . . .'

Von Rodalbe interrupted him impatiently.

'These strategic theories are none of our concern here in procurement, even if they are the concern of the Afrika Korps, which I doubt. It is our task to be able to justify to OKH the allotment of material to the two theatres in which we are engaged. In any case I don't suppose that the SS will be very happy about your proposals.'

Krause swallowed:

'Various other supply matters have been agreed in principle: 22 Air Landing Division has been promised, as well as the new Storm guns.'

'Then you are well supplied.'

'It could well be that the Tiger battalion will be made up from SS. The reichsführer himself believes that such a move could be politically desirable in the solution of the Jewish question. The roots of any Zionist state in Palestine must be eliminated; as you know we have sympathizers in Jerusalem, Beirut, Damascus and Baghdad, Tehran even. A move of this kind would encourage our political allies.'

Von Rodalbe fiddled with a silver propelling pencil.

'I cannot see, my dear major, what all this has got to do with it. This department is only the quartermaster's stores; give us a properly authorized requisition and we shall supply you. However, I must point out, if we are to have a political discussion, that a dozen of our armies are engaged on a thousand-mile front, from the Baltic to the Black Sea in Russia, and they need every panzer we can give them; the logic of their case is self-evident.'

Krause passed his hand wearily over his forehead, and smoothed back an untidy strand of hair. He had been reluctant to bring the SS into the discussion and was in a way relieved that the argument had clearly left Von Rodalbe unimpressed. In any case, he knew that Rommel had disapproved of the performance of the Totenkopf division during the invasion of France. However, he had done all he could, and clearly to no avail. Suddenly he felt discouraged, and Muller took over with one more attempt to persuade Von Rodalbe. In the meantime, Krause recalled the depressing rumours of RAF terror bombing, particularly the destruction of Cologne, by a force of what was claimed to be a thousand heavy bombers. He half-listened to Muller's somewhat naïve argument.

'Everyone in North Africa believes that the DAK will succeed and that Erwin Rommel will cross the Canal before Christmas, smashing the British before there can be any American involvement. The British are, after all, worthy, but not very formidable opponents. In that event Rommel will be undoubtedly promoted to Field Marshal and exercise very considerable influence in Berlin as a consequence. He is, after all, Wehrmacht.'

'Only just,' said the young captain.

They all pretended not to have heard the remark. There was a silence in the conference room, as they realized that the talk was taking a dangerous turn. It was the kind of open discussion that would have been much better conducted after a dinner party, or in the privacy of the officers' mess, if it was worth pursuing at all.

Finally Von Rodalbe said:

'I'm sorry, I do not appear to have made myself clear, the answer is "no" so far as the Tigers are concerned. However I shall see about the other material, since that seems to be in order.'

For the first time since Krause had met him, he smiled.

'Cheer up; it seems that your film star general has had another victory at a place called Gazala. It is quite typical of the fellow, to allow himself to be surrounded, then breach the encirclement to obtain supply and finally turn the tables on General Ritchie. The English are in full retreat, so, for the moment, it seems, he has no need for additional armour. It is men, not material, that win victories.'

But to Major Krause the wind was still cold and unpredictable. Walking out beyond the zigzag painted sentry boxes to the motor pool where they had left their borrowed staff car, he realized they had once more accomplished nothing.

The El Duda Road

CORPORAL MIDGELEY saw the circle of Stukas above him as the Canadian Ford three-tonner ground to a halt too late. He calculated the risks as he jumped from the tailboard; they were through the minefield, a long way behind it in fact, but you could never be quite sure. He had seen the dive bombers at exactly the same time as the air sentry, who began to thump belatedly on the dented ochre metal roof of the driver's cab. As Midgeley jumped, he thought that the whole Western Desert was a minefield that army after army had sown, as a regular crop, throughout two and a half years of war. The retreating Engineers could have slipped up, or laid anti-personnel alongside the tank track parallels the convoy had been following. In theory the tracks were a kind of optimistic insurance, along the principle that where one vehicle had driven, another could follow; that was not always true.

As he landed and ran, Midgeley could hear the eerie wail of the lead Stuka's siren, a sound that he had learned to hate. He trod lightly, as he ran, always looking for a sudden dip in the sand, or the protruding prongs which identify an 'S' mine, at the same time searching for cover. Ahead of him was the rusting hull of an Italian M.13/40 tankette, still chocolate brown in patches and criss-crossed with dark green stripes, its gun split like a burst pipe; sand had drifted up to the superstructure, partially concealing a broken starboard track. Then Midgeley tripped on a boulder and pressed his face into the dust, as the screaming grew louder. Thomson was still running twenty yards behind him, but the rest of the passengers from the three-tonner had dived unwisely beneath the vehicle.

Thomson went to ground as the first Stuka plummeted down in a thirty-degree angle dive and hovered as the pilot pulled back on the stick. Always that bloody siren, thought Midgeley as, under the tilt of his steel helmet, he looked up to see the light blue and sand-coloured fuselage homing in on him personally; the airbrake shifted on the crooked wings and a bomb slid between the undercarriage struts. The Stuka leader came out of his dive three hundred feet from the ground, as the nose spike of the 500kg Stabo bomb impacted without ricochet, twenty yards behind the Canadian Ford; the blast from the resulting explosion somersaulted it into a smouldering wreck.

The blast lifted Midgeley six inches off the ground and into a small personal world of dust, pain and a tingling deafness as his eardrums compressed, so that he did not see three of the survivors from the burning truck hosed down by the second Stuka's gun pack. The wing of JU 87s continued to rip into the rest of the column of soft-skinned vehicles, which made up a planned withdrawal away from the Cauldron to the west of Bir el Harmat. They included an armoured command vehicle, two wireless trucks, a water bowser, five three-tonners and a recovery vehicle.

Each time the siren came nearer, Midgeley's stomach tightened, for the inevitable conclusion would be the strange blast vacuum that lifted his body up and smashed it down; his only consolation being that the attacks seemed further and further off. Suddenly it was over. He could see the blue sky again, though faintly through clouds of settling dust, and the harsh yellow flames that engulfed the shattered column.

A fly settled on his hand and Midgeley stood up, relieved to be alive, exhilarated even, above the appalling feeling of defeat, and the memory of the line of brewed-up Matildas.

Rommel had done it again. For three days he had listened on the regimental net as the squadron commanders were called away to interminable appreciations and 'O' Groups, and while the situation was discussed at length, the Mark III and IV panzers of 90th Light Division and 15th and 21st Panzer Divisions had circled round the flank to the south of Bir Hacheim, virtually unopposed, like a fencer outmanoeuvring a man with a sledge-hammer.

Midgeley, his ears ringing, walked over to the remains of the column. The Canadian Ford, in which he had been riding, was burnt out, and he could see no survivors among those who lay in its shadow, flames flickering over their khaki drill shirts and shorts. There was the bitter smell of burning rubber, concealing to some extent the stench of roasted flesh.

Gripping his Sten-gun tightly, he walked back and Thomson came up to him. Thomson's gaiter was loose, and his trousers were ripped. At first he couldn't make out what Thomson was saying:

'Where's the bloody Raff?'

'How the hell should I know?'

Some other survivors began to appear from the line of blazing trucks, disorientated and numb. The column, which had been heading for 'B' Echelon, was composed of a variety of stragglers, cut off from their units when a Brigade H.Q. had been overrun. Altogether there were about forty: signal clerks, armourers, medical orderlies, craftsmen. The quartermaster sergeant commanding the column had been killed by machine-gun fire in the second truck, which he had insisted in riding in, since he was fidgety about mines.

Midgeley looked round impatiently. It was the kind of untidy situation that always infuriated him, now that his exhilaration at survival was fading and the immediate fear of sudden death withdrawn. Given half a chance in thirty minutes they'd be scattered all over the bloody desert, dying of thirst, being blown up by mines or simply being captured.

Thomson said:

'So what happens next, Corp?'

Midgeley slowly took out the Zeiss 7 × 50 binoculars he had found in an 88 emplacement they had overrun at Mechili on the way to Tripoli, six months before. He had been very careful about booby traps as he had removed them from the body of a dead Unteroffizier.

Focusing them lovingly, he scanned the horizon line westwards towards what had been the front, looking for the puffs of dust that would mean panzers. But there was nothing. Then again to the south and north.

Thomson said:

'What d'you see, Corp?'

Midgeley slowly lowered the glasses, and the anger at

their situation, which had concentrated into a tight knot in his stomach, suddenly exploded.

'A bloody shambles: dead soldiers, a line of burning transport and a long walk back if the panzers don't get here first.'

Thomson said:

'Well for God's sake, don't take it out on me.'

'Just stating facts.'

There were times when he found Thomson's total reliance on him more than hard to bear, and he added:

'I hadn't noticed that the shooting had stopped, where we are now.'

'Point taken, Corp. I'm sorry.'

'What makes my flesh creep is that I'm lumbered with this shower, now that the fat QSM's bought it. Well, Thomson, you can bloody well start to get them organized by falling in as right marker.'

The dust had settled this time but the smoke still billowed up, a giant target indicator.

'I shouldn't hang about either, Thomson; for all we know, the Junkers 87s are bombing up again at El Adem prior to a return visit.'

Thomson accepted Midgeley's impatience silently as he always did, since he seemed to think that even this dangerous and strange existence was an improvement on the twenty years of uncertainty, near-starvation and squalor he had put up with in Glasgow's Cowcaddens. Thomson started to bellow:

'Alright, you men. Over here.' The scattered survivors began to assemble automatically in a line beside him. Midgeley noted that they had an air of defeat and a look of hopelessness he had seen before on prisoners' faces.

However they lined up, sharply enough. One or two of them had superficial wounds. Corporal Midgeley said:

'I am Corporal Midgeley of the Tanks. This is my assistant, Private Thomson. We are going back to "B" Echelon, and I am taking you lot with me.'

One of the cipher clerks, who was wearing slacks and plimsolls, had a crack across one of his glasses, but looked intelligent. He was pink from the sun and his arms were white, so he could not have been in the theatre very long.

'Where's the MT?' he asked.

'Who said anything about MT? You shouldn't have got clever, you should have worn boots like the rest of us.'

Then he went on:

'Check the bowser, Thomson.'

A soldier in a Polish uniform stood beside the cipher clerk, grinning at Midgeley. He was well-built and in his early thirties, with huge curved eyebrows, which gave his face a quizzical owlish look. One thing, Midgeley realized, made him stand out from the others, he was carrying a weapon, a Bren. Midgeley said:

'You're a long way from home.' The last he had heard of the Polish Carpathian Brigade was that they were inside the perimeter, up north at Tobruk.

'Yes, Corporal.'

The Polish soldier continued to watch Midgeley with a half-amused expression before adding:

'Those very bloody Stukas.'

'What's your name?'

'Starski, Starski.'

The Pole continued to stare until Midgeley realized that his attention was focused on the corporal's Tank Regiment badge.

'I drive Ansaldo Fiat in '39. Command Tank; boom, boom. On Pomerania front near Danzig.'

Midgeley looked Starski over. He was tall and scrawny, projecting a feeling of overall strength; tank crew was certainly in short supply.

'Ansaldo Fiat is a light tank, like the British Mark 2,' Starski added helpfully.

'God help you then, mate,' said Midgeley. 'You're lucky to be alive.'

Starski laughed again, the edges of his eyes crinkling.

'Yes Corporal, you are right, I should be dead, like just now; the armour cracks.'

He gave out another bellow of laughter, as Midgeley decided privately that Starski, like many others was bomb-happy; the experiences of the last three years had been too much for him.

Now Thomson came up to tell him that the water bowser

was peppered with shrapnel, but still half-full, and for the moment Midgeley forgot about Starski.

'Right then,' he shouted, 'fill your canteens. If you left them behind for Rommel, take them off the dead men. Also take a rifle and ammo. Egypt's that-a-way if you want to give the cage a miss. And keep to the track, that way you're less likely to disturb any Eyetie thermos bombs or tread on any nasty fruit tins, or any other fireworks our lads have left behind.'

'S' mines were particularly high on Midgeley's list of the unpleasant. They were a German mine, sometimes visible with three prongs, and activated by a surface pressure of between nine and thirteen pounds. Four and a half seconds after activation a charge was shot four feet into the air before exploding; they had a killing range of up to two hundred yards.

Midgeley examined the two unburned trucks before leaving. These were the bowser and the recovery vehicle at the end of the column. The airburst, which had punctured the bowser tank, had also ploughed shrapnel into the engine and cab, disembowelling the unfortunate driver. The radiator was riddled and metal splinters had sliced through the cylinder head. The petrol tank had suffered no damage, however. Midgeley corrected this by emptying ten rounds from his Sten into the base of the fuel tank so that the petrol sprayed into the sand. He told Thomson to give the same treatment to any other spare jerricans. Both of them were well aware of the value any fuel had to the Afrika Korps.

The big AEC recovery vehicle was not on fire, but the force of an exploding Stabo had lifted all twenty tons of it on to its side. Midgeley severed the main fuel leads. He was conscious of Starski grinning again.

'Hey Corporal, we have some visitors.'

'What is it now Starski?'

'Take a look out there, it's the panzers.'

Midgeley's heart missed a beat as he cursed himself for getting caught up in detail; with only small arms and no transport they were as good as dead or prisoners. The black pluming smoke from the line of broken vehicles was a beacon to any enterprising German column.

'Oh God!' said Midgeley fearfully.

There were six of them in a loose half-crescent, perhaps a mile away. Midgeley made out the silhouettes of four Mark IIIs and a couple of Mark IVs, their angular fighting compartments and turret curiously reminiscent of the box-like helmets of the mediaeval Teutonic knights. There was nothing any of them could do except wait. Midgeley instinctively shared the feelings of the German tank commanders; attacking a column of soft-skinned vehicles was like a harvest rabbit shoot. He could see an officer in the command tank carefully examining the burning column and the ground behind through glasses.

The tanks rumbled on for another two hundred yards before starting to slow down.

Midgeley said:

'What the hell are they up to?'

Thomson said:

'They're stopping, Christ that means they're going to shoot.'

The other survivors had flopped on to the ground as they picked up the bad news, assuming the attitudes of hunched and hopeless misery Midgeley had so often noticed among Italian prisoners. Only Starski was still smiling as he checked a Bren magazine before clipping it on.

Thomson said:

'That there Polak must be bloody loco; he wants to get us all killed, the twerp.'

Eight hundred yards to the west, the panzers rolled to a halt.

'Jesus,' Thomson added, 'and what does that mean? They've switched off their bloody engines; they're going to zero in.'

A cascade of green vereys rose vertically from the lead tank.

'Oh Mother,' said Thomson, 'they're calling up the 105s.'

Midgeley shook his head.

'They should have enough to brew us up twice over. You can put that thing away,' he told Starski. 'I've seen that before, it means they're out of juice; probably ammo too.'

Starski began to laugh again, a great billowing roar.

'You can thank your lucky stars,' Midgeley went on.

'Fucking roll on,' said Thomson. 'I hope you're right. Not even enough benzine to make it to this column.'

'They don't want to take any chances, more like, any more than we do. He's seen there's nothing for him here.'

'With one little PAK we make boom, boom,' said Starski. 'Kaput, finish.'

'What the hell's his mob?' Thomson enquired. 'SAS?'

'Better go and ask General Anders. He says he was a tank man.'

'Did they have them in Poland?' Thomson looked him over disapprovingly, but Starski only grinned.

'Anyway what's he doing out here in the blue; could be fifth column.'

'No, he's fighting Germans like you and me.'

'He'll scrounge a PIAT next, and then we really will be in trouble.'

Thomson laughed a nervous high-pitched laugh in reaction to the fact that they were still alive and that the panzers hadn't moved and the muzzles had not swung searchingly towards them before broadcasting death. The others were gradually losing their bleak condemned expression.

Screened by the burning column, Midgeley led the way into the desert, his ears straining for the swish of a shell or the deep rumble of advancing tank engines prepared to run them down, but all he heard was the chink of Starski's Bren and the steady plod of Thomson padding behind.

Berlin. Hotel Central

'It seems that we have struck a brick wall,' Muller remarked. 'We cannot return with promises only, this time; it has happened too often before. But,' he shrugged, 'as both of us know ...'

Krause stared beyond the palms through the plate glass window, out into the Unter den Linden. Strips of brown paper had been criss-crossed over the glass as a precaution against air raids.

'There is another way.'

Muller sighed wearily.

'I don't see how. We've been through all the official channels.'

'Ah, but Colonel Muller, you must know the story of the 50mm panzer gun.'

Muller sighed yet again; any informed tank officer knew the story to their cost. After the capture of France, Hitler had ordered Army Ordnance to upgun the Panzer Mark III to a long, high-velocity 50mm piece, but they had installed a short low-velocity version instead.

'Who doesn't? The Führer didn't like it. Whoever gave the authority is with an Ostarmee penal battalion right now.'

'But with a substantial bank balance in Zurich.'

Muller frowned:

'I know nothing of such arrangements.'

'It would be very simple; the contractors quoted the same price for both guns. Let's say 20,000 modifications were anticipated, that would cost a lot of marks. A nice contract.'

'It has cost a lot of soldiers' lives.'

'Take the Stuka; originally Swedish. Reichsmarschall Goering's wife has a Swedish passport so the connection's obvious. Now the plane is manufactured by us under licence;

who gets fifty per cent of the patent royalties, I wonder? Certainly not Father Christmas.'

Muller said:

'But what do we have to offer?' And then as an afterthought and as though the discussion was becoming improper, he added 'Major.'

'That's where I come in. If we approached the supplier direct, it is more than likely that we could by-pass procurement.'

Muller passed his hand wearily across his face; he was at a loss in this world where people made fortunes out of life and death. He was, of course, aware that certain NSDAP officials went to considerable lengths to pull strings in order to assume command of the new protectorates which now formed part of the Third Reich. It was well-known that the SS trafficked in human lives with profit. Even on the Eastern front, men like Karminsky were busy protecting themselves against rivals and consolidating their fragmented empires.

'You're sure you can handle it?'

'I can only try. The implications are clear for all of us. If Erwin Rommel broke through into Egypt and swung up to Persia, think what the consequences would be. Field Marshal Von Kleist is already in the Caucasus, but if we reached Persia first?'

'To the winner the spoils?'

'We would no longer be a sideshow, a forgotten army.' Muller said nervously:

'If you think you can pull it off, I suppose anything's worth trying.'

'Oh, I think so, with a little bit of help; but don't worry, it needn't be from you.'

The telephone number Krause rang was answered by a maid with a French accent, which was very avant garde in the context of 1942. The flat was in Moabit, a fashionable part of Berlin, but like so many things in the Third Reich it was not entirely as it seemed.

'Fräulein Nehring?'

'Who's calling?'

'Major Krause from North Africa.'

Krause thought back to the old days before the war: Lotti Nehring was still the darling of cinema audiences throughout Germany. She was both discreet and politically adept; the mass exodus to Hollywood had proved useful professionally. Krause glanced at his watch, it was eleven o'clock and she wouldn't be up yet. Then the phone clicked.

'What have you brought me from Africa?'

Lotti's voice was sonorous and vibrant; Muller could imagine her lying back between the satin sheets, dark and luxurious, quite different from the squeaky, empty-headed, plaited peasant girls that Goebbels usually favoured so much.

Krause knew Lotti well enough not to beat about the bush.

'A problem, which if you help to solve, can be to everyone's advantage, Liebchen.'

'You sound like an agent; well, just so long as it isn't a part. They've offered me the lead in "Baron Münchausen". But I had to turn it down.'

'You have a role to play but not that kind. But I do have something for you, Liebchen, a souvenir.'

'Come round for lunch. Let's say in two hours.'

Krause allowed himself a smile as he returned to the gloomy Muller.

'I've made a start.'

'I wish you luck.'

'That won't be necessary, Lotti knows everyone; she moves in circles where even the angels must be circumspect.'

Krause paused for a moment.

'Just one thing, if I pull it off, will you confirm the command?'

'I don't understand.'

'The battalion, the Tiger Abteilung.'

'Oh, I see.' Muller regarded his empty coffee cup. 'Well, yes, that can be arranged.'

Suddenly Krause replaced his playboy façade with a hungry intensity.

'It's important, I don't want anything to go wrong. I want to run the whole show from here to Libya, it's too important. I want to see they get to Africa myself.'

Muller shrugged:

'When you get the tanks to Cyrenaica, I am sure that Erwin Rommel will recommend you personally for the Ritterkreuz.'

Krause had realized for some time that he was a black sheep so far as OKH was concerned. His career had been unblemished up to the time he had left cadet school in the late twenties, but he had been unwisely over enthusiastic in welcoming the advent of the National Socialists at a time when Hindenburg had been quite outspoken in his dislike of Hitler.

However his connections with the party had led to a junior command in Spain in 1936, and two years later he had been seconded to Erwin Rommel to help establish the Wehrmacht training programme for the Hitler Youth.

These were political appointments, but he had found that his way had been blocked in his attempts to join the SS; the party preferred to use him as a Wehrmacht officer. The various unpleasant incidents that occurred between the Nazi organizations and the Wehrmacht in the late thirties heightened his unsatisfactory position. He was, as it were, neither one thing nor the other. As time went on his position became increasingly difficult, since it was clear that Rommel, who was no politician, was becoming disenchanted with the régime.

It was Krause's restless ambition that led him to swim in the murkier waters of National Socialism, since his own family background of lower middle class shopkeeping did little to advance his cause with the traditional Prussian, military, landowning élite. However, it turned out that with all these disadvantages he was a surprisingly adept politician.

His political instinct had given him a considerable insight into the undercurrents of the regime. The Jewish persecutions that had grown into an everyday event gave him a certain cause for self-congratulation, for at least his racial background was quite impeccable. He became aware that there were many who could not be so overtly confident, even Heydrich, the sinister eminence grise of the SS, whose racial antecedents had so mysteriously disappeared. Even so, he realized that in a society based on racial perfectionism, nobody was safe, and there was a ready-made excuse permanently present to remove any freak or odd-ball, or even someone who was over-ambitious.

Krause, therefore, made it his business to locate the skeletons that lay in most people's cupboards, certainly in the Wehrmacht and in those circles of prominent people to which he forced access. His own supreme self-confidence, which others saw as lack of imagination or insensitivity, made him utterly ruthless in opening doors in other people's houses; even someone who was as charming and influential as Lotti Nehring.

The fact that Lotti was Austrian tended to make him suspicious in the first place; the Danube was notorious as a racial hotch-potch.

Krause had been on his way to Spain when he had first met her at one of the innumerable parties thrown at the time of the Olympic Games, when Germany was engaged in an enormous public relations exercise. Many had grasped at the apparent change of atmosphere in hope, unperturbed by the Führer's refusal to acknowledge the athletic supremacy of Jesse Owens.

It had been a party to celebrate a German victory of the Gold in the riding events at a private villa belonging to the Minister of Sport at Charlottenburg. The party, of course, was very proper, like a diplomatic function, except that at most diplomatic functions there is something to talk about, and on this occasion most people avoided any topic which was not to the credit of the party. Flirtations were, of course, an alternative.

Krause had developed a superior, patronizing attitude towards women, in line with current thinking.

If racially pure, women were protected darlings, their destiny only to be the bearers of the race. The old-fashioned morality had been replaced by a mixture of racial purity and promiscuity. After all, the Führer had instituted financial incentives and decorations to any woman who produced racially pure offspring from whatever source. In spite of this, Krause was shy of women; when he was introduced to Lotti Nehring, he had difficulty in saying anything sensible.

She was certainly a very attractive woman, with the kind of Teutonic romantic sadness and inviolability that had influenced the view of such men as Count Masoch. She was of medium height, with dark brown eyes, and a mouth which could at any moment revert from a smile to an habitual wistfulness. Krause had, of course, cast himself in the role of successful warrior, clicking his heels and being patronizingly correct to underline his masculine superiority, and at the same time hiding his lack of assurance.

It was his certainty that fascinated her.

'Oh well, I must go to the studios tomorrow.'

Then Krause realized that he was talking with The Lotti Nehring, the darling of the German box office. Of course, that put her in a different class. She put her glass on one side, since she was not a heavy drinker.

'My dear Lotti, I knew I had seen you before.'

Suddenly she had become a very important person, giving access to the upper echelons in the party, the really top people.

'Oh yes.' She said it without reproach or boredom; she was so used to being in the public eye that it no longer interested her.

'And I must join my regiment.'

'You North Germans, how you love war.'

'You forget, "The Chocolate Soldier" was written by a Viennese.'

'That was after the Prussians had beaten us. You seem to forget we have not had a victory since before Austerlitz.'

'All that will be changed.'

'Why people can't be content to re-create it on the screen?'

'Ah well, life is real you see, a nation must defend itself.'

'I can see that happening,' Lotti said ironically. 'Your Führer has been casting his eyes in our direction.'

'We are all of us Germans.'

'Are we?' Lotti replied quietly.

'I know I am. I can trace my family back to the Thirty Years' War on both sides. We come from Schwabia.'

'Then you are very lucky. We all know what a marginal case Austria is; Turks, Slavs, Bavarians even.' She laughed.

There was a poignancy about her that attracted Krause, in spite of himself.

'I can see you need a lesson or two in social philosophy.'

'How is your career, Captain?' She asked abruptly changing the subject.

'Well now, I cannot say it is good or that it is bad. I seem to be at an unfortunate point somewhere in the middle.'

She looked at him reflectively.

'If that's the case, it is possible that I could help.'

Krause's ambition overcame his immediate inclination, which was to thank her politely and do nothing more. It went against the grain, emotionally, to be under an obligation to a woman, so he said:

'I'm sure we can both help each other.'

'I'm sure we can.'

Lotti had been amused by the apparently open manner of the young officer and above all by his apparently naïve self-confidence. Everything in Berlin was getting more and more complicated since the enactment of the Nuremburg Laws. In the shadows were the Jews, desperate as only the trapped can be, not knowing why they had suddenly become the outcasts of the human race. In the back streets, there were Jews moving into the slum areas, selling their possessions at give-away prices, scrubbing pavements under the supervision of the SA, skulking past notices which forbade them to go to the cinema or sit on a park bench, grotesquely appearing in the vulgar cartoons of 'Der Angriff', generating an awful feeling of uncertainty. She avoided railway stations, frightened of the scenes she might be forced to witness. The uncertainty, the inexorable insecurity, increased her own nagging sense of guilt, since she was fully aware that in a remote parish register near Saint Anton there was an entry which had all the force of a suspended death sentence.

Usually, of course, she projected her public image of the sad, sophisticated, very feminine fraülein, who could outglitter and outcharm the best of Hollywood or Paris, especially Paris. Why is it, she asked herself, that German women are such cows? 'Küche, Kinder and Kirche', are all they're fit for.

Lotti remained at the studios with an open field, since the majority of actors and actresses who were any good, had made their getaway to more tolerant environments. She remained fascinated by Berlin, however, for she knew that it was German. On the other hand she recognized that she was an incurable, who might, at any time, break out with the symptoms of the final stages of a fatal and inescapable disease. She nursed her ghost, her shadow and to some extent her guilt, in silence. That is, until she met Krause.

When they became lovers she took an apartment for both of them in Tegel, the working-class suburb, because she did not want unwelcome publicity. The fact that Krause was apparently racially impeccable did not escape her, it was to some extent another slice of insurance.

She never knew how Krause had found out, maybe he had slowly read it in her reactions, or lack of reaction to what was being perpetrated daily in the streets around them, the smashed shop windows, or the yellow Star of David armbands. She suspected that he had found out, although she wasn't able to prove it until much later.

Physically their relationship was adequate, but what Lotti really wanted was for Krause to lie on the bed with her for hours on end just holding her, more like a frightened child than a woman. She did not want to be possessed or overwhelmed, just to feel secure. To begin with, Krause put it down to the exacting nature of her work.

'How were the lights today?'

He had learned that twenty thousand watts makes one perspire and feel tired just as much as being the constant subject of attention.

'They are very difficult, they make me feel, oh, so tired. Come and lie down with me, Liebchen.'

Krause also found that her public image was just as strictly controlled as her actual work. Her social life was really minimal, except for visits to open fêtes to aid the Sudetens, or some other worthy cause. But he also knew she knew the party hierarchy, though it was something she wouldn't talk about easily.

'They're running a security check on you, darling.'

Krause was shocked for a moment.

'They won't find anything. Why? Because of you?' She nodded and laughed.

'I'm important propaganda material, didn't you know? Especially with the Anschluss – the union of Germany and Austria. You see how important they think you are.'

Meanwhile, Krause had taken steps to confirm the opinion that he had been gradually forming that his mistress had something to hide. It only took a week-end at the public record office to find the dubious surname. Of course, nothing could really be proved one way or the other, but any bureaucratic enquiry was likely to provoke scandal. His motives were not, inevitably, disinterested; he was aware from the start that he was making use of Lotti, simply because he regarded that as being a natural relationship. He would advance his career at some time with her help. Now, if she did not agree he could make her. There was another factor; Krause was running out of time.

As the months went by, it became common knowledge that the Führer was intending to run the army down after victory in the east. Krause suspected that the Wehrmacht would recommend his early release, and he had missed the boat with the SS.

Krause had never made serious use of the power he knew he could exercise, awaiting the most advantageous opportunity. After all, he could have avoided his posting to the DAK with her help, but on the other hand he was an admirer of Erwin Rommel and believed that he could succeed in Africa. But now, with the Tiger Tanks, the time had really arrived.

They had had an interrupted, casual relationship for some years now and Lotti had never pressed for its formal extension; she was aware that the woman must produce a certificate of racial purity. While she did not think that this would prove to be an insuperable difficulty, it was a risk she was unwilling to take, feeling the cure to be worse than the disease.

She was therefore used to Krause's sudden arrivals and departures in and out of her life, and these eruptions, uncertain as they were, gave a certain stability. By 1942 things had gone from bad to worse with the increase in air raids.

Lotti thought that they were worse than the trains, and somehow as unjust, as though she was being punished for being innocent. The retribution the air raids caused was quite indiscriminate; the bombs fell on the just and the unjust. Admittedly Berlin had hardly been touched, but there were hair-raising stories from the Ruhr, and what was worse, there were no signs of the RAF discontinuing their offensive.

She was therefore glad to receive Krause's telephone call, and ordered what she called a special lunch. She was equally glad that he was serving in Africa rather than the Ukraine, since she had difficulty in imagining what life would become without the certainty of his occasional presence.

Food did not interest her particularly. However she thought it would be amusing to tease him by offering Beluga caviare and champagne; she also had a box of dates placed on the table.

Krause arrived punctually at 12.30 and she flung her arms around him, happy to feel his solidity.

She had dressed simply but attractively in a mid-calf morning dress, as a tiny gesture towards the war effort. She also wore the gold swastika bracelet Krause had once given her, since it contrasted well with the black of her frock.

Krause had never asked her for anything except her love, but today she sensed a purpose in his visit.

'You should have sent me a postcard from the Pyramids. Africa – the very name's romantic.'

'It's much better created in the studio, Liebchen. As with most other things the truth is not always bearable.'

Lotti took a step back before recovering her poise. His remark suggested a crisis of some sort; was he going to leave her? Had he found another woman? Krause looked approvingly round the apartment. A couple of things were new, a Persian rug that had found its way back to Berlin from the Russian Front and a signed photograph of Lotti with Dr. Goebbels at the première of her last film. If anything, the apartment was a little too modern and it bordered on the decadent. The most acceptable style of furnishing was always traditional, reflecting in its solidity and craftsmanship the truer Germanic virtues.

'Well,' she said a trifle anxiously, 'and what is it you have brought me besides yourself? Liebchen, it's so good to see you. The air raids are so frightening.'

Krause waited for a moment before replying:

'I want you to help me, you've said you would often enough.'

'Anything, anything, Liebchen, but no politics. You can't imagine how difficult things are getting, with everyone at each other's throats. I only survive because people want to see me.'

'It's not much; all I want is a movement order.'

'I don't understand.'

Lotti poured out a glass of champagne and began to drink it nervously.

'Listen, there are some tanks we need in North Africa. Don't tell me you can't fix it.'

'I mustn't, I mustn't if it means politics. No politics please. Oh Liebchen, how glad I am to see you. How's your poor wound?'

Then she added:

'What have you brought me this time?'

The major produced a small packet wrapped with red, white and black ribbon.

'A war trophy.'

'Oh.'

Lotti stripped the ribbon off with a nervous smile and removed the wrapping to find herself holding a small silver case. When she saw the Hebrew letters, she put her hand to her mouth, uncertain as to what she should say.

'There was a Jewish position we overran. Yes, they have Jews fighting in North Africa. I thought you would like to have it as a reminder; it has a special meaning to some, even though it's only Jewish trash.'

Heliopolis

WHILE Major Krause was waiting for the results of his string-pulling, Corporal Midgeley was also in a similar state of latency or suspended animation. His regiment had been so badly knocked about in the Gazala Witches' Cauldron it had been withdrawn from the line. That is, what was left of it. What puzzled and exasperated Midgeley was the fact that practically every unit had fought bravely within the general framework of the Gazala boxes. Casting his mind back to the briefing, he had attended with Captain Phillips, he suspected that the theoretical control exercised over the battle would only become actual given a static situation.

He realized that he was somewhat unique in his critical view, but experience had been his tutor, and more and more he was tending to rely on his own judgement. The difficulty was that the army system was based on a code of obedience which tended to discourage individual decision-making, particularly within the framework of an armoured regiment.

For the moment, however, Midgeley was happy to be riding in the back of a three-tonner from the holding regiment, where he had been ordered to report, to Cairo along with Thomson and Starski.

Half an hour after they had left the burning transport column, they had been picked up by another convoy also heading towards the wire, that marked the boundary between Libya and Egypt.

One of the things that Midgeley noted was the amount of men and equipment that was apparent, the further they withdrew from the front line. It was as though they were moving away from the apex of a pyramid and the further they descended the thicker the ground was with khaki.

Where they were now, watching the countryside like tourists, Egypt seemed like a great arsenal, with base workshops, huge store dumps, gun parks and line after line of MT; the whole of the British military war effort had been channelled into this surviving outpost of empire.

Thomson knew all the sights and, with the fear of death removed, was in high spirits:

'Look yonder, there's the tropical glasshouse.'

'Don't tell me,' said Midgeley.

It was a wire compound adjoining a Service Corps vehicle park but the wire, at least twenty feet high, was screened with sacking.

'Where's the firing squad?' asked Midgeley.

'Don't joke about it,' said Thomson, 'it can still happen if they find some poor, lost squaddie wandering behind the lines.'

Midgeley's remark had triggered off the nagging fear that lurked at the back of Thomson's mind. Authority in any form was to him malevolent, whether official or backed by the bicycle chain and razor of the back streets. In Thomson's grim Clydeside world someone was always waiting to get him. The fact that Midgeley was an NCO yet also seemed to be on his side most of the time never ceased to amaze him. His world had been peopled by warring gangs, only to be distinguished by their degree of hostility and viciousness.

He had had one job before the war, working as riveter's mate at John Brown's yard when they were building the *Queen Elizabeth*; his earlier memories were of the dole queues and dodging the rent man. He was aware, nevertheless, of another world to which he never could gain access; they had started to build in 1937 the gleaming concrete pavilions of the Empire Exhibition, to him an intelligible blueprint for the future.

He had visited it more than once, appalled at his own insignificance in the shadow of the buildings that housed the dominions and colonies and the various exhibitions of industry and art.

When war was declared most of the lads in his street had vanished into the Infantry if they were graded fit; or into the Service Corps or Ordnance if they were not. What diverted him from this sausage machine was that he owned an ancient Sunbeam motorbike, painfully acquired through endless scrimping and overtime in the shipyard. It had become the centre of his life and he had stripped and re-assembled the faltering engine time after time. A chance admission to this knowledge at his sketchy interview had immediately labelled him as a mechanic. Therefore, instead of ending up as a POW at St. Valery or Boulogne after the fall of France, he had been posted to Salisbury Plain and shown how to load a two-pound tank gun; that and other things.

The three-tonner hummed on in silence and slowed down as it passed an endless convoy of medium artillery.

'Guns,' said Starski and grinned.

'They should be up front,' said Thomson. 'Christ we could have done with the sods the day they massacred our lot.'

The road now edged towards the desert and Thomson suddenly said:

'There's a cage nearby.'

This time the wire rolled on interminably; but there were only a few prisoners huddled in a corner; just sitting.

'It's like feeding time at the zoo.'

Their look of helplessness moved Midgeley, but he remained silent.

'For you, Fritz, the war is over,' Thomson shouted as they rolled by.

'Don't get clever,' Midgeley said. 'It could happen to any of us, and we'd be glad of it.'

'Count me out,' said Thomson.

'Prisoner no good,' said Starski.

'He's the expert, he ought to know,' said Midgeley.

On the way back to the holding camp they had had a blow by blow account of Starski's war experiences, after he had scrounged a bottle of Alexandrian wine. Having been decimated in the Polish corridor, his regiment had been ordered back to Warsaw, and he had arrived there just in time to be captured by the Red Army.

After two years of working in a coal mine, close to the Arctic Circle, Starski had been released when the Germans had invaded Russia and had been 'repatriated' to the Middle East.

'No good prisoner; better finish. We don't take prisoners.'

Thomson sighed and turned away.

'We do though,' said Midgeley, but Starski began to mutter to himself and roll his head.

'Cheer up, Starski,' said Thomson. 'We're trippers in the mysterious East. Five years ago the plutocrats would have spent a fortune getting here on a cruise and it's all for free now. Take a look.' They were passing the Gizeh pyramids.

'Shit,' said Starski, 'a lot of old stone. It's too damn hot.'

Nobody would quarrel with him over that.

Suddenly they were in Cairo. Midgeley had seen the ramshackle streets before, and they were still strangely comforting in contrast to the endless miles of empty space he seemed to have lived through, punctuated by sudden death. The truck drew up outside the Kasr el Nil Barracks.

'This is it,' said Midgeley.

The three men climbed out of the back of the three-tonner.

The street was dusty and dirty but Midgeley didn't notice it. There were a group of Egyptians chewing sugar cane and wearing ghalabeers and the three were immediately surrounded by a selection of hopeful entrepreneurs anxious to dispose of their stock of brass ash-trays, fake antiquities and dirty books. It was curious, Midgeley thought, how little the Egyptians were involved in this war. It was clear that they were not a particularly warlike people, but their lack of involvement seemed to be total, apart from the subsidiary industries that had sprung up, such as the disposal of battlefield loot, robbing the dead or raiding British supply depots. To Midgeley, the Egyptians were some kind of accident who happened to be living at one end of a war. They didn't even seem to care when the British soldiers sang rude songs about their pleasure-loving king.

Starski brushed aside the salesmen, there would be plenty of time for that later. He said to Midgeley:

'A Tommy told me you could get vodka in this town at a place called Shepherd's bar.'

'He was having you on, that's not for the likes of us.'

'What do you mean?'

'Starski, old chum, Shepherd's bar is for officers only, you have to have a tie.'

Starski said:

'After all that sand I need a drink.'

Alcohol was a commodity that was not hard to find.

Thomson was still not very sure about Starski. He had preferred Evans, simply because they had survived together. Besides being a foreigner, so far as he was concerned Starski was 'x', the unknown, except that he seemed intent on taking risks.

They went to an Arab cafe and sat down, pink and scrubbed in their neatly pressed KD. Their belts were blancoed the light green of the Tank Corps, even Starski's, who seemed to have seconded himself without any regard for the technicalities.

'I'll have a beer,' said Midgeley when the owner appeared. 'You better get them zhubib.'

'Zhubib, zhubib,' said the owner.

'Yes and a Stella.'

An Arab in a ghalabeer was nonchalantly scattering water over the cafe floor to make it cooler.

Starski leaned back and said:

'This is the life.'

Thomson said:

'Better than the coal mine. Christ, back in the UK they give you the option, put on the khaki, or go down the mine.'

'Coal mine is shit.'

'I'll believe you, thousands of Stakhanovites wouldn't.'

The cafe owner arrived with a bottle of zhubib, a more potent variety of Pernod.

Starski didn't have too much trouble putting away half the bottle, but then he had a special technique.

'It is like vodka, except there is aniseed. In Poland we drink vodka so.' He filled the glass neat to the brim and tossed it back.

'I'll believe anything,' said Thomson. The heat, the strain of the last few weeks had marked his escape route towards oblivion. The more he drank, the happier he became.

Starski said:

'Let's go to Shepherd's.'

'He still doesn't understand,' said Thomson. 'It's out of bounds to ORs, they even have a redcap patrol.'

Starski ignored him.

'Where is this Shepherd's?'

Midgeley had been watching the people walking along the pavement; most of them were in uniform, but not many of them looked like soldiers. There had been various kinds of cavalry and many of the supporting arms. They seemed to be quite happy strolling in the sunlight, oblivious of the fact that Rommel's panzers were now knocking on the gate to Egypt.

'I am calling a taxi.'

Starski got up unsteadily, joined unwisely by Thomson.

Midgeley said:

'You have been warned.'

Starski said:

'Who wants trouble? I only want a drink.'

One of the strategic advantages that the British had, was virtually unlimited supplies of petrol from Abadan, where it was shipped to the oil refineries at Suez. A proportion of it found its way into the civilian market and the Cairo taxi service.

Starski seemed to be quite drunk as they climbed into the taxi.

'Look,' said Thomson suddenly. 'Real white women.' Two nurses were walking down the street.

The taxi driver did not seem surprised when Starski told him to drive to Shepherd's.

Midgeley said:

'Why do you want to drink the whole time, God, I could do with a square meal.'

'What?' said Thomson. 'Gyppo food, all that oil and spices.'

Midgeley said:

'You're all bloody mad.' The idea of breaking into Shepherd's did not appeal to him at all. It would be filled with a bunch of 'B' Echelon from GHQ, with pips up, re-enacting 'Vile Bodies'. The class system no longer interested him after a year in action; he could only judge people on their reactions under stress and whether or not they could do an adequate job, whatever their title, everything else was a lot of balls. So far as he was concerned the people in Shepherd's were civil servants in uniform who didn't count.

Starski lingered outside Shepherd's staring at the Egyptian waiters. A cavalry officer wearing a scarlet forage cap looked at them curiously as he was on the point of going in, and Midgeley remembered to salute just in time. The captain came over to Starski, who had omitted the compliment.

'What's your unit, soldier?'

Midgeley said:

'He won't understand you, sir. He's Polish.'

'Oh? Don't they teach him English in the Tank Corps?'

Midgeley said:

'You'll have to excuse him, sir, he's just been up at Gazala, we found him wandering in the desert, all his mates were killed, he's bomb-happy.'

The officer looked uncertain. Midgeley decided that he didn't like the look of him, probably a new posting. He was too fat and clearly fancied himself in the poncey uniform. Well, he would have his nose rubbed in it if he found himself commanding a Valentine, awash with blood and guts and a phantom driver. The knowledge that he was almost certainly right gave him some satisfaction.

'The fellow's drunk,' said the officer sourly. 'I don't know what the hell you chaps are doing hanging about Shepherd's, there's lots of other bars.'

'Ah, but you see, sir, there aren't many west of Kilo 99.'

'Alright Corporal, I'll let him off this time.' The captain made his way into the hotel.

Midgeley had noticed, out of the corner of his eye, that a couple of rozzers had been eyeing them. They looked very regimental with their closely cropped hair, tailor-made shirts, cheese-cutter redcaps, white blancoed belts, revolver holsters and lanyards.

'Jesus,' muttered Thomson, 'we've bought it this time.'

The pair of them strolled over to where Midgeley was frantically signalling for a taxi. One was a sergeant and the other a lance jack.

'Pay books,' said the sergeant, who had a soft West Country accent, 'and then let's see your passes for luck.'

'We're waiting for our officer, sergeant,' said Midgeley desperately.

'You're fucking not, Corporal, we've been watching you;

you're making a fucking nuisance. What about that shower?' He pointed to Starski. 'What is it? The wild man of the woods of Long Range Desert Group?'

'He's from the Polish mob; he's come with us down the line.'

'Oh yeah? It'll be jankers or whitewashing coal, at a minimum, if he wants to be clever. What's your mob, soldier?'

Starski grinned at them.

'Feld Gendarmerie?'

Starski moved very fast, delivering a punch to the sergeant's gut that left him coughing helplessly against the wall, his red cap in the dust.

Then Starski butted the corporal just below the heart, making animal sounds. The corporal collapsed.

'Christ,' said Thomson. 'Let's get out of here.'

They scrambled into a taxi.

'You shouldn't do things like that,' said Thomson feebly. Starski spat out of the window.

'Why not? They're the same in any language.'

'I'll tell you why not; we could end up de-fusing fucking mines or cracking rocks inside the glasshouse perimeter. The rozzers never forget a face.'

'Balls,' said Starski, 'we won't see Cairo again.'

'I hope to God, I do.'

'Next time, it is Tripoli,' said Starski definitively, 'finish Germans, you'll see.'

'You know a nice place,' Thomson asked the taxi driver.

'I know number one berry nice blace. Just your ticket, soldier. Lots of Janes.'

The three of them almost died laughing.

Midgeley was fastidious about his sex life and he had never joined the queues outside the Egyptian whore houses in Sister Street, wanting something a little more polished. Nonetheless at that moment he found he had a burning urge to copulate. He didn't analyse the drive too deeply; perhaps, after seeing so much death, he was wanting to compensate. The taxi man drove for some distance before entering a street that was marked 'out of bounds'. Nonetheless, Midgeley suspected that it marked a well-beaten path. Soon the taxi turned off into a maze of side streets to draw up at a place called 'The Blue Cockatoo'.

'Fifty ackers, Lord.' Midgeley gave him the money.

Then they got out and went inside.

At first it didn't seem much. It was badly lit and a chain curtain made from bottle tops hung across the door.

'This is more our style,' said Midgeley. 'Egyptian working man's club, I almost feel at home here. A place for everything and everything in its place, back to the servants' hall.'

A couple of girls in frilly satin evening dresses eyed them as they went in.

'We're one light,' said Thomson.

'I'm pissed off with drinking,' said Midgeley. 'I want to eat.'

'Go ahead; so who's stopping you,' said Thomson.

The room was gaudy and gimcrack, as though the owner had invested as much as he possibly could to make it look expensive, and that wasn't much.

'Bring on the belly dancers,' yelled Thomson and started to shout:

'Singing Nelly put your belly close to mine.'

'For Christ's sake,' said Midgeley, 'I can't take you anywhere; they'll throw us out.'

'Balls. Who cares a toss anyway. Stana schwoia King Farouk . . . Bardin . . .'

The owner came over and said:

'You want?'

'Tomato omelette,' said Midgeley. He had been dreaming about this meal for the last three weeks in the desert.

'Berry kois, berry good.'

'OK. Tomato omelette. Steaks?'

'Alright,' said Thomson. 'Steaks too.'

They also ordered a bottle of zhubib for Starski and the girls came over. They looked nice girls, young and well-scrubbed.

'What's your name?' Thomson asked without ceremony.

The girls laughed.

'Me Jane from *Daily Mirror*.'

'Me Tarzan.'

Midgeley was mildly irritated at Thomson's habit of noisy masculine self-assertion.

The other one said:

'Irene.'

'Goodnight Irene, goodnight Irene; I'll see you in my dream,' Thomson shouted.

'What about me?' Starski asked rather plaintively.

'You can have Deanna Durbin. You find your own girls,' said Thomson.

The girls ordered two John Collins for themselves.

'Hey, you Breetish soldier. Kill any Eyeties.'

'They've got the wrong war,' said Thomson, 'that was way back in '41.'

The girls laughed. It seemed they would laugh at anything. Both were short and fat, like well-fed farmers' daughters. They had slightly crinkly hair.

Jane said:

'We know King Farouk.'

'I'll bet,' said Thomson who was starting to sober up. 'Wait a minute, pull the other one, it's got bells on it.'

'You have many wives in England, Johnnie?'

'In different rooms, one for each day of the week.'

Irene pouted, pushing out her over-painted lips.

'You make fun. Tell me, do you think I look like Esther Williams, if I wear a swimsuit?'

The owner decided it was time for them to have some suitable background music and put on a worn 78 of Lilli Marlene.

When the omelette arrived, Midgeley found that he could hardly eat it; there was a hard feeling of excitement inside him, similar to the feeling that he had when he went into action. At the same time he was storing away every detail.

'Christ,' said Thomson. 'You look intense Corp. I can tell you got a beat on.'

'Haven't you? Haven't we all? Look at Starski, he's panting for it.'

'Poor old Starski, and he hasn't even got a dancing partner.'

'Does he want a partner?' asked Irene.

'Christ, we all want partners, I can tell you.'

'What's the matter? You had a bad time?'

'Something like that,' said Midgeley, suddenly remembering the blazing Matildas back in the Cauldron.

'OK we fix; we gib you good time.'

'I can't wait,' said Midgeley.

Starski filled another glass of zhubib and proposed a toast: 'Arseholes to the panzers,' before downing it in one gulp.

'We gib you berry good time,' said Jane reflectively.

Another girl soon arrived for Starski. She too had crinkly hair and a nice smile. The girls started to fidget impatiently.

'What's up? What's the hurry?' asked Thomson. 'Do they want to do us now?'

Starski was getting sentimental.

'Once I had a wife in Gydinia. It was a church wedding. She is strict Catholic.'

'Fuck off,' said Thomson. 'Who wants to talk about marriage at a time like this? How did you get invited anyway?'

Starski only laughed.

After a time the tension became unbearable; even the girls were caught up by it.

'Where do we go?' asked Midgeley.

'Upstairs; do you want a bath as well? It is one hundred piastres extra.'

'First things first, maybe later,' said Midgeley.

Although the house seemed solidly built from the outside, the woodwork was antique and the stairs creaked as they went up them. Midgeley felt the tension rising inside him again until he was ready to burst. It wasn't so much that he wanted to fuck; but he wanted to get rid of this terrible tension and he knew there was only one way.

The girls took off their clothes in the room upstairs. It was all very democratic and Midgeley, as he struggled with the leather laces of his boots, considered the difference that clothes made.

Once the clothes were off, there was nothing more to hide, just in the same way there could be no more evasions. Midgeley, the fear of death standing behind his right shoulder, knew that he was going to fuck the pants off these girls. It was worth risking everything to do just that, even the barbed wire and armed sentries round the VD ward. It was as though he had to prove to himself that life was basically good, and that there was more to being born than trundling across the desert in a prison of petrol and explosive waiting for the end of the world. He didn't really care who it was, but he had Irene first.

None of the soldiers felt like being private about sex, even Thomson, that was another extraordinary thing; it was in no way secretive and they were all sharing a common experience. Midgeley had it off every possible way and the girls didn't object, even when he indicated that he wanted a blow job. They ended up by switching round. It was as though they had broken into an 'excuse me' at the NAAFI dance, but a hundred times more meaningful.

At the end of it all Midgeley felt drained, yet curiously alert, relaxed yet slightly taut. Most of all he felt alive; it was a good feeling.

'I wonder if that bugger Anderson gets it?' Thomson enquired, when they were waiting for the bath. Irene had brought them little cups of bitter-sweet Arab coffee.

'That's probably half his trouble. No, he just likes camping about, being superior. After going to a public school his moral sense has been confused, he's caught up in all kinds of pointless rules and regulations. He'd probably think he'd be thrown out of the regiment if they ever caught him on the job. Conduct unbecoming and all that.'

'Poor sod,' said Thomson and lit another cigarette.

'Poor sod nothing,' Midgeley replied, but he wasn't really interested in anything about Anderson and his futile honour code, what was more important was whether they would get the new M3 Grants when they re-equipped, or end up with clapped-out, battle-weary Crusaders, that were likely to drop their tracks every fifteen miles.

Morava Valley

Special Transport Train Wehrmacht Z/Pkw/18970 rumbled across the cantilever bridge that crosses the Morava river, two hundred kilometres to the south of Belgrade, into the station at Nis, just as dawn was breaking. It was therefore possible to read the slogan; 'Räder müssen rollen für der Sieg' – The Wheels must turn for Victory – painted on the engine tender.

It said much for the determination, or obstinacy, of Colonel Krause that he had got this far, forcing the journey by night with the special authority, given by the signature on the movement order, in the teeth of the Rail Control Office: a subsidiary administrative department of the Commanding General Serbia.

Their anxiety was understandable, in view of the increasing partisan activity in the western mountains that lined the railway running from Croatia, on the Austro-Italian frontier, to Macedonia on the border of what had been formerly Greece and Yugoslavia.

At Nis, the train came to a halt with a signal against it; but this was not a preliminary to clearing the line and switching the transport train south to Leskovac, the next town on the route, and away from the alternative track up the Dragoman Pass due east to Sofia.

In the station itself, thirty-eight low loaders, carrying the menacing silhouettes of the Tigers, ground to a halt, cushioned between a dozen box-cars and carriages to the front and rear of the train. In the half-light, five hundred tank crewmen and administrative back-up, cooks, fitters and armourers, stirred under the dim station lights and went back to sleep.

Colonel Krause glared at the gorget and orange tabs of the Oberfeldwebel from the Feldgendarmerie.

'What the devil's going on?'

'Beg to report trouble down the line, Herr Colonel.'

'Eh, trouble? What kind of trouble?'

'The usual trouble, terrorists.'

Krause's sallow face grew pink with suppressed rage. He was under a priority directive from the Reichsminister himself to take the newly formed 550 Independent (Heavy) Tank Battalion to the Piraeus in the shortest space of time and ship for Benghazi, and here was an NCO blocking the route. He wanted neither transport officers nor terrorists to foul things up, let alone NCOs from the Feldgendarmerie. Then they were joined by a transport major.

'I'm going on,' Krause said cripsly. 'I've got orders.'

'I shouldn't advise it, Colonel.'

'This is neither the time, nor place, for good advice. Now we've been stopped, I want an armoured engine and an engineer detail, in case we really do get held up. Also please get on to Luftwaffe liaison, I need air cover.'

After he had seen the movement order, the major knew better than to argue, and went off to telephone.

Krause shouted out:

'Dieter come here, I want you.'

A young captain commanding the forward tank company jumped from the train; he was wearing the black panzer uniform and floppy beret.

'Now listen to me; there are some terrorist bastards down the line, so it's alleged, and we may have to take care of them. Have all the Tigers ready and crewed; tell the tank commanders to fire at discretion if they have a target; and I want a machine-gun mounted on every turret.' Dieter went off to relay the order.

The back of the train was taken up with box cars carrying spare battle tracks and ammunition. Prior to shipment, the Tigers had to be fitted with special narrow transport tracks, otherwise they were unmanoeuvreable. Krause had also taken the precaution of loading up with 50,000 gallons of fuel; he knew about the Italians and had no intention of finding the battalion helpless and immobile once they arrived in North Africa.

'Also I want the Quad 20mm flak guns made ready,' he shouted to Dieter.

'Yes, Colonel.'

Fifteen minutes later, the train pulled out of the station into the early morning mists. In normal circumstances, the countryside would have been beautiful, but to Krause, the valley was oppressive and unsafe after the open little plain surrounding Nis.

It was forty-six kilometres to Leskovac, an hour's journey, at the speed they could travel at. Above the cloud base, Krause thought he could hear the vibrant hum of Messerschmitts. Once a Storsch broke through the cloud and circled low over the train. Krause had taken up his position in the First Company's command tank at the front of the train; the wirelessman was netted into the Luftwaffe frequency and Serbian Movement Control. For a time he heard nothing, and then the first piece of solid news came through:

'Hullo, Mayerling, there's a cable cut, the telegraph between Skopje and Vranje by the sixth kilometre marker.'

Krause took up the microphone:

'Mayerling here, keep me informed.'

The train continued to snake along the valley of the Morava river, the contours on each side becoming more and more acute, so that the double line was forced to keep criss-crossing the river. At each bridge, as the Oberfeldwebel had said, there was a pill-box with fire lanes cleared through the surrounding undergrowth.

Beyond Vranje the sun chased away the folds of mist, so that was not possible to see the Jabos darting backwards and forwards across the valley as they screened the train. Then the radio spoke again.

'Mayerling, there's a column.'

'Not our people?'

'X Group is beyond the railway and across the river; these damned terrorists operations are never easy to contain.'

Krause made no comment, as the duty officer went on to address the Messerschmitts:

'Better chase them off, Blue Staffel. Search and destroy.'

Krause said:

'Are they coming or going?'

'Who knows? At any rate they are keeping away from the railway.'

The train was passing through mist again, since the track now climbed towards an area of high broken country that marked the beginning of the borderlands between Macedonia and Greece. Krause was pleased when he checked their position on the map, for once they had crossed the old border at Dojran there was no likelihood of their being attacked inside Greece. The twin locomotives strained up the gradient with their heavy load, and began to lose speed, so that now it was possible to examine the undergrowth at the side of the track, and even look up the wooded slopes that enclosed them.

Suddenly there was a great hiss of steam from the two locomotives, as they applied their brakes and came to a halt. Krause peered forward and saw that they had come to a rockfall at a bend in the river. It all looked very normal, and would account for the disconnected telephone lines. A mass of red earth and rock had slithered down the side of the valley, right out across the track, part of the landslide ending in the Morava river. The hills were blanketed in silence and, now that the mist was down, it was impossible to rely on the fighter bombers.

Krause hurriedly reported what had happened.

'I'll divert "X" Group. Be careful, there hasn't been any heavy rain over the last few days, so why should there be a landslide?'

'I'll be careful,' said Krause. 'You can bet your life on that.'

A flat truck and a crane preceded the first engine. The engineer sergeant clambered from it and took one look before turning to Krause:

'That's going to be a pick and shovel job, Herr Colonel.'

Krause raised his glasses and carefully examined the railway verges in the drip, drip, drip of the fir trees, but could see nothing suspicious and no disturbance in the ground.

He called up the forward Panzer Grenadier Section on the command channel.

'Leutnant Woll.'

'Yes, Colonel.'

'There's a job for you . . . you'll need . . .'

He never completed the sentence, since what was required

became self-evident as they all heard the high-pitched chatter of a PPSH 7.62 Russian sub-machine-gun, followed by the hiss and crump of a light mortar.

Then he heard Woll comment:

'You can say that again.'

'Watch out for mines . . .'

It was probable that the verges, at least, would be sown with mines in anticipation of a rapid deployment across the flat ground that ran towards the river.

'Keep to the upper slope.'

Krause remembered that Woll knew his job, since he had served with the 'Gross Deutschland' on the Don. He switched to the command channel:

'Odd numbered panzers in the first Company fire to the right, and even to the left, to give the hikers covering fire.'

A hail of bullets lashed through the undergrowth, shaking the trees and shrubs with an invisible wind. The tanks mortared the areas of dead ground with their grenade launchers.

It was not long before Krause decided that it was either a suicide attack or a mistake, some terrorist being sufficiently unwise to pull the trigger accidentally, when the safety catch should have been on. As was to be expected, the first to fire started a chain reaction. No terrorist group would be crazy enough to take on a battalion of tanks, even on transporters. For a moment he wondered whether this might not be a deliberate act of sabotage planned from London, but since the movement order was only seventy-two hours old, how could London possibly know anything about it? Nevertheless, Krause was glad that the petrol tankers were almost half a kilometre behind.

He spoke to Woll:

'How many?'

'Probably no more than twenty or thirty at the outside. I think they've guessed they've bitten off more than they can chew.'

'They would be pretty stupid not to.'

However, two of their attackers apparently had not. Each carried a slivovic bottle filled with petrol, resin and tar and a rough fuse, and had crept along the back of the rock face to the rear of the Panzergrenadier Company, where it directly overlooked the centre of the train. Thirty feet below were ranged the open hatches of the Tigers, where the machine-gunners stood waiting for something to happen, since Krause had given them no orders to batten down.

The first partisan was known as Mikael, since he had abandoned his name with his previous life; he was thirty-eight, and until April 6th, 1941, had had a successful conveyancing practice in Belgrade. The destruction of Belgrade by Luftwaffe Stukas had caused the deaths of his wife and two children, along with 17,000 others. The facts of life, or rather death, had left him no alternative but to join the partisans, where he had not immediately been made welcome. The second partisan was a fourteen-year-old boy, who, a week earlier, had been compelled to witness the execution of his father and the ritual rape of his mother and two young sisters by a Bulgarian patrol, who suspected that the village had given aid to Tito. The boy had been spared because of his extreme youth. He had been with the partisans six days, during which time he had spoken only once.

The partisan group had, it is true, intended to block the mainline as a diversion, to allow the group spotted by the Jabos to make their getaway after attacking a small artillery field park and maintenance depot at Buyanovac, ten kilometres away. They were all amazed and frightened by the size of the fish they had caught. Krause had been correct in thinking that the initial burst of fire had been unintentional against such odds. Unintentional was perhaps the wrong word, since the perpetrator had been the fourteen-year-old boy.

The first Molotov cocktail was dropped lovingly by the boy. The aim was accurate and the passage through the turret hatch only partially deflected by a sudden movement by the machine-gunner. The bomb exploded with a roar inside the tank, igniting 92 rounds of 88mm ammunition, together with some two hundred machine-gun rounds. The resulting explosion ripped through the battle compartment and the driver's compartment, reducing the crew to mincemeat. The machine-gunner was, however, lifted by the force of the blast, his trousers burning, thirty feet into the air, like a curious, spark-trailing, rocket; during his ascent his body was dismembered by the violence of the explosion, so that he was no longer recognizable as a human being, and the shreds of his body were scattered through the trees.

Strangely, the explosion that rent the inside of the tank only twisted it on the flat truck, such was the strength of its 100mm armour, and the adjacent tanks suffered no serious damage.

The second Molotov cocktail was not so accurately placed by the ex-lawyer and it exploded against the open hatch, covering the body of the machine-gunner in flames, although he was already dead, killed when a glass bottle fragment severed his carotid artery. However, the running flames of petrol eventually ignited the hydraulic fluid, which controlled the turret traverse mechanism, jamming it hopelessly with the main armament fixed drunkenly at an angle of forty-five degrees, so that it projected well over the side of the line. In this case, only the driver was badly burned around the neck and shoulders and the gunner was able to bring the fire under control with the fire extinguishers. Thirty seconds after the first attack, both partisans were killed by three accurately placed stick grenades. The grenade which killed Mikael exploded against the rock face and caused a shower of fragments, one of which blinded a panzer grenadier who had instinctively started to run back towards the sound of the explosions.

These were the only casualties.

Quite naturally, Colonel Krause was furious that a couple of ragged civilians should have damaged his expensive equipment, and vented some of his emotion on Woll.

'I hope there won't be any more surprises like that.'

'No Colonel, those two were heading away, I didn't have enough men to cover the rocks.'

'Well, they can help to clear the line. We have a boat to catch.'

As he turned away the engineer sergeant told him that they would have to use oxy-acetylene equipment to sever the long barrel of the Tiger, jammed at an awkward angle, well beyond the track. Otherwise there would be a serious accident at the first tunnel they came to.

Special Transport Train Wehrmacht Z/Pkw/18970 was not the only train to be affected by this incident. Six months earlier, the plenipotentiary of the Reich in Greece's Office had taken steps to resolve the local Jewish question along the lines laid down in various secret directives. This did not present any overcomplicated problem, since the Jewish population in Greece was largely centred in the major towns and, therefore, was easily identifiable.

Train number eighty-seven had already begun its journey to the Polish resettlement area of Auschwitz from Thessaloniki, when the line had been cleared to allow freedom of passage for the Tiger tanks. The Jews in the cattle trucks had already been in transit for two days with a minimal amount of water and without the doors being opened. Conditions had become, not unnaturally, indescribable. The train was shunted on to a siding outside Skopje, where it waited.

By the time Z/Pkw/18970 had rumbled south, half an hour later, two more passengers had died; one from suffocation and another from a pulmonary embolism; one woman had become insane.

Krause had almost forgotten about the terrorists, as the tank battalion rumbled on through the pine forests. The valley reminded him of the countryside around Garmische Partenkirchen, where the Wehrmacht/Hitler Youth summer camps had often been held. Naturally he was angry that one of the Tigers would require considerable attention, and that the other would have to be dropped off at the Piraeus. He consoled himself with the consideration that any route was preferable to Italy, with the inefficiencies, graft and politics of the Commando Supremo in Rome and the risk of substantial delays at the Naples docks.

Wrinkling his nose, he lit a Hannover as they passed that other terrible train at the Skopje siding; the stench was unbearable even at twenty-five metres, but the rumble of the tank transporters, in some measure, blotted out the awful inhuman clamour that escaped from each of the cattle trucks, and somehow reminded him of the buzzing of flies. For a moment he remembered Lotti and then shrugged, flicking the butt end of his cigarette unfinished on to the ballast below.

The forest on either side was silent. The mountains beyond looked cool and damp. Once past Skopje they could almost relax. There would be very few terrorists.

South of Alam Halfa

CORPORAL MIDGELEY could feel a thin film of sweat mixing with the dust on his forehead and then drops began to form. It enraged him but there was not much he could do about it. To open the visors of the Grant would bring only temporary relief and increase the drift of dust. The 75mm breech block beside him was warm to the touch. The metal walls around the sponson were filled with racks of black-nosed ammunition, also warm, and covered with a thin film of dust, their caps ringed red, yellow and green to indicate HE, smoke or armour piercing. Without moving his head, Midgeley could feel the heat radiating through the curve of the two and a half inches of armour plate, cooked by the desert sun.

Long experience had made his movements subconsciously deliberate within the confined space, although the Grant was roomy against other tanks in which he had had to fight. He was squeezed to the right of the driver between the breech shield and the starboard wall. Behind him sat Morton, the loader, ready at a moment to take a round from the rack and swing it smoothly into the breech block as Midgeley pressed his eyes to the gun sight, his hands on the elevation and limited traverse.

The Grant's gun had the disadvantage of a maximum fire field of fifteen degrees to the right or left. What was more important was the formation of the beads of sweat. For one thing, they attracted flies which were an added distraction and lowered the safety factor. As he commanded the gun, this particularly interfered with the use of his periscope, Azimuth indicator and elevation quadrant. He knew that if he was called on to lay the gun with his instruments, a few vital seconds would be lost as he wiped away the film of sweat, which must be done with care, before applying his eye to the eyepieces, Since traversing must be accomplished within strict limits, this could mean the difference between life and death, for in this kind of warfare, he who saw first and fired accurately would win. There would be no second chance with a PKW 25.

The tension that this sequence of thought produced gave Midgeley the same taut feeling in his throat and across the pit of his stomach he used to get when he went out rabbit shooting at the farm in Warwickshire before the war. There was only a more exaggerated realization that a momentary indecision would result in disaster with the target missed. The difference being that the other gunner would get it in first.

After a year in the desert, he was all too aware of this probability. He had seen many burned-out tanks, apart from the recent Matildas, and was familiar with the consequences of failure. Under these conditions his own personal discomfort became secondary and only relevant insofar as it affected his efficiency. He could comfort himself with the thought, for what it was worth, that other men in earlier centuries had fought in equally onerous conditions. But even the collision of armed knights, in armour that was too hot even to touch, would be determined by the one that struck first and accurately.

And so he cleaned the eyepieces once more, with the little strip of towelling he reserved for that purpose, and wiped his forehead yet again, before intently searching the white glare that opened out beyond the constriction of his periscope prisms.

The desert spread out into nothing ahead of them. Somewhere to the north-west lay Gazala, the zenith of a line that had been outflanked by Rommel. To the south, the stony ground rose to a scarp, which ran brokenly westwards, a jagged line of ancient rock that was as fretted and filagreed as a weatherworn cathedral.

Since before dawn, the Grant had stood in the shadow of a buttress which cast a harsh black shadow, across it. Westwards, the scarp sank back into the plateau, rising haphazardly in spines of low-lying rock three or four miles below the horizon line. It was this feature that interested Anderson, the troop commander. In fact it interested them all a great deal, since the gently undulating plateau, at that distance, could well provide cover for a battery of German 88's.

Morton, the loader on the other side of the gun, had the bovine ability almost to cross the threshold of sleep, at times like this. Yet Midgeley knew that he would respond correctly and instantly to any command he might choose to give. Then with relief he heard the order to stand down over his head-set. Dawn was two hours past and the desert had changed long ago from pastel pink to the white shifting brilliance of the morning.

However Morton's apparent torpor concealed a state of mind that even Anderson, who was supposed to be an expert in these matters, had been unable to fathom. Morton had been on leave at his home in Bootle during Liverpool's May week blitz of the previous year. Going to the pub one evening to try and locate cigarettes he had become involved in Merseyside's worst air-raid. The consequences of which, in his case, had been quite traumatic.

On that particular evening the BBC Light programme had been interrupted once more by a local announcement: 'An air-raid warning has been sounded, an air-raid warning has been sounded, an air-raid warning has been sounded. Message ends.' Then Tommy Handley resumed his light-hearted triologue with 'Funf' and Mrs. Mopp, as the air-raid sirens began their inharmonious warbling moan.

Nobody left the pub. But the tension rose as the business-like bark of the ack-ack echoed like exploding tyres and was followed by the inexorable drone of the Dorniers and Heinkels. After this everyone grew quiet or began to make unnecessary jokes as the first stick of bombs fell and the lights flickered.

'When you hear the whistle you're OK,' said the man standing next to Morton in a pork-pie hat, rather nervously. 'I don't like public shelters, filthy places. What I say is, if it's got your number on it you've had it whatever happens.' Morton said nothing. It was his first air-raid since he had been called up a year earlier and had spent the intervening period in camps from Yorkshire to Dorset. Nevertheless he had a strong urge to return to Jamaica Street, ten minutes walk away.

The next stick of bombs was closer and rattled the glasses behind the bar. Morton picked up his forage cap and stumbled into the black-out.

Outside the streets were in total darkness except for the faint glow of the flickering searchlights that picked their way across the sky, and the sudden flash and crash of exploding bombs. An AFS fire engine ground slowly along, its headlights filtered blue by the slitted masks.

Morton groped his way along the pavement through the silent streets. The silence was punctuated by the crash of exploding bombs and the patter of shrapnel on the slate roofs. On the corner of Castle Street, Morton was flung to the ground by a nearby explosion. Immediately he heard an erupting roar as the gas main ignited and the whole scene was starkly lit by blue-yellow flames. Deafened by the explosion, and shaken by the blast, he picked himself up in time to see two parachutes slowly swinging through the red sky. At first, he thought that these were escaping enemy bomber crew, but he was quickly disillusioned.

The first parachute disappeared among the roofs before erupting as a tall red target indicator column. The second parachute was a one thousand kilogram bomb, principally composed of six feet of Dinitro benzine and ammonium nitrate, which exploded on impacting with the cornice of the Baptist chapel that stood at one end of Jamaica Street.

In a second Morton's world changed to an inferno of blast-flying bricks and glass. Nursing his cut hands he began to run up the familiar hill to Jamaica Street.

Half of Jamaica Street had ceased to exist. The road was a four-foot rubbish tip of joists, plaster and window sashes, so that as he turned into it the regular line of back-to-back houses suddenly became foreign, if not hostile territory. Number fifteen had become just another heap of rubble. He was crying as he began to search the smoking ruins for any sign of his mother, his father, and his sister Lil.

In this way Morton lost his family five weeks short of his nineteenth birthday. Up to then he had not taken the war seriously. It seemed more of an adventure and escape from the monotony of factory life that inevitably lay ahead. The SB 1000 parachute bomb had changed his life as surely as the lives of the fifty-seven dead, shocked and disabled it had left behind.

After compassionate leave, when he had stayed with an aunt in Southport, he had acquired a curious air of fatality, as though he had nothing further to live for. In the regiment his moodiness and his bad luck made him into something of a Jonah. However he had survived several battles in the interim. Midgeley had done his best to shake him out of his withdrawn silence to become an efficient loader, though sensing the seam of negative fear that lay beneath.

'There's no point,' Morton would say. 'The family was the bloody lot to me, we were that close. I mean, of course, I would get my own place sometime but it was so sudden like. It would have been better if I'd scrubbed round the fags, at least we'd have all gone together.'

In the end Midgeley adjusted to Morton's moodiness, as he adjusted to most things when he had to.

Anderson crouched down through the turret hatch.

'OK, men, we can brew up. Fleming can stay on wireless sentry.'

Midgeley straightened instinctively when the troop commander's legs vanished through the hatch above him, resenting his ease of exit, although there was a second hatch immediately behind the gun crew. Removing his head-set he carefully manoeuvred himself back and up.

'We can put out the net, Corporal.'

The dun-coloured hessian rags would break up the metallic, angular outline of the Grant, that stood in high profile above the rock, reminding Midgeley of a mobile castle. He moved expertly behind the turret to the engine grating, and carefully began to unstrap the netting that lay along the starboard sand shield above the track, draping it over the White Knight assortment of ironmongery, welded to the forward faceplate, and the spare track links on either side of the hull. Armour-piercing shell was activated by any obstacle, and the added thicket of metalwork increased the odds in favour of survival where the hull wall was only one and a half inches thick. The netting gave the illusion of shade.

When he had finished at the side, Thomson, who manned the turret armament, helped him unroll the netting forward across the 37mm gun and the 75mm barbette, draping it forward. As they worked, he heard voices and recognized them as those of the squadron commanders and the colonel. They were coming in on the 'A' channel of the SCR 508 set. Nobody seemed unduly worried about keeping wireless silence.

'No sign of Jerry, Tom, from where we're standing; no tracks, but there's a line of shot-up transport to our right; looks Italian, could have whiskers growing on it; there's also a beat-up German half-track.'

'Any mines?'

'Mostly hard standing . . . unlikely.'

'Nothing moving up front?'

'Wide open and no dust; the ground's broken but not too much cover. We're boxed in to the south.'

'Relaxez-vous, then. We're still waiting for the infantry.'

'Shouldn't they have been with us at first light?'

To the north a battle was supposed to be taking place near Bardia and Sollum. The tank regiment was holding the flank.

'What sort of infantry?'

'I don't know, Tom, probably the Free French.'

Midgeley and the others were there to protect the southern approach to Egypt, in case Rommel decided to throw the kind of counter-blow he was so fond of and hook round and through to the north; rolling up their rear to the Trigh Capuzzo and the road to Alex.

Fleming, the radio operator, had opened the starboard port so as to be within earshot of the wireless, and taken a jerrican from the line strapped above the exhausts. He was now filling a blackened ration can with three inches of sand preparatory to pouring in the petrol. Having completed this operation, he carefully positioned the ration can against a stone in the shadow and threw a lighted match on it, before placing a mess-can of water on top of the improvised stove. At that distance, with his steel-rimmed glasses and ascetic sharp-cut features, he looked like an intellectual monk, in contrast to the youthful flabbiness of Morton and his glistening Brylcreemed hair. Brylcreem was the only pleasure Morton seemed to allow himself. At Heliopolis he had declined Midgeley's invitation to visit Cairo and had simply sat on his bed studying his Bible and Scripture Union card.

Midgeley watched them, trying to gauge their respective moods; it was typical of Fleming to leave his post and begin to brew up in order to ruffle Anderson. Then he became aware of a distant hornet-like buzz. He did not change his position and neither did any of the others. Only Thomson asked anxiously:

'Is it one of ours?'

'Sounds like a fucking Storsch.'

'Could mean eighty-eights. A spotter plane.'

'Where's the bloody Raff?' Fleming asked impatiently.

'How the hell should I know? Screwing a bint in Alex most likely,' Midgeley replied.

'You should know all about that,' said Fleming, with the slightest hint of monastic moral superiority.

'Shut up, you two,' Anderson snapped nervously, in a forlorn attempt to release the tensions they all felt. But his edginess was just another irritant.

The long-winged plane dipped lazily to their right, as though it was giving a harmless air display before releasing balloons or bags of flour. Half-relieved and half-fearful, Midgeley heard the 508 set again; for a moment he wished they would stop, in case the observation plane was listening.

'There's a Jerry on the swan in my neck of the woods searching for targets.'

'I'll get through to Air Support.'

'Yes, Tom, please do that small thing. There's . . .'

The squadron commander's voice was abruptly cut off by a sound like a snapping guitar string, followed by an unreal cacophony of squib-like explosions. Then Midgeley heard another voice shout:

'Christ, Mother . . . let me out of here.' And then an agonized scream. The set went dead as Midgeley heard the colonel say:

'Better get the medical jeep and the padre forward, Chris. You have his map reference.'

Another voice said incredulously:

'This is BOSCO to Sunray. I think Jumbo's been brewed up.'

'We'd rather gathered that.'

'Can't see properly for the bloody smoke. There was a green sighting tracer.'

'Well bloody well don't move, young man, or you'll catch the same dose.'

'Fucking roll on,' said Fleming loudly in his best upper-class accent. 'What a way to start the day.'

Midgeley tried briefly to focus his mind on the crew in Jumbo's tank, recalling that he knew one of the sergeants in 'A' Squadron, who had admitted to being a pigeon fancier. He felt a tight knot of rage and fear in his gut. Morton, on the other hand, didn't seem to have taken any of it in. As the Storsch droned off, Fleming bent over the boiling water in the mess-can and threw in a handful of tea and sugar. Midgeley said:

'It must have been an eighty-eight.'

'You've got a gift for the bloody obvious,' Anderson snapped.

They heard the wireless again:

'There's three hurt. I'm taking them back to "B" Echelon.'

'I wish to Christ it was me,' Morton said unexpectedly.

'Get on to Recovery. You're in charge BOSCO. Where was he hit? What happened? Sitrep please.'

'This is BOSCO to Sunray.' The young officer's voice sounded formal and strained. 'Could be anti-tank bearing green seven to ten. There's a ridge where Jerry could be holed up.'

'Could be . . . could be? Could be holed up bloody anywhere. I'll try and raise the Hurribombers again.'

Midgeley felt that soon, too soon, very soon, they would be told to move. There had to be panzers up there, and they would have to run the gauntlet, with their high profile, of that eighty-eight anything up to ten miles off, as helpless as a beetle crawling along a railway line. Suddenly the Carnation milk in the tea turned his stomach.

'Where's the Gunner FOO we need twenty-five pounders.'

'Char's up,' Fleming shouted. 'Always time for a second cup.'

Anderson was standing nonchalantly in the shadows; he was the sort of officer who took a professional pleasure in seeing that his men were attended to first, with the kind of patronizing undertone that Midgeley couldn't stand; particularly as somebody would be expected to hand him his mug.

But at least the Storsch had vanished. To the north a flight of Hurribombers skimmed across the desert at five hundred feet.

'Jammy bastards,' remarked Midgeley. 'I bet they'll brew up sod all. I hope to God someone's marked a bombing line, or they'll be having a go at us.'

'I bet they're Polaks,' Fleming shouted from inside the tank. 'Bomb-happy Polaks. Next thing we'll have the whole Luftwaffe storming down our necks, just after we've been invited to dig in hull down.'

Starski said:

'Feelthy Breetish. Feelthy Breetish.'

Starski had not moved from the driving-seat since Anderson had given them the order to stand down, because it made very little difference to him whether he was inside or outside the tank. Fleming took no notice of Starski's comment; neither did Anderson appear to hear these remarks and put down his mug for someone else to pick up.

'I'm going forward; I've a hunch about that eighty-eight.'

Midgeley had to admit that Anderson looked very military in the brown suede sand boots, striped coloured scarf and goatskin coat, fashionably dressed in the tradition that had developed under the first successes of 1941 against the Italians. He could not, however, see what good it would do; it seemed a somewhat theatrical gesture, but he realized that Anderson was a master of drama. At least, he didn't apparently want anyone else to come along.

'D'you want me, sir?'

'No thanks, Midgeley, I can cope. You better be on hand here in case there's a signal.'

Anderson strolled off westwards gripping his ash walking-stick and picking his way carefully round the boulders, his pistol holster bumping against his thigh. He disappeared and re-appeared twice between ridges.

'Where the hell's the mad bastard off to now?' Fleming asked. Although he had shaved that morning, the patina of dust on his face gave the effect of five o'clock shadow. Fleming hated officers, probably, thought Midgeley, because Fleming had failed to get through a WOSB himself. What made it worse for everybody was that Fleming's father had been a brigadier in the Indian Army. Fleming removed and polished his steel-rimmed glasses, his features pinched and pointed with permanent discontent. Fleming felt his situation keenly.

'Maybe he's kidding himself he's on some scheme behind Lulworth Cove.'

'Poncey bastard.'

Midgeley said gently:

'Well, he can usually look after himself; that time in a minefield, he walked us out.'

'He wants to prove something, they all do, that we're shit and he's the bee's knees. It doesn't stop him from being a poncey bastard. What are we supposed to do? Once they spot him out for a stroll, they'll start focusing their binoculars really tightly.'

Midgeley shrugged. Although he secretly agreed with Fleming, this was the kind of risk they were always running.

'Come to that thirty odd tons of bloody Grant isn't so easy to bury.'

Midgeley didn't want to think about it; an error of judgement made by someone five years ago and thousands of miles away could still spell out personal disaster.

The Grant lay behind the boulders under the camouflage net like a strange stage prop, inert and meaningless until the men who worked it climbed inside. Thirty tons of iron and steel overpainted in matt dun ochre, with little patches of orangey-red where the primer was coming through. Midgeley was constantly amazed at the amount of room the Americans had allowed for the crew of six. Compared with a Valentine or a Matilda it was like the Ritz Hotel. The only personalization that had been allowed by Anderson was a name, chosen by Anderson, which Midgely secretly disapproved of. Being essentially a theorist and an academic, Anderson had borrowed the title of one of the 1916 Mark VIII's at Bapaume, calling it 'Jabberwocky'. He had explained this by telling them that tradition was the lifeblood of the cavalry, and that they were motorized cavalry. Midgeley would have preferred something more down to earth and homely, like 'Vera Lynn' or 'Coventry', his own home town. He said to Morton:

'While he's away, you better check the sump and the oil seals.'

'That's not my job, that's Starski's.'

'It is now. Besides Starski probably can't read the manual.'

'Bloody hell.'

Midgeley had no wish for anything to go wrong due to lack of maintenance. As an afterthought he added:

'Also the tracks and the idler wheels.'

'I hope there aren't any poxy scorpions.'

'Help you to take your mind off things. Anyway you only get them near water. Think how nice it'll be in that shade.'

The possibility of scorpions was remote in this part of the apparently waterless desert, which could not even support scrub. Nevertheless scorpions were a perpetual fear to Morton. In his days at Jamaica Street he had developed a hatred for the parasites and rodents that waged constant war with the people at the bottom of the scale; rats, mice, nits, bugs, he had a loathing for them all. Not that there had ever been any at Number 15, his mother had been exceptionally houseproud, it was the stories he had heard in Standard Four at the primary school. Here similarly, in the Western Desert, the minor enemies of man were at one remove, but on the other hand more sinister; there had actually been bed bugs in the mosquito nets at the transit camp, and there had also been scorpions, with scorpion spiders the size of a sparrow, and sand snakes; all these terrified him. And yet it was somehow comforting that this lesser fear deadened the hopeless memory of the awful Merseyside air-raid.

Morton carefully unrolled the ground sheet and pulled himself under between the tracks to check for oil leaks; his instinct for order, and fear of immobility, overcoming his distaste for desert insect life. A few minutes later he pulled himself out.

'Nothing.'

'How about the track shoes, Skouse?'

'Good for another two hundred miles at least. They seem OK.'

The tracks of a medium tank had a life of about one thousand miles, before it was necessary to replace them.

Anderson had absented himself for ten minutes now, but somehow it seemed like ten hours. They were all subconsciously straining for his return, not because he was in any way popular, but because his absence constituted a threat to them all.

Midgeley screwed up his eyes, looking over to the right to try and make out the hulls of the other tanks from 'J' troop, but was unsuccessful. The heat was shimmering so much that it was impossible to be certain of anything. Once he thought he heard what could have been the rev of an engine.

As he waited for Anderson to come back, Midgeley shaved, taking the piece of smooth concave glass from his pack to give an edge to his razor blade. Blades were in short supply. The razor blade was almost his only personal possession, that and a couple of photographs of the family and the farm. He had a high regard for his privacy and didn't want to compare notes with others about his people and girlfriend. Possessions didn't count for much, bundled, as they were, into the crew-box at the back of the tank. The necessities were either free or in short supply.

When they had disembarked at Suez, after rounding the Cape, since winter was ending they were issued with khaki drill. Apprently the ordnance depots did not recognize the fact that, at night, temperatures still dropped to forty and below.

It was alright in the tank, but at the first opportunity, Midgeley equipped himself with a pair of battle-dress trousers and a clean Afrika Korps smock he had found in a half-burned-out laundry wagon, after an air-raid on the coast road beside El Hammam. It made him feel uncomfortable wearing the German uniform and he was always careful to put on his beret and web belt when he was on guard, but at least it kept him warm.

As he shaved, his reflection shimmered brightly, dulled by the yellow sides of the can. It told him little that he did not know already about himself. He was in his early twenties and that made him an old man by wartime standards, at least anywhere near the front line. His face had a calm, reflective look, the result of many considered decisions that had resulted in life for him and death for others; just which piece of ground to move behind, when manoeuvring hull-down, and just where to cross an open stretch of desert when there were eighty-eights about.

One of the first and most important decisions he had made had been along the St. Omer–Bourbourg Road on May 27th, 1940. The Mark One Matildas, with which he had been, were finally abandoned near Arras, although not before they had acted as a brake on the German advance towards Dunkirk and the Channel coast. They had engaged the SS Totenkopf Division, without proper replenishment and without the tank transporters which would have enabled them to withdraw.

Since their maximum range was eighty miles, it could have been expected that they would have been abandoned very much earlier by the BEF under the hammering pressure of the Stukas and Rommel's armour.

At first Midgeley had tagged along with the reconnaissance company, but the Whippet light tanks had run out of fuel and were also abandoned west of Béthune. A CSM told him to find his own way back to the coast.

'You're a likely lad, Midgeley, get out of it while you can, and take my tip, don't listen to any bullshit about surrender, not with those SS Totenkopf buggers about; once you're in the bag, you're better dead.'

Midgeley found an abandoned rifle and two full ammunition pouches and requisitioned a bicycle he found in a bombed-out estaminet. It took him a day to reach St. Omer, which he found crowded with 'B' Echelon, drivers, cooks and storemen, who had had a role in giving logistic support to the men in the front line. They were a rabble because they were leaderless and in a totally unpredicted situation.

Battle sounds continued from the direction of Hazebrouck where a line regiment was still maintaining a holding action.

'Over there,' said the redcap at the checkpoint.

'Is there transport?'

'Do as you're told, son.'

There was a group of dispirited, demoralized Other Ranks in a sawmill yard. A service corps sergeant was busily taking names under the eyes of an engineer captain.

'What's going on?' Midgeley asked a signals corporal.

'They're jacking it in. There's no point; we're cut off from the coast.'

Midgeley heaved his bike over the wall at the back of the sawmill and wheeled it off across the misty fields. The next morning he got to Gravelines and rode in to Dunkirk along the hard damp sand the receding tide had exposed.

He only knew how right he had been afterwards. Apart from the ugly rumours about the SS massacres of the Norfolk Regiment, if he had obeyed the order to surrender and given in, accepting his fate with all the others, he would have been pacing the wire somewhere in Silesia, breaking up scrap truck axles with a sledge hammer, or building the Autobahnen. It had been so simple to cross that wall with his bike, but none of the others had even contemplated a decision which seemed perfectly obvious. The lesson of that blue-skied May morning had been burned into his soul.

He wiped his face with his towel. His mouth was sensitive and intelligent, the obscenities which were a feature of active service passed him by, although he rationalized them as the fighting soldier's assertion of life in the face of continuous death. He had earned his corporal's stripes through calculated thought, together with an ability to bring together, in a short time, groups of illiterate, disgruntled conscripts; men who had been pitchforked into a situation that they usually resented, thousands of miles from home, and who also brought their problems with them.

Midgeley caught his reflection once more. He had arched eyebrows above clear blue eyes, that were almost feminine, but he was self-contained rather than sexually aware, so that any homosexual overtures that had been made to him were simply disregarded. His chin was determined, but he often expressed himself indirectly to measure the reaction of the person to whom he had given a command.

Next he changed his shirt. His turnout was as near spotless as possible, since water was available for drinking, cooking and washing in that order. It made him angry that the inside of the tank accumulated the body smells of five men who slept and sweated in their clothes. He had served with a number of armoured units and respected the purpose of cleanliness. A demoralized soldier, who does not care what he looks like, is working against himself. If he does not accept his own value in the framework of the battlefield, the enemy certainly won't. This brought him another memory of Dunkirk; Sergeant-Major Bennett marching his company of grenadiers down to the beaches in regimental order alongside the milling, disorganized columns of the defeated British Army. It was not just sentiment, in his opinion, but an assertion of will; the Grenadiers would survive and have their brasses polished, even if all hell was let loose against them.

It was for this reason that it was automatic for him, when circumstances allowed, to shave, wash his clothes in petrol, crease his trousers by sleeping on them, replace his buttons and use all the little tricks he had picked up, which contributed to his own self-confidence and therefore his survival. There was one thing in particular that he disliked about the desert; it was difficult, if not impossible, to have a proper wash.

Morton said, his black hair Brylcreemed back above his white, townbred face:

'The officer's taking his time.'

Midgeley thought that Thomson should take over from Fleming as wireless sentry, and said so.

Fleming climbed out of the Grant with a kind of passive resignation.

'The batteries are fading.'

'Now you tell me.'

'I can't help it, can I?' His cultured voice was prickly with the refusal to accept responsibility.

'Why can't they send some more up?'

'You know as well as I do, I couldn't break wireless silence just for that.'

'Well for Christ's sake what happened last night when we were in leaguer? You know it's your job to get the batteries changed, Fleming.'

'Yes, but we were late in and Sergeant Nicholls didn't turn

up last night, did he? And neither did the cooks. They don't want to know, now we're all out playing blitzkrieg.'

There was six hours' life in a freshly-charged battery. Since yesterday, theirs had been running for slightly over that limit.

'You'd better get on to Squadron, they'll pass it on to Nicholls.'

'What do I do? Send a carrier pigeon or book a Don R?'

'Think of something; you could go for a walk, for example.'

Fleming licked his lips uneasily. Midgeley went on.

'What's happening anyway?'

'Only wireless silence. I caught the BBC news though, there's a big battle we were winning yesterday outside Bardia.'

'I'm glad to hear it,' said Midgeley. Bardia was some fifty miles to the west of the position they were holding. 'These bloody war correspondents will believe anything.'

'I wish they'd kept fucking wireless silence this morning,' Thomson said. 'Jerry's bloody crafty with his intelligence. I bet that Storsch was switched into our net; that's how 'C' Squadron bought it; I'll bet.'

'These officers are all so fucking casual,' said Fleming, 'they seem to think it's a scheme half the time. Like Anderson's flaming, poncey bedroll; it's a wonder he didn't bring a Windmill girl wrapped up inside.'

Anderson's bedroll was a source of irritation to all of them, reflecting, as it did, the privileges of commissioned rank. It was, in fact a goosefeather sleeping bag, covered in oiled silk. This slid tidily into a canvas valise on which Anderson's name had been neatly stencilled; the rest of the crew slept under dusty, torn, army issue blankets.

Midgeley didn't make any comment, although he agreed mostly with what Fleming had said. However, he was still half-reassured because over the last half hour there had been no shots, no sudden roars of exploding HE, no whine of mortars.

Fleming was still brooding about Anderson:

'If he was such a genius he should have done something about the wireless last night. Maybe he's got too bloody clever and disappeared up his own arsehole, like the Egyptian shite hawk in the ballad, never to be seen again.'

Midgeley said:

'Maybe the shite hawk's the answer to the Stuka.'

They all laughed nervously, for it was a standing joke; any decrepit bi-plane with RAF roundels that drifted across the sky was acclaimed sarcastically as the answer to the Stuka. So far, the British had not come up with an alternative to that demoralizing weapon, although the Hurricanes and Spitfires saw them off quickly enough if they caught them dive-bombing. Fleming said:

'In the end, they'll maalesh the whole fucking issue, that's what I read in my crystal ball. We'll be sent off to nowhere again to await contact; Christ where's the Free French shower, and another thing comrade, I don't see any anti-tank portees and not even a twenty-five pounder. I'm all in favour of the mighty cannon's roar.'

Everyone knew that the most effective answer to the eighty-eight was the British twenty-five pounder gun.

'Aren't we all,' said Midgeley.

He peered carefully forward once more into the shimmering heat haze. The desert was empty, or rather the desert seemed to be empty. Death could suddenly strike, silently and without prior notice from ten miles off. Or a dot in the sky would turn into a wing of Stukas. If they were to go forward, the little boulder in the track ahead would suddenly erupt, to smash the suspension and track, and gouge holes in the thin armour that lined the base of the tank. Immobile, a tank was an iron coffin, hardly capable of any adequate self-defence, and the only thing to do was to bail out. Midgeley always preferred the ambush, the stalking game, to the head-on charges apparently favoured by cavalry officers in perpetuation of Balaklava and High Wood on the Somme. Midgeley always looked for cover, the only thing he wanted to perpetuate being himself.

Thinking such unpleasant thoughts brought Midgeley back to Anderson. Anderson was a carbon copy of the local gentry back in Warwick, although the edges were a little more blurred. He was probably going to end up as a provincial solicitor, having started off as the son of a successful businessman. Armoured regiments were now less fussy about whom they accepted. Perhaps it was this that annoyed him about Anderson; much of the time he seemed to be acting a part which, underneath, he knew didn't really suit him. The unfortunate thing was that most of them recognized it.

He guessed that was one of the reasons why he had been assigned to Anderson's tank by Captain Phillips, the squadron commander, who wanted some sort of reliable back-up in the event of an emergency. Probably he was not overconfident about Anderson.

Glancing through the draped camouflage hessian he caught the flash of something silver, three or four hundred yards out ahead. It could be a bayonet, and if that were so then there would be infantry forward. He looked again to the extreme right and the spine of rocks, where, on the horizon, he thought he saw a plume of dust. It was difficult to tell since, by now, the desert actually seemed to merge with the sky at the horizon line.

Midgeley called to Thomson:

'How's the set?'

'Running out of steam, Corp.'

'Did you get through to Nicholls?'

'There's not enough power to transmit.'

'Bloody marvellous,' said Morton uneasily. 'No bloody officer and no bloody wireless. Next, it'll be no bloody POL and then no bloody water.'

'Turn down the gain,' said Midgeley, 'at least we want to stay in the picture for as long as possible. We could always try flag-wagging.'

'Yes, Corporal.'

'In the meantime I suggest you rig a jumper lead from the engine batteries.'

'That may not work, they're twenty-four volts.'

'Just do it, Fleming, just to please me. Then we can tell them back at Squadron about Anderson.'

There was a whisper of distant signals on the 508 set receiver. The batteries were dying.

'What now?' Fleming asked.

'We'd better hoist the bloody pennants for a start. Green, yellow and red read: "Enemy in Sight".'

'Christ! Where are they Corp?'

'Eyeties about four hundred yards ahead. Won't they be pleased when Starski turns the ignition key.'

'What about the officer?' asked Thomson.

'What about him?'

'You reckon he bought it?'

'No, my guess is they jumped him, and he's heading for the Duce's nearest barbed-wire hotel.'

Thomson persisted:

'Is it ice-cream vendors out there, or real soldiers? Could be the fucking panzer grenadiers. The master race.'

On their right they heard the sudden distinctive roar of engines. Midgeley said:

'Who knows? That's the starting gun; now climb aboard and and tell Starski to get going.'

'Fleming's trying to sort something out with the RT.'

Fleming had taken a pair of jumper wires off the engine batteries and fed them up into the cupola of the fighting compartment. He said:

'We'll have to halve the voltage or we'll blow the set.'

'Think of something, but don't do that.'

Midgeley was aware of an uneasy racing feeling at the pit of his stomach, realizing that he was in command; not only in command but virtually on his own.

'We'd better keep up with the troop, Starski.'

'Alright Corp.'

While Starski warmed up the radial engine, Thomson and Morton helped Midgeley meticulously secure the camouflage netting and strap it down firmly in a collar round the cupola.

'Right driver, retire.'

On their flank a dozen of 'C' Squadron's Grants moved forward, scurrying westwards in leapfrog, the first line halting hull down under the cover of a stony ridge.

The Grant had a fixed 75mm gun which could only be traversed outside a narrow arc by moving the tank, although there was enough latitude in the sponson casement to bring it to bear across ten degrees. Two .303 medium machine guns were mounted in the cupola beside the 37mm.

A green verey arced up against the sky from the nearest

Grant a hundred yards away. Starski saw it through his open visor and said:

'That'll be for us. That's Sergeant One Hung Low.'

Midgeley was glad that the 'B' set was giving no trouble and that there was still enough power to keep communications functioning inside the tank.

'It would be that mad bastard,' Fleming shouted.

Midgeley liked Sergeant One Hung Low, respecting him as a successful realist. His real name was Cooper, and he was a hard case, a tough nut, an individualist who always kept a Bren handy as his personal weapon, since it was the only automatic, capable, in his experience, of stopping a man.

The 340 h.p. engine roared in reverse as the rubber track shoes ground back down the thirty degree slope and 'Jabberwocky' pitched and bucked away from the natural depression, behind the emplacement of boulders where it had been lodged. Midgeley leaned down to Morton and said:

'You'll have to lay and load most likely, so put one up the breech.'

'What sort Corp?'

'HE. If there's anything it'll be infantry. I'll give you the wire soon enough if there are AFV's.'

Fleming said:

'Why can't we sit this one out, Corp? After all now the officer man's vanished and the radio is U/S have we got to go on playing heroes?'

'You think we should wait for recovery, do you? Fancy scrounging radiator water? These other sods will press on to Tripoli for all we know. I should forget about playing Beau Geste.'

Thomson said:

'The corporal's right, Fleming. Who wants a one-man war? Not this soldier.'

Fleming said:

'OK, OK. I only asked, whoever's laying and loading's got a big responsibility.'

If he was expecting support from Morton he was unlucky. Morton had relapsed into his usual pre-battle gloom, with a fatalism which denied any kind of protest.

Midgeley said:

'Everyone's important. You'll be alright if you fix that set and there's no time to argue. It'll be a piece of cake. After demob you're on your way to a BSc so just extract your digit.'

Fleming shut up after that.

The fact of the matter was that Midgeley had only revealed part of the reason for his decision. While it was true that he didn't fancy being cut off from the rest of the squadron, his emotions were stirred by a mixture of fear and a kind of gnawing urge to action.

This state had been partly induced by the fact that he hadn't had a letter from Pauline. Usually letters arrived in batches of six at monthly intervals. Last Wednesday there should have been something. Morton had had a letter from his aunt, so the mail bags couldn't have all gone down in the same Malta convoy. There was a particular kind of uncertainty that he hated and that was uncertainty involving sex. He wasn't sure whether he loved the girl or not, sometimes she had a harsh, proprietary manner that he resented. She was a doctor's daughter and it had been the contrast between her brittle virginal exterior and the secret fire that burned within that Midgeley had, for the most part, enjoyed. She would never have given in, had she not known of his overseas posting. The fact that she still bothered to write to him meant that it still worked for her, and that was the most flattering and powerful reassurance. No letters might mean that it had ceased to work, or that she had found someone else, and Midgeley could no longer console himself with his memories, out here, a million miles from nowhere. His pride and his urge to self-assertion could not bear the threat, so he was more than willing to bury himself in activity.

He was able to ignore Fleming's comments, standing on the tank commander's shelf with the hatch open, absorbed in a mixture of fear and exhilaration. This was always the commanding position, the picture that the war photographers preferred, of the confident, dominant commander, with the wind ruffling his hair on top of his mobile castle, riding aggressively into battle. Midgeley also realized that it was the most exposed and dangerous position.

The pennants still fluttered from the aerial but Midgeley

reckoned that, by now it was stale news, and that the advance was the result of some new tactical assessment. There had been no reaction from the rest of the troop, although Midgeley guessed that the others must have realized that their wireless was out of action. Everyone was much too busy trying to make out what was ahead, nudging forward at a steady fifteen miles an hour, while cautiously trying to keep what cover there was between themselves and the hostile silence.

As the line of armour progressed, it was clear to see that they were on the extreme left flank of a loose crescent of tanks. Midgeley carefully watched the ground ahead and told Thomson where to go, keeping to the hard, windswept limestone, rather than the sinister, unpredictable sand where mines might be buried. The desert rose and fell in a series of uneven ridges, the crest limestone with the dips between sand bunkers. Sometimes Midgeley ordered Starski to halt halfway up a reverse slope, as he did not wish to present 'Jabberwocky' too frequently as a target. Suddenly a smokeless, dull, red flash flowered from the left-hand scarp, followed by a resonant, occluded thud. One Hung Low's Grant wavered and slithered round from the force of the projectile, into a little rocky outcrop.

'Hell's teeth, hold it Driver,' Midgeley shouted. 'There's a PAK.'

'Must be close,' said Fleming. 'Oh Mother, it couldn't be more than three hundred and that would be pushing it.' Midgeley could hear his teeth chattering down the intercom.

The attack by the anti-tank gun seemed to be a signal for the whole of the desert to open up in front of them with small arms fire and machine-guns. Midgeley's throat went dry and his stomach tautened with fear.

'Jesus,' Thomson shouted. 'We need those Free French bastards or some guns to make it safe.'

'Drive on,' Midgeley ordered.

Midgeley considered the nature of the attack from the edge of the scarp to their flank. It indicated a defilade and the automatic tactical reaction would be for the line of English tanks to veer to the right, away from the anti-tank gun.

On the other hand it was an unnecessary attack, quite conspicuously so. A good commander would not have shown his hand so early. It was almost calculated.

'Driver, bearing red two forty.'

That course would bring them back towards the scarp, contrary to the direction the anti-tank gun had shepherded the main body.

'Fucking roll on,' said Fleming. 'Into the valley of death . . .'

'I marked it,' said Morton suddenly.

'They'll mark us more likely.'

'Give them a three-quarter-second air burst.'

It was almost at the acceptable fuse limit, but the muzzle velocity was over two miles a second.

'You're cutting it fine.'

'Just do as I say, Morton. Shoot in your own time, but be quick, we're closing range.'

'I'll give them anything you tell me.'

There was a very definite tension inside the tank, they were all afraid. A rifle bullet ricocheted off the front armour and Midgeley pulled down the hatch, using the periscope as the roar and recoil of the 75mm gun slapped through the Grant, and the empty case crashed down on to the steel floor, filling the fighting compartment with explosive fumes. A dirty puff of smoke cottonwooled near where Midgeley had marked the red flash.

'Try two degrees over left. Keep the bastards' heads down.'

Now the slope ahead was silent as though the infantrymen that were facing them regretted the attention they were attracting. To their right One Hung Low's tank crept forward, it could not have been badly hit.

'He's a trier,' Fleming commented, 'I'll say that for him.'

Midgeley watched One Hung Low trying to catch up with the crescent now half a mile to their right.

'Christ, he's a mad bastard.'

'What about the Teller mines?' Starski asked.

'The ground's too hard.'

'Always a bloody optimist, aren't you Corp?'

By now they were on the edge of the scarp, climbing

slowly up the ridge. A group of olive-overalled figures detached themselves from the ground and headed left. Thomson gave them a burst with the .303 machine-gun.

Thomson's stomach was also taut with excitement and he too was afraid. Some of the figures dropped as he traversed the gun.

'The buggers have got the wind up.'

Fleming said:

'Maybe our new leader isn't such a stupid cunt. Maybe he did some good with those airbursts.'

As he spoke there was a clang and a shock wave that sent them all sprawling as a solid shot penetrated the frontal armour at an angle to the left of the barbette, drilling two neat holes in the front and side of the tank. Midgeley's ears rang with the crash. Starski began to mutter fiercely in Polish.

'Keep shooting for Christ's sake Morton,' Midgeley shouted.

They were now sweeping along the ridge, following the rest of the armour. Midgeley scanned the ground ahead through the periscope. Everyone was very quiet. Midgeley was puzzled, for there had been no second shot in their direction. As he watched the scene ahead One Hung Low's Grant dipped and swayed through a belt of sand and then abruptly halted in a puff of dust, pivoting on its starboard track. The hatch covers opened.

'That was a mine, I told you so. Oh Christ!' said Thomson.

'Keep firing,' Midgeley shouted excitedly.

One Hung Low's tank lay silent, indifferently askew. The mine had shattered the first bogie and the herringbone. As Morton bracketed his airbursts over the ground a hundred and fifty yards ahead the small arms fire stopped.

'Now what?' Fleming asked.

To the north and away from One Hung Low's Grant, the other tanks were still advancing but curving off to the north and ignoring the infantry pocket. Midgeley wondered whether they were not letting themselves in for something rather worse. It was as though they were being channelled into a fire lane, flanked by the ridge with its anti-tank guns screened by infantry. There might be worse things at the end of the channel. Midgeley said:

'Keep going, Starski.'

'Bearing is different.'

'I know, press on along the scarp.'

'Christ,' said Fleming, his teeth chattering again. 'I'm not a bloody volunteer, you know. I haven't put in for any gongs.'

Nevertheless the tank rolled on; Starski jinked it in a zig-zag path.

Midgeley calculated that the positioning of the PAK anti-tank gun was not without significance. It could mean that the minefield would grow thinner against the scarp, since, probably, the German engineers had not had enough time to do a proper job. The anti-tank gun had been a device to head them off, and it could even be a bluff, the corridor to the north was probably mine-free. The scarp itself would most likely be held by Italian infantry.

'Fire smoke, Morton, fire smoke.'

From what he could remember there was not very much wind. Already the crescent to the right was blurred by the dust trails thrown up by the advancing line of Grants. He wanted smoke to overrun the infantry ahead. It was a calculated risk to go out on a limb, but he preferred it to the risk the others were running.

Morton obediently dropped a cluster of smoke shells to their left.

'Steer 200 green, Starski.'

By taking that bearing they would gain a little cover from the re-entrant masking the ridge beside them. They passed a thicket of rusting wire and a pile of jerricans. The shooting ahead seemed to grow panicky with the smoke.

'What about the fucking mines?' Fleming shouted.

'Why should you worry? There's smoke if we blow a track.'

'You are a fucking hero.'

Midgeley made no comment.

'Just stick to the high ground, Starski.'

'Like a leech.'

As Starski inched along, Midgeley could feel all their fear from the fighting compartment.

Ahead, there was nothing to see but smoke. As the Grant rumbled on, Midgeley quickly ran over the events since dawn, the interminable waiting, the silence, the solitary Storsch, Anderson and the radio traffic that drew no fire. More and more it seemed to him that they had been lured into a trap whose teeth were anti-tank guns and panzers. Midgeley alone had refused the invitation and they were now overrunning the infantry positions. So far, there had been no mines; probably the Italian sappers, through lack of material or time, had concentrated on the left-hand side of the corridor.

Thomson said, putting a bold front on it:

'I see weapon pits. There's nobody in them.'

Midgeley said:

'We must be in the middle of the bastards, put down HE.'

The Grant rolled over a wide belt of wire and Midgeley told Thomson to keep his finger on the button of the .303 machine-gun as he glimpsed more olive-overalled figures slipping back through the smoke.

But he did not see the PAK 75 until it was almost too late. The emplacement was ringed with a half-circle of stones, the long barrel of the anti-tank gun rakishly parallel to the ground.

At the moment he saw the menacing silhouette, with its crouching gun crew, the muzzle brake was tipped by a blinding white flash and the shock wave of the penetrating solid shot smashed him against the turret race as it entered in front of Fleming, slicing through the sloped armour to the right of the barbette. The shot, at a velocity of a mile a second, flashed across the fighting compartment to the filter panel, shattering the water expansion tank and ripping another hole through the engine louvre as it continued. The Grant slewed wildly under the impact as Morton toppled headless off the layer's seat. The tank filled with smoke as the rear ammunition rack began to smoulder, the white-painted interior hull walls now sprayed with a fine patina of blood.

The fearful clang of the penetrating shot had almost deafened Midgeley. He worked the 37mm gun wildly beside Thomson, as Fleming sprayed a CO_2 hand extinguisher to dampen the flames that already had begun to flicker dangerously across the ammunition rack, while Starski, moving the engine into higher gear, charged the emplacement twenty yards ahead.

Midgeley felt the starboard track crunch into the metal of the PAK's six-metre barrel, as the Grant hovered for a moment on the edge of the emplacement before its twenty-three tons screamed down on to the shield and breech block. Underneath he could hear screams from the crew.

Then Starski moved the engine into bottom gear through to neutral and then reversed, systematically crushing the emplacement and everything that was in it, as he shouted:

'Kaput, Germanski soldat, Kaput, kaput.'

Midgeley bellowed:

'Stop that, Starski, go forward.' But Starski took no notice, systematically ploughing the remnants of the gun into a shambles of stone and blood. Midgeley heard the ineffective clatter of small arms fire against the hull and turret, as impotent as rain against a concrete roof. He traversed the 37mm gun and started to spray the ground ahead. Just as suddenly, Starski moved into second gear and advanced grinding down the trail.

Through the dust and smoke, Midgeley could see a group of vehicles, which were now ablaze, one of them disintegrating in a fountain of exploding ammunition that plumed out smoke trails.

Midgeley shouted down the interphone:

'Press on, Starski, they'll have this position marked on their range cards.'

Starski, singing in Polish, obediently went forward, his face white, and beaded with sweat, following the tracks that marked the path of the blazing vehicles.

'Jesus,' said Fleming. 'D'you want to win the war single-handed? Where we off to? Agheila?'

Midgeley could see that he was white with shock. The floor of the tank was sticky with Morton's blood, and he looked down with revulsion at his own blood-covered overalls, feeling sick. Then he shouted:

'We'll have to stop for replenishment.'

He skirted round what was uppermost in all their minds, Morton's mutilated body flopping beside the gun at every lurch of the Grant. Only Starski didn't seem to notice. Starski stopped the engine. In the silence that followed they reacted nervously, overwhelmed by the confusion of the last five minutes.

Fleming tried to make a joke:

'What happened to the rest of him?'

Thomson said:

'He always was an untidy bastard.'

Fleming suddenly became serious:

'Why can't we find the others?'

Midgeley shouted in exasperation:

'We've been a sitting duck once; I don't want to try it again.'

'You must be mental Corp, we don't stand a chance. We could have brewed up; we could all be dead.'

An image of all the burning, destroyed tanks he'd ever seen, focused in Midgeley's mind; wisps of smoke rising from the started plates like steam, the red-hot glow inside as the fighting compartment became a furnace, exploding ammunition and petrol. He opened the hatch, under which he could so easily have been trapped, a charred corpse. The fumes and smoke began to filter out. He pulled himself together.

'How's POL?'

Starski said:

'Eighty gallons.'

'You see,' Fleming shouted, 'we don't stand a chance like this, eighty gallons will get us nowhere. We're fucking no hopers away from the squadron, we'll end up just like him.'

'He's a reminder we can do without. OK, we'll clean up.'

It took time to manoeuvre the headless corpse out through the loader's hatch, they groaned and swore as they eased it through with a kind of desperation, in case the pall of smoke suddenly lifted and they were left exposed to whatever else lay concealed beyond. There was blood everywhere, now stickily congealing and attracting hordes of flies.

After they had dug a shallow grave and buried what had been Morton in a groundsheet, Midgeley ordered them to clean up the tank as he carefully put away Morton's dog tags.

'What with, Corporal? What with?'

'Bloody petrol, what else.'

Reaction had set in now, after the exhilaration of survival underlined with fear. Midgeley watched them as they mopped the walls with scrim dipped in petrol, its pungent smell partly obliterating the sweet odour of death. Only Starski seemed to be unmoved. Then he suddenly said:

'You English, what the hell you know about war?'

None of the others felt they could give an adequate answer.

Midgeley noted that the clouds of smoke from the burning transport lines had blotted out the sun and induced an artificial twilight. When he looked at his watch it was only nine o'clock.

Piraeus

Colonel Krause hardly noticed the pastel, shoe-box houses scattered over the whiteness of the burned-out landscape as he alternately brooded and gave orders, during the twelve-hour train journey between Gevgeli and Athens. It was quite unnecessary for him to have sat huddled in a corner of the first-class compartment that had been reserved for his use, since he could have easily gone ahead in the Junkers 88 transport that had taken the advance party south from Salonika. However, he had refused to be separated from his tank battalion after the partisan attack, ordering Grunen, his second-in-command, to sort out whatever confusion that might lie ahead at the rail head. He further reminded himself that he must conserve his energies for the probable risks of the sea crossing to North Africa.

The passage from Athens to Benghazi, a distance of four hundred miles, would take anything up to two days. At one time it would have been a hazardous undertaking. However, with Malta almost neutralized and the British fleet penned up in Alexandria, the transit of convoys across the Mediterranean, escorted by the Italian navy and with Luftwaffe protection, was easier than it had been for many months.

So he had chosen the comfort provided by the Compagnie Internationale des Wagons Lits, relaxing for the first time in many weeks within the purposeful vacuum of the railway journey, as the train traversed the mountainous ribs that edged out eastwards from the spine of Greece.

Not that there was much to see except for the shoe-box houses, olive trees, dusty roads, fields of ripening maize, and peasants with dogs in the broken-down villages. For a time Krause puzzled over the Greek script at a railway station, at once alien and classical. He could not make head nor tail of it; it was like Russian.

At first the thin and listless people watching by the railway would stare at the train, amazed at the spectacle of the 38 low-slung flat trucks, with their grotesquely sinister freight. Then, after a moment, they would quickly turn their heads away. They rarely waved, although the panzer troops often whistled at the sallow-faced Greek girls, sometimes taking snapshots when the train went slow enough, as though they were on holiday.

For a moment Krause allowed himself to be romantic, but correctly so, remembering the Berlin Olympics; for Greece had been, after all, a candle of civilization in darkness, a constantly beleaguered bastion against the Eastern hordes.

The train ran more slowly now, as though this had something to do with the fact that they had almost reached their destination. They were now passing through the suburbs of Athens by Nea Liosia, which seemed more like a sprawling village than part of a great city, and which extended southwards to the hump of the Acropolis enclosed by smooth, dome-shaped hills. But the train veered south-west towards Tavros, rumbling over the Kifisos girder bridge and then through the naked olive groves downhill to the natural harbour of the Piraeus, landlocked on three sides.

The locomotives slowed to a crawl as they reached the Wehrmacht Field Army Tank Park, where four eighteen-ton half-track Zugkraftwagen recovery vehicles would winch down the damaged Tigers to the high gantry, which was capable of swinging out the turrets.

Krause at once saw Grunen beside a kübelwagen, but instead of sitting in the shade, he was pacing nervously up and down, which indicated to Krause that there were problems.

Krause jumped off the train as it slowed down to walking speed.

Behind the gantry and the accompanying jumble of mechanical litter that always seemed to surround field workshops, stood a row of tents ready to receive tank crews or troops in transit. There would be no question of that, so far as Krause was concerned, they would embark immediately. Grunen came up at once, his long horse-like face wearing a worried expression. As he saluted he said:

'I'm certainly glad to see you, sir.'

'Well, tell me the worst.'

Beyond the tents, Krause could just make out the thicket of derricks and masts that marked the limit of the Piraeus harbour.

'You better come right away, sir. The Italian crew are refusing to sail.'

'I thought we had been assigned a German Transport.'

'It had already sailed for Crete, before they had our signal! The *Brescia* is all they could offer. She's a modern ship with a good turn of speed, but . . .'

'. . . but no crew.' Krause finished the sentence for him as he climbed into the kübelwagen. Grunen nodded to the driver and they tore off towards the harbour, raising a cloud of dust.

Grunen turned anxiously to Krause.

'The matter's been taken up at the highest level. The Italian general has telexed Rome for instructions.'

Krause turned away to hide his irritation. If they were to be involved in a diplomatic incident they could be waiting until Christmas.

'What happened exactly?'

'The *Brescia*'s captain says that his crew has had enough; apparently they suffered one or two casualties on the voyage to the Piraeus.' He paused. 'The crew have barricaded themselves inside the port area, they've locked the gates that give access to the *Brescia* and thrown up a barricade. Apparently they have some small arms and ammunition, although they have not, as yet, used them.'

'How long do they think that they can get away with it?'

'They are asking that the *Brescia* makes passage for Brindisi immediately, since they do not wish to return to North Africa. They say they have with them a number of Marina Mercantile survivors from ships that were attacked and that they should return to Italy at once.'

'Who is the Italian representative?'

'We have been dealing with his deputy, Colonello Umberto; General Vallone is at the moment inspecting a proposed seaplane installation at Rhodes. You can see the position we are in. I can hardly line up an Italian crew against a wall and have them shot.'

'It might come to that,' said Krause thoughtfully.

If Grunen was disturbed by his colonel's opinion, he certainly hid his feelings well. By now the kübelwagen was bumping across the uneven pavé that made up the dockside road. They passed a Flak emplacement where bare-chested gunners were playing Skat.

The harbour was crowded with naval traffic and two E-boats swung against the jetty, their long, sleek hulls, painted in broken white, poised across the glittering water. Krause said:

'What escort do we have?'

'I was able to arrange that pair of sharks.'

'The E-boats?'

Grunen was obviously proud of his achievement.

'They are returning to hunt off Cap Bon and are quite happy to keep us company.'

Close by them rode U-372. It was a picturesque scene and there was a studied silence enveloping it, as though the problem of the *Brescia* and its mutinous crew did not exist.

Grunen had been right to describe the *Brescia* as modern. It was a fast cargo ship of 13,000 tons laid down at Genoa in 1936. Krause noticed that the dazzle camouflage of the forecastle was blackened by fire and that her superstructure plates were riddled with shrapnel. Her Breda anti-aircraft guns were unmanned, and he could see no air sentries.

'It looks as though they've given up the war.'

Grunen said:

'We've been propping them up over the last year; if it hadn't been for the Duce, they'd have ratted months ago.'

Beyond the perimeter fence, the sheds and bollards, the crew loitered in little groups in the shadow of the *Brescia*'s side, waiting with uncertain expectancy the outcome of their action. A roughly constructed barricade of concrete blocks and torn-up railway lines had been set against the dock gates to reinforce them. The barrier was surmounted by the Italian flag. The gate was manned by a nervous young Kriegsmarine guard with a fixed bayonet. Krause said to Grunen:

'See that the Tigers are brought down here and de-trained at once. Did you arrange an Engineer Abteilung?'

Grunen nodded, not too certain of the implications of the colonel's order, although he was aware that Krause had insisted on technically qualified staff being on hand to supervise the loading of the tanks.

Krause went on:

'It seems quite simple, I wonder you hadn't thought of it; unload the tanks off the transporters and drive through.'

Grunen hesitated before saying:

'It had crossed my mind, Herr Colonel. But I must point out that we are unlikely to get much co-operation.'

'Who needs co-operation, just get the tanks to the quayside.'

Krause now noticed the Mercedes parked in the shade to one side of the dock gates. Beside it stood a Wehrmacht engineer general and an over-decorated, swarthy Italian officer wearing dark glasses. Making up the trio was a short, fat man in white ducks and naval cap that Krause immediately identified as the *Brescia*'s captain. The colonel made his way over to the group and saluted. The engineer general returned his salute. Krause detected a certain indifferent arrogance in the bearing of the Italian colonello, who carried a fly whisk and wore patent leather boots. The Wehrmacht engineer general looked as dynamic as a retired station-master recalled to duty in an emergency.

'I am afraid you have arrived in the middle of a delicate situation, Colonel.'

'If you can call mutiny "delicate", Herr General.'

The Italian ship's captain, who was called Bertini, tried to adopt a conciliatory manner.

'I am sorry, but the transport you require is not available, Colonel. These men are refusing to make another trip across the Narrows. We spent four days unloading ammunition at Benghazi under constant bombings. Then they were ordered to Athens, with many survivors from other ships that were not so lucky, the *Foscarini, Venice, Beatrice Costa, Mortello* . . .'

'Yes . . . yes . . .' said Krause impatiently.

'There is a shortage of plasma in North Africa and some received bad burns.'

The Italian colonello interrupted:

'So you see, Colonel, it is quite impossible for you to proceed. In one day, two days maybe, perhaps they will come to their senses. But in the meantime . . .' He shrugged.

Krause said:

'We all run risks when we are at war.'

Captain Bertini said:

'Twelve hours we were attacked by Blenheims and Marylands. The forward hold received a direct hit, and many of the wounded sailors were killed.' He paused once more before adding with a look of embarrassment, 'We were sent to Piraeus with a special cargo, a number of crates for delivery to Berlin.'

Krause said indifferently:

'So?'

'The crates contained statues, Roman statues from Cirene. The men are bitter, they say that if they had been ordered to Naples all this would never have happened. They say that they do not risk their lives to act as removal men for the Third Reich.'

The Italian colonello said behind his dark glasses:

'There will always be misunderstandings between the best of allies; it is inevitable like a quarrel "nella famiglia".'

Krause was unsure how to react, certain that the Italian colonello was laughing at him. The fact that the *Brescia*'s crew did not like running errands for Goering in Berlin was none of his concern, besides it was an everyday occurrence.

The engineer general said:

'Unfortunately I am powerless to intervene. It's a matter for Supremo Commando in Rome. I'm sorry that there are no other ships available that are capable of carrying your battalion.'

Captain Bertini obviously still felt it his duty to explain the circumstances which had led his crew to act in the way they had done.

'Herr Colonel, you must understand that these men have seen ship after ship sink around them and even under them; this last attack was too much. We should never have been ordered to make the longer passage; the survivors we took on at Benghazi should have been given places on the hospital ships.'

Krause had heard about the hospital ships; the Royal Navy took them in for examination to Malta. It was rumoured that General Cavallero, appointed by Commando Supremo for supply liaison with the DAK, had, on occasion, filled their bilges with petrol on the outward voyage from Naples. Very little surprised him about the Italians.

'You must understand, Herr Colonel, when the English bombers attacked it was terrible. Now they will not listen to me, they wish to return to Brindisi; they say the hospital facilities here are insufficient.'

'They won't have to listen to you.'

The first of the Tigers was now being shunted into the siding parallel with the fence and the dockyard gate, its flat car edged gently up to the ramp and Krause could make out the low steady rumble of the Maybach engines. The sailors, waiting in their little groups, did not react at first. Krause asked the engineer general:

'Is there nothing you can do?'

'I have mounted a guard.' He laughed nervously. 'But since they obviously do not wish to leave, it hardly seems relevant. As you can see they have barricaded the dock gates. Certainly, we could not use force.'

'It is a matter on which I am awaiting instructions,' the Italian colonello interrupted. 'They are refusing to handle any kind of cargo.'

His glance fell significantly on the siding. The Tiger stood poised on the flat car and then, with a roar, the driver engaged first and slowly nosed forward to the ramp, then the tank dipped, its engines purring, before slowly turning towards the dock gate. As Krause watched, a slight smile hovered across his lips.

The Italian colonello said:

'So you see, you will have to be patient.'

Even as he spoke, his smug and somewhat arrogant expression started to change to one of alarm, as he incredulously watched the progress of the tank. It had also, by this time, attracted the attention of the Italian sailors at the quayside, as it ground on inexorably towards the dock gate.

One of these men, who was wearing a black fascisti shirt, ran forward to the gate in front of the tank, waving his arms above his head scissor-fashion, as though this would somehow dissuade the tank driver from advancing as it crunched into the locked gate and the barricade. The crowd behind murmured half-angrily, half-fearfully. The Italian colonello said:

'I shall hold you responsible...' But the rest of his remarks were lost in the dominating roar of the engine.

The crowd behind the gate was in two minds, surging forward as though in support of the solitary figure standing on the barricade, but quickly backing off as the sixty-two tons of moving metal reared up and then bore down on him. He either misjudged its speed or its driver's intentions. One moment he was standing, fending it off with his outstretched hands, and then the rubble must have slipped. A moment later his screams were lost in the grinding of the tracks on the mound of broken concrete as he scrabbled along the cobblestones, dragging his crushed leg behind him; blood spurted from the great artery in his thigh and he fainted. Seeing what had happened, the crowd sighed angrily in disbelief, surging fearfully but sullenly back from the massive thrust of the approaching Tiger.

The tank stopped and the driver switched off the engine, the gunner traversing the turret backwards and forwards with impersonal menace, following the movement of the crowd which began to break up.

Krause turned to the Italian officer with a smile and asked:

'What was that you were saying, Colonello?'

Point 289

THE desert shimmered, a great opalescent landscape of light. It was curious, thought Midgeley, how the desert did not change, only the light; and with the light came the heat that melted the rock and sand into a sea of whiteness.

To the east a ripple had disturbed the whiteness and he had identified it as a dust cloud. It could only be a German column, but whether five or five hundred vehicles it was impossible to say. Rommel was adept at confusing the issue by using a decoy column of five captured three-tonners mounted with aircraft engines and propellers, whose resulting dust trails were designed to give the impression of a whole panzer regiment on the move.

They had left the position which they had overrun some hours before and it was now afternoon. It was strange how the battlefield had assumed the appearance of nothing more sinister than a scattered rubbish dump, once they had crossed it, with a litter of German shell baskets, cases of tins haphazardly spilled open and burnt-out vehicles. Starski had wanted to search for loot, but there was hardly anything worth taking; the Italians they had overrun had brought little with them, largely because they had nothing. The Pole found a few rings under a burnt-out truck but he couldn't decide whether they were gold or brass.

Midgeley said to Thomson:

'What d'you think the Axis are doing?'

'It's what you're doing that worries me, Corp. You want to win the war single-handed? Where are we going next? Afrika Korps HQ at Agheila?'

'Whichever way we go, it's not going to be easy.'

Midgeley raised his field glasses once more and swept across the horizon, pausing for a moment at the ruins of what had once been an Italian colonial fort. Now the walls were broken and gaping up to a height of not much more than seven feet.

'That's where we go,' he said decisively.

The fort was a roofless shell with an outer and an inner wall. Once it had been nothing more than a small police post beside a dried-up well.

'Pressing on regardless?'

'Have you any other suggestions?'

They had found sixty gallons of petrol scattered round the battlefield and Thomson had brought it in, while Midgeley, Fleming and Starski had cleaned the inside of the blood-spattered tank with petrol and scrim. The petrol in some measure cancelled out the unspeakable perfume of death. Midgeley, however, was not satisfied and insisted on it being done all over again.

But there was an obvious reason for making for the fort, since it provided the only available cover against the distant column. For now they had left the scarp, where they had overrun the anti-tank gun, the desert was featureless and level.

Thomson reluctantly climbed back into the hull of the Grant, obviously preferring the safe, though exposed, anonymity of the desert. Midgeley said to Starski down the intercom:

'Drive slowly and keep down the dust.'

'Yes, Captain.'

Although Starski was being funny, Midgeley realized that the others, however reluctantly, accepted him as decision-maker and leader.

Thomson had got one of his spare socks from the crew box and stuffed it into the forward hole drilled by the armour-piercing shot. He did not like to be reminded that two inches of sloping armour could give so little protection.

Midgeley continued to watch the dust cloud as the Grant edged up to the abandoned fort, quite certain that the building was deserted.

The northern wall had a gap in it and Midgeley ordered Starski to drive in facing east, so that they could, if necessary, withdraw quickly. Then he traversed the turret so that the 37mm armament faced the cloud of dust that was approaching. He made Starski manoeuvre the tank until they were in exactly the right position, with the 75mm facing in the opposite direction and to the rear, at an angle of sixty degrees against the corner of the ruin.

'OK then, let's get out the net.'

They draped it loosely on to the mud-baked floor of the fort. Thomson wrinkled his nose when he saw it had been used as a latrine. Mixed in amongst the rubbish was a crumpled copy of *Oase*, the DAK newspaper, a British steel helmet with a hole in it and an empty Bren gun magazine. Thomson weighted down the edge of the net with rubble until it stretched at an angle like the pitch of a tent, concealing the vertical contours of the Grant within it.

Then they pegged down the netting on the desert side of the Grant, so that at close quarters it stood transformed into a wide low-angled pyramid that, beyond two hundred yards, would blend into the desert. Once they had finished Thomson said:

'I'm not half hungry, Corp.' He got out one of the tins marked 'AM' he had found on the battlefield.

Starski said:

'Don't start opening canisters anywhere near me; it could be anti-personnel.'

'Nuts,' said Thomson.

Midgeley said:

'The Eyeties pull a trick with water-bottles, it's true.' With thirst a constant problem the Italians sometimes littered their abandoned positions with canteens containing a plastic charge. Unimpressed, Thomson opened the can.

'There's stories about Jerry Peters chocolate bars as well.'

'Yeah, well not this weather,' said Thomson. 'It's too bloody hot for chocolate.' He pulled out a piece of fat, greasy meat.

'AM – Arse of Mussolini, more like,' said Starski and laughed.

'Very funny,' said Thomson.

Through the stillness, Midgeley began to catch the distant rumble of engines and carefully peered out through the camouflage netting, between the dangling strips of sand-coloured hessian. The dust cloud in front had now divided; one part hooking eastwards to the battle area they had just left. Midgeley estimated that it couldn't be more than a squadron, sent forward to secure the line they had broken through. The dust cloud, still on the far horizon, would be the main body, probably re-grouping after attacking the British armour, from which they had become separated.

Midgeley told Thomson to man the 37mm and fire only if he told him to. Then Midgeley carefully loaded the 75mm. At the most there would be time to get in three shots.

'You're not seriously taking that lot on?'

Thomson asked nervously.

'It's hard to say, there could be a game of chicken.'

Sometimes a line of opposed tanks would creep forward and then halt, waiting for the enemy to fire or retreat. Midgeley felt confident, however, that with the camouflage net out they would remain unseen. With the Grant's main armament firing towards the west into the rear of the panzers as they passed the fort and the 37mm trained forward, the German reaction could well be one of avoidance, if they could not locate a target.

'Remember, only fire if I give you a shout down the intercom.'

'You needn't worry about that.'

Midgeley watched the column as it began to move south of the wrecked Italian fort, spearheaded by three BMW's and followed by a couple of 222 half-tracks. These vehicles screened the main body and bounced along at top speed. One of the BMW motor-bikes detached itself and circled round the fort, the side-car machine-gunner swivelling his MG42.

Midgeley could feel the tension building up inside the tank and said down the intercom:

'For Christ's sake, Thomson, keep your finger off the firing button.'

'Alright Corp, alright. Why don't you do the same?'

Midgeley ignored the comment; he had allowed himself one good shot to make up for the burning Matilda. Through the gunsight, he watched the light armour bounce across his line of fire and vanish into the distance.

Then he looked westwards to where the heavy armour should be. He at once made out a crescent of Mark III and

IV panzers; slightly behind them and to the rear, two tractors followed, drawing 88mm guns. Bringing up the immediate rear was a self-propelled gun.

Midgeley took a long look at the 88's. They were very similar to the 3.7-inch anti-aircraft guns he had seen in the Delta. In transit, their long, slim barrels were parallel to the ground, their cruciform trails raised vertically against the shield and gun platform. In that position they were totally helpless, although they could be unlimbered, the platforms winched down from the wheels and laid on target in less than three minutes.

He had not seen the self-propelled 7.5cm gun before, lurching forward like a monstrous, out of balance tank, its stubby snout protruding from a huge gun shield, and ringed with a dozen white circles to register each confirmed kill.

Behind were the troop carriers of the panzer grenadiers, soft-skinned trucks and two captured British Bren gun carriers. As the tanks came closer, Midgeley could see that their engine compartments were draped with scarlet swastika flags, which could mean that the column had air support.

Of all the vehicles in that column, the 88's would be the greatest prize. German armour quickly lost its confidence and aggression without its reassuring screen of anti-tank guns.

Remembering the line of burning Matildas, Midgeley felt a flame of anger flicker inside him.

The heavy armour continued stolidly on at twenty miles an hour. Soon the lead tanks were lost to sight, hidden by the shattered fort walls, from which Midgeley estimated they would re-emerge a minute and a half later.

He called to Thomson urgently down the intercom:

'Forget about the 37mm. Come down and help me load this thing.'

Behind him, he heard Thomson squeezing his way into the loader's position.

'I want armour-piercing and then HE.'

'What fuse?'

'As short as you can make it for the HE.'

He registered the criss-cross sight graticules, waiting for the tractors, followed by the 88's to traverse his sight. Taken from the rear, one shot should kill each gun at the junction of the recoil cylinders and the gunshield.

Moments later, the first tractor began to move painfully across his line of vision, its huge canvas awning flapping slightly. Five seconds later the graticules criss-crossed exactly at a point forward of the breech block and Midgeley pressed his foot down on the firing pedal. The whole of the fighting compartment shook, as the 75mm breech flew open to discharge the empty shell case. Thomson, slapping in the next round, tapped him on the shoulder to tell him that the gun was ready once again amidst the cordite fumes.

Already the first 88 had erupted in a shower of shattered metal and as the second gun veered away uncertainly, Midgeley wildly traversed to keep it in his sights. Suddenly it stopped. Midgeley stamped the firing pedal again and saw the gun slew over on its side, twisting the tractor towing-bar with such violence that it snapped, flipping the tractor over on to its canopy as one of its tracks continued to revolve.

Again Thomson tapped Midgeley on the shoulder, as the corporal exultantly watched a dirty orange and black puff of airburst spray the area surrounding the shattered guns. The first tractor began to burn.

Midgeley was now aware that the soft-skinned vehicles had changed direction in front of the fort and had begun to scatter, raising a massive dust screen that obscured the whole of his front.

He now watched, with detachment, a scene of utter confusion. Inside the dust cloud, he could make out the sharp, crisp back of 50mm guns as he realized that the Germans were firing indiscriminately at nothing. The dust cloud gradually drifted south.

Starski had also been watching in amazement the turmoil outside his visor; there were small dust clouds everywhere, lit, from time to time, by the flash of exploding shells. At the centre lay the broken 88's, ringed by a circle of dead gunners.

Suddenly a Mark III panzer emerged from the murk. It was on fire, but still moving. A fuel line had been severed by a splinter that had entered the engine compartment. The tank came to a stop as one of the crew hurriedly climbed out with a fire extinguisher to deal with the blaze.

Midgeley watched fascinated as the tank rolled away. But the engine temperature had risen so much that the fire spontaneously re-ignited and after a few seconds the fuel tank exploded in a dull, dark patch of red. It was not possible to see what happened to the crew, as a column of black smoke erupted with the explosion and drifted back towards the fort, making Midgeley cough.

'What happens now?' Thomson asked.

'Stay put, have a kip. The last thing we do is move.'

'You've got to be joking.' Thomson made the remark automatically, for he could see the sense in staying as they were.

'If you want to pass the time,' said Midgeley, 'you could try removing the last of Morton's signature off the walls; come to that you could get rid of all that bloody white paint.'

Tanks newly supplied from ordnance depots were invariably coated inside with a layer of glossy white enamel. Although artistically pleasing, the paint was extremely dangerous in action, since minute fragments would chip off at the slightest outside impact. Some tank crew had been blinded in this way.

Thomson, of course, knew all this.

'You've chosen a funny moment.'

'You want something to do, there's lots of time now; get your jack-knife and start scraping.'

Only Midgeley knew how scared Thomson was, the others were sufficiently occupied with their own feelings. Fleming, the professional complainer, had said nothing since the tank had entered the fort. He too got out his jack-knife. Starski, however, did not leap at the opportunity.

'Come on Starski,' Midgeley said, 'check the tracks, check the oil seals and the fuel lines; get on and do some maintenance.'

'It's a new tank to me. How?'

'Check the bloody manual, we don't want to get caught by 21st panzer just because there's a piece of fluff in a petrol filter. And Fleming, get busy on the wireless.'

Fleming, the failed WOSB candidate, had now recovered sufficiently from the events of the morning to begin to question Midgeley's authority.

The fact that Fleming's younger brother had been commissioned into the Indian Army added to his subconscious sense of grievance. He had tried to analyse what it was in his character that made him officially unsuitable to command. However hard he looked he could not see that it was a streak of hypercriticism of others combined with an intellectual superiority, a defence mechanism, that deprived his nature of warmth.

Intellectually, Fleming considered it logical to put some distance now between himself and the panzers.

'When do we move on, Corp?'

'When it gets dark.'

Fleming projected a disapproving silence, as though this state of affairs could only be tolerated due to Midgeley's superior rank.

'Where to, though?'

'Well, we can't go back to where we've just come from. Not with all these Jerries swarming all over the place.'

'I suppose it's likely we'll be shot at wherever we go.'

'Right, so I'm heading north.'

'Tobruk?'

'What's to stop us?'

'Oh, I don't know, just a couple of panzer divisions and half a million Eyeties.'

Fleming paused again, this time considering how ironic it was that he should have been posted to Egypt. For he had hated India, what he had remembered of it.

Everything in England, where he had spent the long school holidays with an aunt in the Lake District, had seemed so controlled, well-ordered and rational; at any rate compared with the irrational extremes of the East.

Midgeley bit his lip, Fleming somehow always ended up by irritating him, perhaps it was this underlying current of competition.

'If you know some other way, let me in on it. Maybe you'd like to try your luck back over the minefields.'

Fleming answered:

'How do we know they don't have Thermos and Teller mines where we're going?'

'Jerry doesn't seem too worried.'

In rational, logical terms, of course Fleming was right, but it was this argumentative smugness that Midgeley resented.

'Anyway,' Midgeley went on, 'if we blow a track we're carrying spare links.'

Fleming said:

'We've been plum lucky so far, except for that poor sod Morton. However I'm afraid I don't believe in luck.'

Midgeley said:

'Forget it. Lightning doesn't strike twice.'

'Even when it's a twenty-four hour storm?'

Everybody was silent, including Starski; they all knew it was true. There was something depressing about the memory of Morton. Twenty-four hours ago he had been sitting with them, and they had the feeling that he was trying to get to the bottom of what they had been up to in Cairo; and now, twenty-four hours later, he was dead.

By the time evening fell, the self-inflicted battle among the panzers had dissipated; it was a time when Midgeley normally felt uneasy, since the German tanks often made a final attack of the day out of the sun with the light in their favour, putting the gunners in the British tanks at a strong disadvantage.

This time, he felt slightly more at ease, although he did not look forward to a night march which could involve crossing derelict and forgotten minefields. On the other hand to keep in the same position would invite disaster on the following day, as the Germans would not rest until they had dealt with the source of the afternoon's attack.

Just before sunset, Midgeley told Thomson to help roll back the camouflage netting. The desert was now empty except for the ruins of the 88s, the Mark III panzer and a German wireless truck. Thomson said:

'Time for a brew up, Corp?'

'What's the water situation?'

Midgeley did not have to stress the fact that being out on a limb meant no supply. He went on:

'When did you last check the jerricans?'

'I haven't.'

Two minutes later, Thomson returned with the bad news that four of the jerricans had been punctured by shrapnel.

'Did you put two inside the turret like I said?'

'Yeah, Corp.'

'I suppose that's something, there's no drinking water from the radiator in this battlewagon.'

The M3 Grant had a Wright Continental nine cylinder air-cooled radial engine.

Thomson grasped at Midgeley's sleeve.

'What's that over there?'

Two shadowy figures were moving fifty yards away near the blown-up Mark III panzer.

'Looks like the bloody tomb robbers.'

'If it's souvenirs they're after, they won't find much.'

'Anything goes with those buggers.'

The war had provided a secondary industry for the Arabs of North Africa; anything near the battlefields had a value, from signal cable to gold teeth.

'Starski will be pleased. Shall I chase them off?'

Midgeley knew that Starski was anxious to look over the results of victory on his own account.

'Hard luck on Starski.'

Starski emerged from underneath the Grant carrying an inspection lamp; Thomson said:

'Looks like the Gyppos have beat you to it, this time, Starski; finish the souvenirs.'

'Wait,' said Starski. 'Listen.'

From the west they heard the rumble of a half-track and then came a weaving pair of dimmed headlights.

'Now we have some company,' said Starski.

As the half-track passed the fort, a white success flare lit up the desert and showed that a German recovery vehicle was nosing towards the burned-out Mark III panzer. The night sky blazed with magnesium light, further revealing the Arabs grouped around the German tank.

'The Jerries won't like that,' said Thomson.

'Too right,' said Fleming, 'but neither will the Gyppos.'

Green tracer arched across the Arabs, splashing against the armour of the knocked-out tank. By now the recovery vehicle was almost half a mile off from the Grant, lost in the darkness.

One of the Arabs was caught in a beam from the recovery

vehicle as he started to run, carrying what looked like a section of exhaust pipe. For a moment he hesitated before he was cut down by a burst of machine-gun fire.

'Time to be on our way,' said Midgeley.

Starski said predictably:

'It is much too bad the Gyppos got there first.'

'Robbing the dead; better you than me,' said Thomson and laughed.

The Cyclades

Colonel Krause watched Point Maleas slip away in the soft afternoon light; in an hour or two the mountains of the island of Kithera would become a blur, as the *Brescia* crossed the straits between Peloponnesus and Crete. For the moment they were safe from aircraft attack, since they were under cover of the Luftwaffe bases at Heraklion and Maleme. But every mile they sailed southwards would bring them closer to the RAF, whose medium bomber squadrons formed a chain along the Libyan coast and back to the Canal Zone. The British constantly fought for air superiority over 'Bomb Alley', the stretch of sea between Cyrenaica and Crete. Once they had passed Crete, the *Brescia* would change course to the west across the gulf of Bomba towards Benghazi, an area patrolled by British submarines and surface vessels as well as the Malta bomber squadrons.

Krause was aware of all this, as the *Brescia* slipped easily through the glassy shimmering water. He was aware of it because he had read about it; but he did not really take it seriously, considering that these alleged threats were merely the excuses Commando Supremo had manufactured over the brandy to cover up their own shortcomings. It was, in any case, his first trip by sea, since he had always flown to Africa before.

From where he was on the bridge, he could see the lines of Tiger tanks and soft-skinned auxiliary vehicles laid out neatly on the upper deck below, where dungareed crews were busily overpainting the drab grey olive with sand-coloured waterpaint, in anticipation of their arrival in the desert.

Since their departure from the Piraeus, the *Brescia*'s crew had remained sullenly aloof, their wider experience of what the future could bring, in this apparently peaceful sea, contrasting with the boyish anticipation of the young tank soldiers.

To them, it was still all a big adventure that so far showed no sign of being dangerous.

Behind Krause, in the forward rear cargo hold, lay the fifty thousand gallons of petrol Krause had prudently pumped aboard, together with the spares. Even this had made insufficient draught, so that the ship still rode much too high. Angrily, Krause had had to agree to postpone sailing for two hours, while pig-iron ballast was added forward to give some appearance of trim. Even so, the *Brescia* rode high out of the water, and to any experienced eye was out of balance, with two and a half thousand tons of armour chained to the main decks.

Captain Bertini was silent, but polite, recognizing that Krause was a man with an inflexible will, who would take any risk to achieve his end, as he had amply demonstrated at the dockyard gate. The Italian colonello had lodged a formal protest after the incident to the German authorities, in other words the engineer general, but Krause had been too busy to be interested in that kind of protocol; he would have been much more impressed if the Italian had threatened him with a pistol.

Of course, Krause had a self-evident defence; since they were at war, the Italian crew's action was essentially treason against the Third Reich.

The ship's captain accepted the fact that Krause stayed on the bridge, in silent command, without question, in just the same way as he had been forced to accept the incident at the dockside. He resented Krause's presence, secretly, but he was not prepared to argue about it, at any rate until such questions as placing the ship in danger arose. Anyway the ship was in danger precisely because Krause and his heavy tanks were there.

Krause stirred at the rail, the breeze ruffling the hair under his DAK cap. He was wearing new panzer camouflage overalls. Looking at his watch, he estimated that in sixteen hours they should make port.

Captain Bertini said:

'The weather forecast predicts fine weather.'

He did not say 'good' weather, since that implied a calm sea, which would make the *Brescia* an easier target; a gale always increased the margins in favour of survival.

'If we make the crossing by night, it does not matter.'

Bad weather, on the other hand, meant clouds which would obscure the moon. The captain silently prayed for cloud and for squalls and for rain, which he knew would never come. Somehow he knew that the moon would hang, bold and orange and round, that night, like a giant carnival lamp. Then the torpedo planes would come.

'Herr Colonel?' he asked, not quite sure what Krause meant.

'We have good company.'

Krause nodded to the two E-Boats that screened the *Brescia*, circling like dolphins round a whale.

'Ah yes, the Kriegsmarine.' Captain Bertini forced a smile.

'Also, we have air cover,' said Krause reassuringly.

The Italian captain was not particularly impressed by his optimism, remembering only too well the number of Italian ships he had seen go down, and the number of men he had seen die. So far as he was concerned, it was the Italian merchant sailors who were the sacrifice in the Mediterranean War, dying, day in, day out, because the Italian navy had refused to commit itself in a major fleet action since Matapan. Automatically he felt for the grappa bottle in the cupboard above the chart table.

'Would you like a drink, Colonel?'

'No, thank you, it is too early.'

'I always have one, before I go into action.'

Krause glanced across the smooth empty sea.

'I don't see any enemy.'

'Do not delude yourself, Colonel. They will know that we are on our way.'

Krause had given little thought to the Mediterranean crossing, regarding it as merely the final step to his objective. He had always put down the shortage of supply, in North Africa, to Italian mismanagement, rather than allied bombs. Of course, there were some losses, but the risks and figures were no doubt equally exaggerated. Anyway, since the Kriegsmarine U-Boats had arrived in the Mediterranean, things had changed very much for the better. Krause had summed up Captain Bertini as a melodramatic windbag, a definition he was inclined to apply to most Italians.

'Captain, I think that you are over-anxious.'

'I can see you don't believe me.'

Bertini stared at the grappa bottle, thinking, but I have seen death far more often than you, my friend; death in the inferno of an exploding munitions ship, in an unnatural sea of burning petrol, in ships abruptly turning turtle ten seconds after a bomb stick drilled holes through the keel. In fact, death did not affect Captain Bertini any more, because he had seen so much of it, so that he had not even flinched when a blazing Wellington had crashed into his bows, with a full bomb load, before crumpling into the sea. He had watched it all happen in a kind of frenzied detachment. He could see that Krause was evidently no expert on this subject. The panzer colonel was drumming his fingers on the rail in a disinterested fashion.

'In war, anything can happen.'

Captain Bertini got up, hardly taking in the banality of the remark, and looked at the sea. The hills to starboard were a purple blue, back lit by the sun, so they had a golden aura. Captain Bertini loved the sea and could never quite understand why it had to be like this. At Benghazi, they would be bombed again; they always had been before, and that would mean more death. It seemed so pointless, the war should have ended a year ago, even earlier, and now one of his sons was in the Ukraine, with Italian VIII Army, thanks to Hitler and the Duce.

The E-Boats slid round the *Brescia* throwing up sprays of liquid silver. It was all very pretty, so far. Colonel Krause said somewhat heavily:

'In this war, we are all comrades.'

Captain Bertini nodded glumly.

'I love Italy, the Roman tradition. I have some records of Caruso, at home.'

After what had happened in the Piraeus docks this attempt to make friends was so obvious it was almost insulting.

Fratelli, the only other ship's officer the *Brescia* could currently boast of, now appeared on the bridge to relieve the watchkeeper, and caught the end of the conversation between the German colonel and his captain. Fratelli glanced to where Krause was standing and then quickly looked away, since he did not wish to draw attention to himself.

His interest in the war was purely selfish, as he was able to make a sensible profit every trip from the black market goods he sold in North Africa. However, this trip, because the *Brescia* had been ordered to Athens, he had nothing to sell. Athens was as clean as a whistle, they did not even have bread; people were starving in the streets. Everything in Greece tended to end up in Germany. Normally, he felt a certain calculated warmth towards the Germans, as any businessman might do, in some measure, towards his customers; besides, they paid well, since the everyday articles of Europe, although they were in short supply, were total luxuries in Tripoli and Libya. It was this entrepreneural instinct that gave some purpose to this senseless war. Now he was angry that he would have to risk his life at the whim of some pig-headed German panzer officer.

Fratelli said:

'We should make Crete in half an hour.'

Bertini said shortly:

'Yes, Fratelli. How are the crew?'

Again, the lieutenant glanced at Krause and then looked away.

'They will be glad to be back on dry land.'

Krause turned and smiled indulgently:

'In war, everyone takes risks if they do their duty.'

Fratelli absorbed the remark in silence, registering the fact that Krause had a tendency to talk like the mottos that might be found in a box of sinister Christmas crackers.

Fratelli said:

'I've been torpedoed twice, Colonel, and I really don't want to repeat the experience.'

Krause changed the subject by asking:

'When will you man the Breda positions?'

'When it's necessary, and we'll know all about that when it happens. It's submarines I worry about.'

'Submarines?' Krause looked incredulous.

'Don't worry, Colonel, they're likely to attack nearer the coast.'

The *Brescia* slipped through the flat sea as the shadows lengthened. Krause noticed that the crew were wearing life-jackets and he turned to Captain Bertini:

'What about life-jackets for my men?'

The captain replied:

'There are rafts and floats for your men.'

Krause hid his uneasiness at Bertini's stony expression, realizing, too late, that this was a question it would have been better not to have asked. Fratelli grinned sarcastically in the background as Krause went down the companionway to the cabin he had requisitioned.

* * *

The moon rose early that night, leaving Captain Bertini's prayer unanswered. However, two hundred miles to the south-east, three Albacores rose from the deck of HMS *Illustrious*, like moths attracted by a lamp. The *Brescia* and its escort had, indeed, been reported by a Sunderland flying boat, patrolling Bomb Alley that afternoon. The fact that the *Brescia* was not in convoy but escorted by E-Boats had caused a flutter of speculation in the carrier's operations room, which had resulted in the decision to attack.

The Albacores had curiously little difficulty in locating their target, perhaps it was the bright moonlight. Captain Bertini, who was still on the bridge, had half-anticipated their arrival, and had stood the gun crews to, when he heard the distant droning of their Taurus engines.

The Albacore bi-planes were not difficult targets, since the maximum attacking speed was no greater than one hundred and fifty miles an hour.

Captain Bertini ordered the release of an 'attack' rocket, as the Albacores were making their approach. The fact that its despatch was delayed by the fumbling signalman affected the course of the attack, for, as a result, the E-Boats opened up with their 20mm armament later than they might have done, spitting out four long arched trajectories of green tracer from each mounting at the last moment, which threw the Albacores off balance. Two of the torpedoes went astray in consequence, and the other, though on course, passed under the *Brescia*'s keel, where the duplex pistol of the twenty-one inch torpedo, normally activated on impact, or by a change in the magnetic field, failed to explode.

One Albacore, turning too late and too slow, was caught in a cross-fire of the E-Boats' tracer, when four 20mm shells ignited the smoke and flame floats stowage behind the rear gunner. The other two torpedo planes made off as abruptly as they had come, into the night sky.

Krause, who had run to the bridge at the first sound of gun-fire, was almost exultant.

'Well done, Captain,' he shouted, as though Bertini had had something to do with what happened. 'We got one of them.'

Bertini shrugged, merely noting sourly to himself that thanks to this German he had been compelled to witness further deaths.

'Will they return?' Krause asked excitedly.

'No Colonel, but we shall need all the air-cover you can raise once it's daylight.'

Krause went off to arrange the necessary priority signals and when he had gone the captain put his arm round Fratelli. He was shuddering. Fratelli reminded him sometimes of the boy in the Ukraine.

'Well, it's started again. Albacores this time.'

Fratelli nodded gloomily; he liked the captain.

'They were from an English carrier.'

He did not add the secret thought that, so far, they had been let off extremely lightly. Sensing Bertini's mood he went on to say:

'That German colonel thinks that's all there is to it; but so far he's seen nothing.'

Outside the sea was dark and cool with traces of phosphorescence. It was difficult to imagine that if one of the Albacore's torpedos had struck they might all have been fighting for their lives in that quiet, peaceful water.

Magdalena

When the sun rose, Starski was almost asleep for the third time and this was obvious to all of them, because as his leg muscles relaxed, his foot released its pressure on the accelerator pedal and the engine stalled. Starski, however, had insisted on continuing to drive. Midgeley, too, had been awake all night, standing braced within the turret port, in the cold air, peering forward at the flickering headlight beams.

As they had moved northwards, there had been lights around them across the desert, bursts of vereys or the white, probing fingers of parachute flares, lifting and falling on either side. Sometimes, too, there were headlights moving purposefully in one direction or the other, crossing the path ahead, or behind, the Grant.

The vehicles, like the lights, were almost certainly German, but at night there was usually a tacit truce, and they did not go out of their way to investigate any others over-closely, involved as most of them were in the business of recovery, replenishment and supply.

Nevertheless, Midgeley was anxious to avoid the risk of running into a German Laager, which was why he was prepared to stand hour after hour, collecting bruises from the jolting metalwork.

The further north they travelled, the more conscious Midgeley became of their fuel situation. Next to running out of water and mechanical breakdown, this was the worst eventuality. For a tank to be immobile in the desert was the equivalent of removing an infantryman's weapons and handcuffing his hands behind his back. They all knew that an immobilized tank was a death-trap.

Midgeley sensed that the tank crew had suddenly united, after the destruction of the 88's, for it was the first taste of major victory together. The fact that their target had been what they had feared the most and yet they had wiped out that source of death, and survived, induced a subtle change, a relaxed and more buoyant attitude. They had survived, even if they were swanning about the desert in the middle of the fluid battle that was taking place unseen on every side of them.

Fleming was the only exception to the new feeling, as though Midgeley's success made him even more critical. It was in the nature of a private and secret vendetta to which neither of them would admit; so private in fact that none of the others would notice the vendetta being conducted by Fleming.

As the dawn light broke over the desert, revealing stunted shrubs and tamarisks in a damp, grey setting, Midgeley carefully examined the surrounding landscape. Now he could make out that they were crossing the re-entrant to a gentle, sloping wadi. Midgeley shouted down the intercom to Starski:

'What's the mileage?'

'We have travelled thirty-eight miles.'

Thirty-eight miles of creeping, crawling and stumbling through the dark, like a beetle in the black-out. They must have averaged five miles an hour. So far as Midgeley could see, when he looked at the map, they must have crossed the Trigh Capuzzo.

The Grant slowed down and they began to climb.

Midgeley shouted across to Thomson:

'We must have hit the scarp.'

Close to the coast, the desert fell away in a curtain of cliffs. They were approaching the plateau that fell away south, beyond it, from the opposite direction.

Fleming said:

'How about stopping and taking our bearings?'

Without further encouragement, Starski edged into the wadi and brought the tank to a halt, and after doing so, he immediately fell asleep.

Wearily, Midgeley climbed on to the back of the tank and began methodically to unravel the camouflage net, then he pulled the blanket from his bundle and dropped down into the sand.

*   *   *

Fleming shook Midgeley's shoulder and the corporal woke up, automatically feeling for the stud of his web pistol holster.

'What the hell is it?'

Glancing at his issue watch he saw it was twelve minutes past eleven.

Fleming pointed north to where half a dozen kites were circling.

'So what?' said Midgeley.

'It means there must be something, doesn't it?'

'Yeah, unburied corpses.'

Midgeley got to his feet reluctantly. The dead attracted pi-dogs and the kite hawk, everyone knew that, always on hand to clear away the carrion, before the padre arrived with the burial detail. Midgeley peered up the hill that lowered over them, its crest lost in a jumble of rocks.

'Alright Fleming,' he said, 'have it your way.'

Starski and Thomson were still asleep.

'That's a court martial offence,' Fleming commented. Midgeley couldn't be sure how serious he was.

'Just leave them.'

Midgeley picked his way carefully through the rocks, aware of how conspicuous two men could be, passing across that barren wilderness. Moving from boulder to boulder, they reached the ridge at last.

The ground was broken ahead of them, indented by little depressions, but Midgeley could see a group of squat Italian houses standing in the distance. A tall wireless mast stood at one side, although the wire now flapped lackadaisically against the pole. Midgeley searched the complex through his glasses, lowering them when he thought he caught a movement.

'There's someone there.'

'Ours or theirs?'

'Hard to say. I can't see any vehicles.'

Fleming checked his Sten as Midgeley took another look.

'It could be a woman.'

At least it seemed like a woman to Midgeley; then the figure vanished into the buildings.

Midgeley got up and moved forward again.

'Perhaps it's a hospital.'

'Maybe.'

Midgeley raised his glasses and examined the buildings again. They were daubed with the graffiti left by the advancing armies that had swept forward and back, ever since 1940. One read NACH TOBRUCH, another VIVA L'ITALIA; a cluster of British divisional signs had been stencilled on one wall underneath KILROY WAS HERE.

'It looks like everybody's village.'

There was nothing marked on the map. No name.

The underlying pressure at the back of Midgeley's mind was fuel replenishment, after their night march; fuel and water; they had to replace those empty jerricans.

It was clearly impossible for the Grant to follow where they had climbed, but looking back, Midgeley could make out a track twisting slowly up from the wadi they had just left.

'Come on,' he said.

But Fleming seemed reluctant to go. Midgeley almost lost his patience.

'What's the matter?' he asked. 'Are you looking for an on the spot commission? Want to take over where Anderson left off?'

Fleming looked at him coldly through his steel-rimmed glasses.

'You didn't even try for WOSB.'

'What's that go to do with it? Jack it in will you, Fleming, I know you're carrying a chip half the size of the Great Pyramid because you've bucked your family's military tradition. But there's nothing I can do about it and I'm certainly not stepping down.'

Fleming followed him down the hillside in silence.

Back at the Grant, Midgeley shook Starski awake and ordered Thomson to take over in the driver's seat. He told Fleming to roll up the camouflage net.

Thomson eased the tank back in low gear. He hated low gear, since the high-pitched whining note that reverberated through the driving compartment seemed like an open invitation to any nearby anti-tank detachment. There were too many folds in the country they were crossing to make him feel entirely comfortable; it was ideal for eighty-eights.

Midgeley took up his usual position in the turret. The slight slope they were now climbing gave him a panoramic view of the desert. To the south lay the point at which they had broken through yesterday morning. Already the haze was beginning to shimmer, but in the distance he could still see two tiny dust clouds that were probably made by armoured cars on reconnaissance; whether they were British or German, it was impossible to say.

The track had obviously been used by both sides, since the edges were littered with jumbles of abandoned material, rusting coils of barbed wire, a derelict Italian truck engine and a pile of dented 3-gallon petrol cans. The track inched up a spine of rock, which gave Midgeley some comfort, since it minimized the likelihood of mines.

The Grant veered round the last bend towards the plateau, its gears grinding and growling. Thomson did not increase speed once they were on level ground. Midgeley shouted to him to bear west when he saw the first belt of wire. Wire stretching in any direction and for any distance was usually accompanied by mines. Once more, Midgeley trained his glasses on the buildings as they circled round; perhaps it would have been better to have come in from the east, because if this had been an Italian post that had been overrun, the Italian sappers would, most probably, have mined the western exits; although if they had been Italian they probably would not have given themselves enough time. To the west of the buildings lay a wide exit on the wire, where the litter grew, dark green Italian great-coats, tasselled forage caps, rifles and packs were scattered across the tyre- and track-marked sand.

Thomson cautiously ground his way beyond the wire as Midgeley swept the area ahead of the tank to mark any unexplainable depressions in the surface that might indicate the presence of anti-tank mines.

After a hundred yards they came to a cluster of vehicles, one on its side. It was here that the kites were circling. There were twenty-eight bodies in drab green Italian uniforms, frozen in the bizarre and unlikely attitudes of death. There was also a faint but sickening stench.

'Maybe it was an air-strike,' said Fleming.

The carrion birds hopped excitedly from corpse to corpse, tearing at the flesh through the loose, faded uniforms.

A long command caravan was parked in the middle of the buildings. Midgeley tensed himself against the sudden crack of a rifle, or worse, the slap of an anti-tank shell against the Grant's armour, but there was only silence beyond the rumble of the tank engine, occasionally broken by the thudding flap of the birds. As they came to a rise, Midgeley saw a body near the caravan, its face coated in a mask of thickly congealed blood. The woman had been flung from the doorway of one of the buildings, and he could see that she was quite dead.

The Grant halted by the caravan in the middle of the buildings. Midgeley climbed out and looked around; a low, throbbing wail came from the caravan. Ignoring this for the moment, Midgeley went over to examine the woman's body.

He now saw that the shattered remains of a door lay close by. The threshold must have been booby-trapped when she tried to go inside. Beyond the opening the floor was stacked with straw-covered Chianti flasks. The first dozen rows had been smashed by the violence of the explosion and red wine was still dripping down the doorstep.

The mud wall of the hut was stencilled with the legend '24 Regimente – Cantina degli Ufficiali'.

Midgeley went back to the tank.

'There's booby traps,' he said.

The tractor which towed the caravan was still in position. When Midgeley examined it he saw at once that the left-hand track teeth were broken and had become disengaged from the idler wheel. Nothing else seemed wrong with the vehicle.

Midgeley was trying to work out what he had been brought face to face with, as Starski came up beside him. The information that there were booby traps made him walk as delicately as a cat.

'Italian bint?'

Midgeley was wondering why a nurses' caravan would not

be marked with a red cross. Going to the door, he pulled it open, holding his pistol. It took him some time to adjust to the inside darkness after the glare.

A group of women lay huddled against the far trailer wall, clinging to each other for reassurance. They wore incongruously pretty cotton floral skirts and low-cut blouses. One had a yellow ribbon in her hair. Most of the girls seemed to be in their early twenties with the exception of an enormous woman in black, very heavily made-up, who blocked Midgeley's way, shouting at him in Italian.

Midgeley was still not quite sure what to make of it. Then it clicked.

'Christ. A mobile Italian whore-house.'

'I always thought that was propaganda,' said Thomson.

There was nothing more to say. It seemed clear that the post had been attacked and the Italians had left in a hurry, at a time when the caravan tractor had broken down. Eventually a girl had gone out to the officers' mess to see what was going on, and had been killed by the booby trap. When this had happened the other girls had been too terrified to move. Not one of them would dare to put a foot outside the door for fear of being blown up. Now they were scared of being raped or shot.

The shock of their arrival made the girls strangely subdued, and the men were equally uneasy and silent, except for Fleming. He simply did not react as though he was in the middle of an impossible situation it was best to ignore. Midgeley licked his lips, his mouth was dry with embarrassment. What had happened in Cairo had at least been logical and in a sense pre-determined; but women had no place here in the middle of a battlefield. It was somehow strangely insulting.

Fleming said:

'What the hell do we do with them?'

Midgeley shrugged.

'Search me. Take your choice.' He left the caravan and started to look round. It turned out that practically everything had been expertly booby trapped. It was just like one of those puzzles in a children's magazine where various objects are concealed in a landscape.

However, the booby trapping was also too well considered, like props carefully arranged to dress a film set, or a set of unrelated treasure hunt clues. Apart from the charges hidden by the hut doors and windows, many desirable objects lay scattered around, apparently at random, a bottle of wine on a window sill, a pair of field glasses in the sand, even a radio, switched on and emitting a faint crackle.

He had seen this sort of thing before, including the corpse rolled over on its stomach to prevent access to paybook and money in the tunic pockets, which, on being moved, would release the firing pin of a British Mills bomb.

Starski joined him and said:

'These were experts. But they did not mine the track.'

Midgeley said:

'Just come into my parlour.'

Starski shook his head.

'Not understand.'

The only petrol they could find was in the tractor's fuel tank, although there was a heap of abandoned DERV drums. Midgeley was equally anxious to find water. He would have to ask the women about that.

Starski said:

'I do not like this place. It is a no man's land. It is always bad when you can be attacked either way.'

Thomson yawned and looked across the plateau into the distance.

'God knows what's happening out there in the blue, though it looks as quiet as Aberdeen on a flag day.'

Midgeley couldn't quarrel with the self-evident truth of Starski's remark. At any moment the Afrika Korps might arrive to reman their lost position, or the English advance to exploit their success. He went back to the caravan.

The women were quieter now they seemed to realize that they were in no immediate danger from the tank crew. Midgeley spoke to the fat woman in black, haltingly fumbling for Italian words and phrases he only half-remembered.

'Acqua? Acqua. Ah! Acqua!'

The woman broke out into a high-pitched, nasal torrent of Italian, from which Midgeley could only isolate the words 'periculo di morte'. Maybe the dead girl had gone out looking for water. The woman dressed in black advanced her enormous bulk and squeezed through the caravan entrance, pointing beyond the officers' cantina in the direction of an open shell dump. Midgeley said:

'Watch it, all of you. Don't anybody start poking around and look out for trip-wires.'

He followed the woman beyond the piles of shells to the sandbagged entrance, to a dug-out beside a vehicle track, pointing to the untarmaced road she said;

'Mina . . . mina . . .'

Thomson immediately fell back a pace.

'Do we have to, Corp?'

'Shut up and fetch a bayonet.'

After three minutes of careful probing, Midgeley came to a Teller mine half-way across the track.

He gently smoothed away the sand to uncover a round metal container, the diameter of a dinner plate. The sand ran loosely through his fingers as he explored the area immediately below it, sucking in his breath as his fingers felt the brick-shaped box of the anti-lift device beneath. Making a depression on one side, he shouted for Thomson to bring him some wire. The anti-lift device was very simple, a block of Nipolite explosive, its firing-pin attached to a mousetrap spring, which the weight of the Teller mine held on safety. Once the Teller mine was removed the spring would be released, whipping forward the firing-pin to explode the anti-lift charge. Midgeley put a piece of wire in the lower safety pin hole and gently placed the Teller mine on one side. Thomson watched him in horrified fascination.

Midgeley said:

'Some of them you can't touch, they can't be disarmed.'

'You jammy bastard, you're king of them all; I couldn't do that.'

'Nobody asked you to.'

Midgeley probed forward again, but discovered no further unpleasant surprises. The entrance to the dug-out seemed clean and there were no loose wires running along the smooth granite. Inside the entrance was littered with stale-smelling Italian blankets, and beyond were ranged row upon row of jerricans. Midgely tried a can, it was filled with brackish, petrol-tainted water.

'O.K.,' said Midgeley. 'That's one problem solved.'

As he spoke they heard a whistle and swish above the stone roof followed by a reverberating crash outside. A few seconds later Starski hurtled down the stairs.

'Bloody Breetish!'

'What is it? Twenty-five pounders?'

'You can bet on it.'

Midgeley said:

'We can't hang about here then. Let's get back to the Grant.'

They all took two jerricans of water and started to run the two hundred yards to the Grant, closely followed by the Italian woman who was shrieking at the top of her voice.

'Did she get the message, Corp.'

'She'd be stupid not to.'

The twenty-five pounders were bracketing the Italian outpost and the air reverberated with the curious whoosh of the approaching shells. Suddenly the Italian woman stopped.

Midgeley only realized what had happened when he heard more screaming. One of the shells had landed at the rear of the caravan, ripping off the end section; inside a girl lay in a puddle of blood, her skirt indecently blown above her thighs. One of the buildings had also suffered a direct hit and the blast and breeze combined, had scattered the contents of hundreds of office files across the centre of the outpost.

'Christ!' said Thomson.

The other four girls were cowering in the farthest corner of the caravan. One of them, biting her fingers with a look of lunatic indifference, was clearly suffering from shock. The touches of pathetic feminity inside were now exposed in the shrapnel-riddled shell of the caravan; one of the patterned curtains lay torn across the shattered window. The three other girls were crying, but the shell-shocked victim sat silent, hugging a teddy bear and ignoring the attempts of the fat woman in black to persuade her to leave.

Something else was blowing from the caravan into the desert. Suddenly Midgeley realized that they were photographs. He picked one up, it was a dirty picture – three hairy bottoms raised, with legs flapping in shiny silk stockings, to encourage the customers. Midgeley dropped it as though it was a live stick grenade. He felt out of place – or was it these women who were out of place – since he thought that by now he was hardened to the squalor and horrors of war.

For a moment, he felt a quick stab of compassion. The girls should have been in that night club in Cairo, entertaining soldiers instead of being killed by them. The older woman continued to scream at the shocked girl, in between the shell bursts, as the other three ran towards the dug-out. In the end she lifted the girl on to her shoulders and ambled grotesquely after them; the girl was still clinging to the teddy bear.

Starski was climbing into the tank and Midgeley followed him. The bursting twenty-five pounder shells were entirely unpredictable. He felt like a fly scuttling about a table as a giant with a power hammer tried to wipe him out. The Grant's engine started up; he slung the water jerricans on to the rack at the back of the tank and it started to move as he clambered through the turret hatch. Thomson was peering out of the loader's entrance, and Fleming was at the wireless as Starski circled round the camp and away from the barrage.

Midgeley was thinking grimly how ironic it would be if they were hit by their own artillery, when he saw that Thomson was pointing at his shirt and looked down. With revulsion he saw that it was covered in fleas, and glancing over to Thomson he saw the same. Thomson, simultaneously, also realized what had happened and started to pull his off, cursing at the top of his voice against the exploding shells, as he reached down for the empty 'flimsy' petrol can they used to pee into inside the tank. Then he precariously pulled down a jerrican of petrol, slopping it into the open can and plunging his shirt into it as the Grant rumbled westwards.

Midgeley followed his example and they both stood naked in the hot metal of the armour.

'Don't tell Starski,' Midgeley shouted, 'or we'll never get out of here.' He should have known it was those bloody Italian blankets.

Bomb Alley

BY dawn, Crete was a faint smudge on the north-east skyline, as the *Brescia* changed course on the five hundred kilometre leg across the Bay of Bomba towards Benghazi.

Colonel Krause had spent a restless two hours before he returned to the bridge, and what he now found there did little to encourage him. Bertini was slumped over the chart table, where obviously he had spent the night, with an open half-bottle of grappa to keep him company. Standing at one side was Fratelli, who did not see Krause come in.

Glancing forward, Krause could see that the Breda position was still unmanned, in fact there was no sign of a watch on deck. The helmsman alone was performing a useful function.

The sea was empty beyond the *Brescia*, dull green and bloodstained with the red glow of the rising sun.

However the E-Boats were still keeping rigorously to their station, sweeping round and round the merchantman, to left and to right; the Kriegsmarine gun crew at their 40mm Bofors positions.

Krause ignored the Italians and went out on to the bridge, looking down aft to where Grunen was making his rounds with the duty officer, to see that the Tiger tanks were lashed down satisfactorily. He waved to Grunen, and his second-in-command obediently came up the companionway to where the colonel was standing, out of earshot of the wheel-house.

Krause said:

'What's happened to the Italians? They're not even keeping watch?'

Grunen replied:

'They must be below.'

'I could have told you that.' Then Krause went on with a look of contempt:

'It seems as though our captain has gone to pieces.'

'Perhaps the affair of last night's torpedo attack has upset him.'

'There's no other reason I can think of. They're all the same, these Italians, spineless, no guts. One single and unsuccessful attack and he goes to pieces. I ask you.'

* * *

To the north-west, a radar-equipped Wellington of 201 Group, Malta, had picked up the blip of the *Brescia* on its ASV set. Within the next few minutes, three Mark V Blenheims were alerted at Luqa Airfield. Three, because at this time Malta's ability to mount air strikes was limited but still maintained. The Blenheims took eleven and a half minutes to climb to 15,000 feet, where the Mediterranean became a slowly moving picture from a school atlas. The loom of Sicily was seventy miles to the north, lined with flecks of white, as sea met shore and crept away south towards the Gulf of Sirte and Africa. It was unfortunate for Colonel Krause and the *Brescia* that they were about to be hunted by Malta Blenheims, who could draw on many months of bitter experience and a sharpened instinct to seek out and effectively attack Axis shipping. The Blenheims flew on.

For the first time Krause was restless; perhaps he had been infected by the tense atmosphere generated by last night's attack. He turned to Grunen and said:

'I don't like it. I don't like it at all.'

He was, of course, used to suddenly unpredictable and hostile situations, when he would act decisively rather than let matters take their course; a vacuum should always be avoided. And yet here he was stuck right in the middle of a vacuum; the Tiger battalion was a sitting duck and he didn't like it at all.

The panzer colonel turned slowly on his heel and went into the chartroom where Bertini was still sitting as he had left him, except that now his glass was full. Krause said:

'Good morning, Captain Bertini.'

Bertini did not seem to hear him. He gestured towards the bottle.

'Bring the colonel a glass, Fratelli. Pour him a drink.'

'No, thank you, it's too early for me.'

Bertini said:

'It's never too early for me.'

He still did not look up.

'Where are we?' Krause asked.

Bertini impatiently jabbed his finger on an empty patch of chart, somewhere north of Tobruk.

'About here.'

'Can't you be more precise? What's our exact position?'

Bertini turned his head slowly and blinked.

'Our position is that we are in the shit, Colonel. D'you think they'll leave us alone after last night? When they find us, how can knowing our position make any difference? It's a casino where they are the bankers; they may find us, they may not, but the odds are that they will, and soon. Let's hope they won't; let's hope they all get killed before they get here. Let's drink to that.'

Bertini's hand shook as he raised his glass.

* * *

Sixty miles to the north-west, the flight of Blenheims lost height as they made course for the bearing quoted by the Wellington's wireless operator. In doing so they passed through a thin drift of cloud that had built up to the south-east of Sicily.

Flight-Lieutenant Morris, who was flight leader, emerged first. Flight-Lieutenant Morris had had six hours sleep in the last seventy-two hours, thanks to the round the clock raids from the Junkers 88 and Heinkel 111 bombers of Fliegerkorps II based at Comiso and Catania in Sicily, seventy miles away. He had turned restlessly on his metal cot in the bomb-proof close to the runway, as the German and Italian bombers returned relentlessly, time and time again, to strafe the airfield.

Apart from his tiredness, below the mercurial stimulus of the benzedrine, he felt constricted, as he always did in the close confinement of the Blenheim's pilot's seat, with the flying instruments cramped over to the left. 'Smash' Phillips, the navigator, sat next to him in the navigator's seat, the knees of his gangling legs jack-knifed up towards his chest, as he clutched the flight plot. Some time soon he would have to assume the role of bomb-aimer, folding down the forward seat immediately ahead and moving down to control the bombing approach.

Morris tried to focus on the blur of blue ahead of them, positioning the nose of the Blenheim away from the sun, towards which they had been flying. At the same time he used all the tricks he knew to stop himself from falling asleep, pinching himself through his flying suit and biting his lip. It was anybody's guess whether they would ever find a target, with himself in that condition.

Phillips pointed and said:

'There's something at red zero ten, moving south.'

* * *

Five miles away the unsuspecting *Brescia* sailed on.

Yet in the chartroom there was a faint, indefinable air of foreboding, even tragedy. Bertini had continued to finish the grappa bottle as Fratelli stood unsmiling. They were waiting, but they did not know what for, except it could only be bad.

'Come, come Captain, this will never do.'

'Where is the Luftwaffe escort?'

The captain belched and his eyes shakily examined the woodwork round the chartroom cupboard, until his gaze switched to the obligatory photograph of Mussolini, framed on the bulkhead.

'Fuck the bloody war,' he said. 'Fuck the Duce.' He turned to Krause. 'And come to that fuck the Führer too.'

Bertini waved his arms.

'Anyway, what are you Germans doing on my ship, Colonel? My beautiful ship, the *Brescia*. If it wasn't for you I could enjoy my life, instead of which you have turned it into a target ship loaded with petrol and explosive.'

Krause stepped back nervously, uncertain as to what precisely he should do next, his hand instinctively feeling for his Walther P-38, before he realized that this would provide no practicable solution. He could not hope to navigate effectively without Bertini, which would only place the entire Tiger tank battalion at even greater risk. Fratelli hardly seemed a satisfactory or co-operative substitute; more at home, Krause conjectured, negotiating black market deals on the Neapolitan waterfront, than commanding a ship.

* * *

'Smash' Phillips settled himself against the perspex floor, through which the sea rippled in slow motion two thousand feet below. The nose of the Blenheim was so positioned that it was impossible to see the wings or elevators and the crew forward had the sensation of being hung suspended in their moth-beaked bubble, between the twin engines. Morris, beside him, had watched the air speed indicator needle hover at 270 mph, as the altimeter hands moved backwards. In spite of the benzedrine tablets, his hands felt numb inside his silk flying gloves and he reached forward to adjust the cold air louvre so that the jet played across his face. Forward, and now only two miles away, the *Brescia* was sailing obliquely across their flight path. Morris throttled back to just over 150 mph; in another minute they would be at the target.

Phillips had done this so often with Morris, he felt no excitement. He had viewed the target with professional detachment, noting that the *Brescia* was riding unusually high in the water. As usual Morris had read his intention and was making a low shallow circuit so that they would attack the target side on. He could rely on Morris' ability to fly on a centre line between bow and stern, so that the bomb salvo would straddle the ship as the *Brescia* sailed across the pattern.

He felt particularly confident when he saw that the cargo ship had no destroyer escort, and had heard no reports from the rear gunner of having sighted Messerschmitts in the area. The long, low swoop of the medium bomber towards the target could however verge on the suicidal, when the approach had to be made through a curtain of rising flak. The new rivets running in a circle round the Blenheim's nose underlined the point; but then most of the aircraft on Malta had been cannibalized or interchanged time after time, to improvise flight- and battle-worthy aircraft.

As they got closer Phillips shouted:

'This should be a piece of bloody cake; it looks about as active as the *Marie Celeste*.'

Although he did not hear the words over the intercom, Morris caught their meaning, though he never stopped to consider why. Now that they were making the approach, he gave the Blenheim more flap, dragging the speed down to something over seventy mph, just above stall point, as tracer started to blink up from the E-Boats.

When he heard the bomber's engines and the helmsman shouting, Fratelli instinctively reached for the klaxon sounding action stations, but the wail was cut off in the string of explosions that followed, shaking the hull and throwing great black columns of water across the deck. Phillips' marksmanship was of a high standard and the pattern of 1000lb bombs he had released, fifty yards from the ship's side, straddled the *Brescia* like shotgun pellets.

The first bomb, which did the least structural damage, penetrated the decking forward of the superstructure, missing the fifth row of Tiger tanks by a metre. Since its use was delayed, it exploded in the third level of the forward hold, killing or wounding forty-seven panzer crew, who were eating sausage and black bread or drinking tepid coffee after 'Kompanie Aufstehen'.

The second bomb crashed through the roof of the officers' flat, sliding along the steel bulkhead that enclosed the engine-room, and finally exploding at its base. The force of this explosion shattered number three engine-room bulkhead, discharging a shower of steel splinters forward of the steam turbines, and severing the main steam feed pipe in four places.

This had two direct results, first, an immediate loss of steam pressure, with a consequent fall-off in speed; while filling number three engine-room with invisible white-hot steam at the temperature of 1000C, instantly scalding to death the two firemen who were on duty.

Finally, a near miss at the *Brescia*'s stern started the rivets on a ten-foot section of plates, so that trickles of sea water began to flow down to the bilges through the opened caulking.

Phillips, now half a mile away, gave a thumbs-up sign to

Morris, who was still fighting to stay awake and keep the nose of the aircraft out of the sea. On the way back he would use locked controls and try and grab some sleep.

Morris suddenly realized that the rest of the Blenheims weren't with them and said:

'Where the hell are Gillespie and Birch? They can't have missed the target.'

It was then that he realized that the intercom wasn't working. Phillips had shouted back:

'They will have a fuel problem.'

Under normal circumstances a Blenheim carried a fuel load of 468 gallons, affording an average fuel consumption at a weak mixture setting of 65 gallons an hour, which gave a range of about eight hundred miles. The squadrons at Luqa worked on tighter margins and every drop of fuel had to be meticulously accounted for.

What had happened was that the other Blenheims had turned back after missing Morris in the cloud. Since then they had been assiduously trying to establish wireless contact. Tired as he was, Morris had inadvertently disconnected an extension cable to his R.30003 set, as he had fumbled at the throttle, and only now, after the attack, had he become aware of it.

Morris plugged in the jack and said:

'Hello Annie two and four, this is Leader, report signals, over.'

'Hello Annie one, where you been? Pete spotted some Geschwader Shmitts along the narrows and we missed the target. We shall sweep for coastal traffic off the Sicily. What's your heading, Leader?'

* * *

The blast from the number three engine-room bomb had rocked the chartroom, scattering maps all over the floor and overturning the table. Glass had been shattered outwards on to the deck. Three of the gun crew of the forward Breda tower had died, moving too late to their posts. Two were killed by blast and the third, smashed unconscious against the superstructure, had been blown clean overboard and drowned.

The starboard charthouse flat was riddled with splinters. The impact of the bomb had thrown Bertini from his chair and through the open doorway into the wheelhouse, where his left shoulder had struck the binnacle. His face had been cut, but not seriously, by flying glass. Fratelli had flung himself on to the deck at the short whistle of the first bomb and lay still with the chart table across his back. Grunen was dead, a splinter had flicked through his brainpan, opening a four-inch cavity at the back of his head. Krause, on the other hand, had survived without a scratch and was the first to get to his feet. The man at the wheel, who had seen the bombers first, lay groaning against the steel bridge rail, nursing a dislocated shoulder.

Krause rushed past the helmsman to take stock of the obvious damage and note any irregularities in the lines of Tiger tanks secured to the forward deck. However, the force of the explosion in the hold only seemed to have buckled the steel deck plates, although they were crumpled like paper at the point of the bomb's impact; white smoke now poured through the hole, through which the screams of the wounded resounded.

Krause was quick to note the loss in power. Although the telegraph registered 'full ahead', it was immediately apparent that the *Brescia* was not moving, but merely rolling in the almost imperceptible Mediterranean swell.

Bertini also noticed this and picked up the engine-room telephone. But there was only silence, the line was dead.

This time Krause ignored him, after checking the Tiger panzers aft. He told Fratelli to get the Breda positions manned;

'We don't want to get caught out like that again.'

In reaction, Krause was quite furious, with himself as much as anyone else, for letting it happen. He should have seen to it that there was a proper watch and that the E-Boat Kaleus had also done their job; in fact the Kriegsmarine Bofors gunners had been inhibited by the low approach of the Blenheim which had been masked by the cargo ship. Not least of all Krause was angry with Bertini and his constant defeatism.

Bertini listened in silence to the reports from the nominal

damage control system. The Italian crew were wild-eyed and incoherent.

Bertini then ordered the pumps to be manned to deal with the leak caused by the starting plate, but he was more concerned about the engine-room, as he looked up nervously to the sky, half-fearful of another attack. He tried to stop repeating to himself that the *Brescia* was now nothing more than a stationary target, an easy prey for any allied patrol, or bomber sweep.

Krause asked Bertini, not without a hint of sarcasm:

'What is the matter, Captain?'

'We have lost power; the engine-room has been hit; I'm going down with the chief engineer.'

Fratelli added:

'And we're taking water aft from a near miss.'

When Bertini entered the engine-room, the steam pressure had, of course, reduced and now only three or four spurts of steam from the damaged pipe plumed upwards. Bertini was nonetheless shocked at what he found; the two firemen, who had been on duty to check the steam pressure and oil flow, lay on the deck by the bulkhead against which they had been flung by the pressure of the invisible escaping steam. They had been literally boiled alive; skin hung in pouches from their lobster-red faces and their eyeballs were hideously white. What was worse, a sweet sickening smell overrode the harsh scent of diesel. Closing his mind to these unpalatable facts, Bertini quickly examined the apparent extent of the damage to the main steam pipe, from the fractures of which hot water dribbled. While he was doing this, Lampone, the chief engineer, lowered the steam pressure to minimum and shut off the turbine access pipes.

'Have we a replacement pipe?' Bertini asked.

The chief engineer, who was a quiet hard-headed northerner from Milan, looked doubtful.

'Mother of God, don't say that we're stuck out here and you can't do anything.'

'The ship's stores were flooded on the last run to Catania; there was some corrosion and the spare turbine parts were stored forward where the first bomb fell into the troop deck. We have only one short replacement section, the others are quite hopeless. This is a special material, don't forget it has to withstand exceptional pressure.'

Bertini absorbed the bad news without further comment, as he made his way out of the engine-room, leaving Lampone to deal with the remains of the firemen as best as he could. On the bridge Bertini made for the charthouse and found another bottle of grappa that had escaped the bombing. Krause was waiting for him:

'How serious is it?'

'We've had it, Colonel. We may drift to North Africa, but we certainly won't get there under power.'

'What is it precisely?'

'We have no replacement for badly damaged sections of the main steam pipe in number 3 engine-room.'

He finished off a glass and poured himself another.

'Now, with your permission, Colonel, I'll give the order to abandon ship.'

'Abandon ship?'

'That's what I said.'

Krause gripped his sleeve;

'Listen to me, Captain, I have civilian technicians with my battalion, who could conjure steel plate from cardboard; do you really think they would be defeated by that?'

Bertini said:

'Impossible.'

'We have welding equipment in our field workshop. I have specialist engineers.'

Bertini said:

'You can do what you like, Colonel, but I can't accept responsibility, an unproved, welded seam is unlikely to withstand any pressure worth mentioning.'

Noticing Krause's expression he paused for a moment; 'however if you want to try . . .'

An aldis lamp was winking from the E-boat on the *Brescia*'s starboard bow, since Krause had insisted on wireless silence. The colonel told Dieter to go down to the engine-room and take the civilian heereswerkmeister technicians from the workshop with him.

Krause guessed that the E-Boats were getting fidgety now that the *Brescia* was stationary. He would make a point of mentioning their ineffective and off-hand attitude in his official report to the Reichsminister. Now the battalion medical officer came onto the bridge and saluted. Secretly Krause despised Dr. Arnim. There was something unmanly about being a doctor; besides he wore glasses.

'Well what is it, Captain?'

'Some of the men are in shock, Colonel; they need surgery; unless they are taken to a base hospital, they will probably die.'

'We all have to do that some time; well, you will just have to do the best you can.'

'Couldn't you signal?'

'I'm sorry, it's out of the question.'

Krause retained his self-control with some difficulty. There was enough of importance to worry about, without this kind of irrelevant detail, about which nothing could be done.

The medical officer withdrew in silence to administer morphine and prepare his casualties by making out labels, and writing the injection dosages on their foreheads, against an evacuation he suspected would never take place.

The *Brescia* was now strangely silent in the aftermath of the attack, with the turbines no longer running. Bertini took the grappa bottle out into the open, glancing again over the vast, clear, open dome of sky, half-fearfully expecting to see a squadron of Blenheims, Wellingtons or Bostons. His left shoulder still ached as he poured himself another drink.

The gun crews sat equally tense in the two manned Breda AA turrets, waiting for more bombers. Bertini drummed his fingers nervously, as he listened to the reverberations, clangings and bangings that came from the engine-room as the army welders heaved their equipment about.

Bertini was aware that he was not alone and that Krause was watching him. He could not avoid Krause any more than he could avoid the war. Krause studied Bertini with that indifferent detachment that made him so hateful. With a gesture, intended to display his contempt for Krause, Bertini began to drink the grappa from the bottle, hoping in this way to ruffle Krause's fastidiousness. He raised the brandy bottle in mock and sarcastic salute.

'All that it needs is one little torpedo,' he shouted. 'Or one little bomb. Smack.' He slapped his hand on the rail. 'Right through the bottom. That way you would get your uniform wet, Herr Colonel.'

The aldis was winking again from the E-Boat.

'What does he keep on doing that for?' Bertini demanded irritably. 'Permission to come on board? Permission to bugger off, would be more realistic.'

Krause ignored Bertini, although he resented everything about him, hypnotized by the four lines of panzers on the foredeck, like a boy with his toy soldiers; examining each one, from a distance, to see whether the covers had been correctly placed over each muzzle brake. He did not want the accuracy of the eighty-eights to be impaired by barrel corrosion.

By this time the E-Boat had drawn alongside and a young kapitän leutnant swarmed up the ladder which had been flung down to him. His youthful face wore a half-smiling, half-patronizing expression, and it seemed inevitable to Bertini that he was the bearer of discouraging news. The Kaleu saluted smartly and clicked his heels. Krause turned to return the compliment, unaware of the tear in the back of his panzer overalls and his smoke-stained face.

'How is your situation, Colonel?'

This seemed a fatuous question to Bertini. Krause shrugged and turned to the captain of the *Brescia*;

'Well? How is it?'

Bertini shrugged and rolled the unlighted cigar he had just taken out from one corner of his mouth to the other.

'It could have improved in an hour or two, I simply don't know. On the other hand we could be sunk without trace.'

'Colonel, there has been a signal; we have been keeping radio watch. I have orders from OKM to proceed to Cape Bon immediately. Another English convoy is trying to get through to Malta. I must go at once.'

Krause said:

'That's quite impossible.'

'I assure you, this is an order I cannot disobey, it comes on the highest authority from Berlin.'

'I am not altogether satisfied with your performance on this operation,' the German colonel said.

The young man smiled;

'I am sorry to hear that, but nevertheless I have my orders.'

'What happens when we lose the escort?' Bertini asked.

'Well Captain, at least I have some good news for you. In twenty minutes, maybe less, you will have an umbrella of your Capronis, and they will see you through. But, in any case, I think that from now on you will be safe. The English are gathering their forces to protect their convoy and so you will be left in peace. I do not think that they will trouble you.'

'I hope you are right, Kapitän Leutnant,' Krause said. 'You are assuming a grave responsibility. As you know I am acting on the direct order of the Reichsminister.'

The kapitän leutnant smiled again;

'But so am I also, Colonel, so am I. However there is one area in which I can extend co-operation, I can take the wounded; that has been agreed. I shall take them to Derna. It is better that way. As for the rest of you, I will wish you good luck.'

He saluted and clicked his heels again, with a certain air of independent and arrogant self-assurance that Krause found infuriating. Krause knew that he was beaten, he dared not break radio silence, and even if he did, it would be hours before he could get the E-Boat commander's order countermanded; even if that were possible. Instead he returned the compliment again, as gracefully as he could.

Ten minutes later, the eighteen most severely wounded panzer crew were swung carefully on to the slim foredecks of the E-Boats and gently positioned midships, behind the spare torpedo racks. Bertini watched the proceedings with indifference while Fratelli brought him another bottle of grappa from the Lazareet.

He was still standing in much the same position, an hour later, after the E-Boats had left, planing away in a great sweep westwards, and creating a bow wave that had gently rocked the *Brescia*. Like its captain the cargo ship also stood motionless, silent except for the hammering of the civilian artificers; as vulnerable as a wounded swimmer in a school of sharks.

Point 389

Midgeley listened incredulously to the swelling strains of 'Lullibelero', that came in faintly over the radio. Fleming was pleased with himself because he had finally succeeded in evoking a faint response from the 508 set, although in the rain of static, this was the only station he could pick up.

'This is the BBC Home Service. Here is the news and this is Alvar Lidell reading it . . .'

They stared at each other in disbelief and Thomson said:

'Jesus, Fleming, you are the genius. Maybe we'll get some real gen at last. Be in touch with the outside world.'

'Shut up,' said Midgeley tensely.

'Last night, Lancasters and Halifaxes of Bomber Command attacked the Hamm marshalling yards in strength, starting many fires and causing heavy damage. Three of our aircraft are missing. The next-of-kin are being informed.'

'In the Western Desert,' they all drew closer, 'heavy fighting is taking place in the vicinity of Tobruk. Elements of the Eighth Army are regrouping in prepared positions along a line south of El Adem.'

'The Ukraine. Heavy fighting continues around Rostov on the Eastern Front. A Red Army communiqué reports that strong German counter-attacks have been repulsed with heavy loss.'

'On the Home Front, the Ministry of Food announces new measures to prevent . . .'

The 508 set whistled and hissed; the freak atmospheric conditions which had bounced the short wave signal off the ionosphere and through the aerial to the barely functioning amplifier circuit abruptly changed, and the signal suddenly dissipated. The crackling grew fainter.

'Tobruk,' said Midgeley, 'Fucking hell, we really are behind the lines.'

Fleming said:

'Don't say I didn't tell you. We'll never make it anywhere, except the Cage. I'd give us another twenty-four hours. Rommel's "B" Echelon'll be swarming all over.'

Thomson said:

'That's a lot of bullshit, Fleming, and you know it. You're always trying to prove how brilliant you are. We've survived O.K. so far without taking orders from you.'

'You're a bloody optimist, Thomson. You should remember what they told us at Geneifa; get away from the main force and you've had it.'

'That was to stop you from becoming so independent, you'd go over the hill.'

Fleming said:

'That's no way to talk. You wouldn't take that tone with Anderson.'

'Well you're not bleeding Anderson, mate.'

Midgeley stood up from where he had been crouching beside the radio and looked across the desert, narrowing his eyes. The heat was a wall that enclosed them to the east and south; the sand shimmering in flat white patches, that looked like watery pools, which came as suddenly as they went.

A truck was moving in the distance, but its image was distorted as though it was being viewed in a fairground mirror, so that it had an attenuated bonnet and a canopy that touched the sky. It was impossible to tell to which army it belonged, or, come to that, if it was just a truck and not a disguised tank, since both sides used this ruse. Midgeley guessed that it was almost certainly German. He looked away and took a bearing on a Jebel to the east and a cross-bearing on the end of the escarpment to the north. Projected back, on the map, the bearings intersected at a 'feature' marked Point 389 on the map. On that assumption they must be some miles west of El Adem and about five miles from the sea. If they made it north to the coast road, they could possibly slip into the Tobruk perimeter; or even join one of the probing columns that the South Africans regularly pushed out beyond the defences.

Midgeley was keen to meet up with a 'Jock' column, since he was beginning to get worried by the condition of the

Grant. Starski complained that second gear was tending to slip, and that the engine was using too much fuel.

Although they had done everything they could to clean inside the tank, there was sand everywhere, and a grimy, stinking patina of oil, condensed breath and petrol vapour had attached itself to the interior. They had not had a proper wash for days, although they had soaked their K.D. in petrol and risked dermatitis. Even on the move, flies remained trapped in the fighting and driver's compartments, which they could never totally dispose of.

More often than not these were not just the irritating Egyptian house flies, which swarmed restlessly across their hands and faces, but a breed of horsefly that bit through their shirts and hose tops.

Looking at the map once again, Midgeley could see that, if he headed north, the track they were following would bring him to an airstrip. He had therefore the choice of crossing this or moving towards the mine belts in the east.

The crew were still digesting the BBC News. It was weird to hear the familiar voice of England after what they had just been through. Midgeley put away the map and said down the intercom: 'How much benzine, Starski?'

'Maybe thirty gallons; she starts to gobble it up.'

The trouble was it could be anything, air filter, plugs, a broken valve, dirty filters; but there was no time now to pinpoint the trouble.

'O.K. then, forward.'

They followed the camel track for a mile or two, moving in bounds from one ridge to the next; each time they stopped Midgeley scanned the surrounding desert with his glasses.

There was nothing to be seen, until a spotter plane idled over, six miles to the north. Midgeley told Starski to switch off the engine.

They sat in silence until the Fiesler Storsch droned away eastwards; in which direction Midgeley imagined he could hear the clamour of distant guns.

Then Starski pressed the starter motor button. The engine turned over once and then stopped. When he tried it again nothing happened.

'Sweet Jesus,' said Thomson, 'that sounds worse than a faulty track.'

Midgeley asked:

'Is it the battery?'

Starski said:

'That we shall have to check.'

To begin with, Starski methodically cleaned and scraped the battery terminals behind his bucket seat and tried again. This time the starter motor turned over, but not the engine.

'Maybe those Eyeties did something to the petrol in that tractor,' Fleming said. 'Maybe it wasn't such a good idea to liberate it.'

'Yeah, I bet they peed in it,' said Thomson.

Fleming laughed with a hint of superiority.

'I bloody mean it,' said Thomson. 'Either water, or sugar or piss, which is the commonest commodity in this fucking wilderness.'

They climbed out in silence and Starski carefully unbolted the engine compartment grill behind the turret.

Midgeley checked the carburettors and reached the same conclusion.

'I was switching to reserve,' Starski explained.

'So we came to the shit in the bottom of the main tank?' asked Thomson.

'That's about the size of it,' said Midgeley.

'It'll be a heavy job clearing the fuel leads.'

'I've no doubt that's what they had in mind.'

Midgeley primed the carburettor with clean petrol; this time, when Starski switched on, the engine coughed and ran for a few seconds.

'Well there's nothing else for it,' said Midgeley. Midgeley and Thomson drained out the main tank, as Fleming and Starski painstakingly followed the fuel leads back to the petrol pumps and then on to the carburettors, carefully loosening the union joints and drawing out the liquid in each pipe section.

It was Fleming that heard it first. He froze and crossed his fingers, for they were, after all, in dead ground; a little depression like a giant golf bunker.

Then the sound of engines came nearer.

'Jesus,' he said, 'that sounds like a jerry half-track.' He half-turned to take up his pistol from the holster, attached to his web belt, which he had removed and put down beside the tank.

Midgeley said sharply:

'This isn't the time to start playing heroes; don't do anything silly; just carry on with what you're at.'

'I don't much fancy being a sitting target, Corporal. We've a duty not to get caught, it's in the Army Act.'

'Don't bloody well argue. You're talking wet. Just keep on with what you're doing, get it?'

'What? D'you think they won't notice?'

'Just do as I say.'

It was too late to clamber into the turret, and in any case they would have to hand-winch the turret round to face the enemy, since they were without power.

All they could do was wait and hope that whoever it was on the other side of the ridge, would not find them; and if they did, would not shoot them up.

A Sd222 half-track reared at the ridge above. It was the sort generally used for reconnaissance, or bringing up supplies, in fact, for any odd job. Midgeley did not look up. It was closely followed by a growling, rumbling 18-ton recovery tractor, its crane cable swinging. Out of the corner of his eye, Midgeley saw the half-track stop. The MG 34 medium machine-gun mounted on the half-track was trained on them but did not fire.

Midgeley continued to replace the petrol tank drain nut, also acutely aware that at least four Schmeissers were aimed in their direction. At any moment a stick grenade could plop down at their feet.

Then he heard sand scuffing down the slope and looked up to see a German leutnant in a DAK peaked hat, goggles and white scarf, waving his MP 40 machine pistol.

'What is the trouble, gentlemen? Have you broken down?'

Fleming shifted his position a little too quickly and the leutnant shouted:

'Hande hoch.'

They all stood up and did as he said.

'What is it then, Corporal, engine trouble?'

Midgeley nodded, aware that this was the critical moment, which, if once passed, would ensure their temporary survival. If the leutnant had it in mind to shoot them, now was the time he would do it. The longer he decided not to, the greater their chances.

'Dirty petrol, eh? You should do your maintenance, like we do. You are a long way from your comrades. Now we are advancing past Tobruk. They are quite gallant fellows, your comrades, but soon we shall be enjoying the pleasures of Cairo.'

Midgeley watched him slowly lower his machine pistol and wave to a feldwebel who had been covering him beside the half-track. The NCO ran over to them; he wore no shirt and his socks were rolled down to his plimsolls. Wisps of his hair had been bleached white by the sun. The feldwebel looked over at the Grant with some interest.

'Amerikanische?'

Midgeley nodded again.

The leutnant said:

'It is a new tank that I have not seen before.' Then he went on in German:

'Put our markings on the panzer, Reuter, there's a good chap.'

Reuter shouted an order to two panzer grenadiers in the half-track who brought a stencil and a tin of white paint from one of the side lockers.

'You people,' said the leutenant, 'can finish off what you are doing.'

Fleming seemed to hesitate.

'Do as he says,' Midgeley ordered.

Starski cleared the petrol from the pump with a piece of scrim and Midgeley checked carefully before the bolts were replaced. He did not support any noble acts of sabotage which would end up with them de-lousing boobytraps after a beating-up.

Meanwhile the panzer grenadiers were engaged in stencilling a white equilateral cross on the sides, the turret and the engine compartment grill.

One of them, who was clearly something of an artist,

added an Afrika Korps palm tree, the bisected D divisonal sign of 21st Panzer, and the parallelogram of a panzer unit.

The leutnant noticed Midgeley watching;

'The spoils of war.'

'Yes, sir,' said Midgeley bitterly. He had an affection for the Grant, since it was, for the moment their only home.

'What are you doing out here?'

'We were cut off from our regiment.'

'There are no British units in this area, then. Is there a minefield?'

'I wouldn't know, not that we've discovered.'

The leutnant gave him a long, hard look, but evidently decided to believe him.

'Well, there are many more things Intelligence can discover at your interrogation.'

Midgeley relaxed slightly. It was encouraging to hear the leutnant considering their future.

'Over there, all of you. Go and sit down on the sand with your hands on your heads.'

Once they were sitting down the Germans conducted a leisurely search and removed their pay books, money, revolvers and webbing, together with Midgeley's watch and field-glasses. They also took Starski's rings, but the feldwebel spat when he looked at them closely and threw them down on the sand. The crew of the recovery vehicle also removed the jerricans of water and fuel from the Grant.

Midgeley's feelings after the tension of capture, followed by the brief elation he felt when he realized that they were not to be shot, now changed to a dull despondency. It had, of course, been too much to hope that they would not have stumbled upon a DAK patrol in the light of the BBC news bulletin, for they must be well behind the line. However he felt annoyed, after everything they had just been through, that they should have been captured simply because an Italian had urinated in a petrol tank.

It was not easy to focus on the future, for all he could see was a long expanse of frustration and boredom interspersed with fear. He had seen enough of the shambling greatcoated columns of prisoners in the Canal Zone, to be aware of that. From now on, he would be entirely at the mercy of other people.

The German recovery vehicle backed away and stopped but the feldwebel and the leutnant lingered, fascinated with the Grant and inspecting its every detail. The leutnant even brought a Rolleiflex camera from the half-track to take pictures.

As all this was going on, Midgeley heard the sound of approaching aircraft; the dull persistent booming of high-flying bombers. In answer beyond the low undulations to the north came the high-pitched rev of fighter engines.

Two minutes later a flight of Macchi-200 fighters, their undercarriages retracting, banked over the group of vehicles and began to climb towards the deep, steady roar of the bombers.

When the first salvo landed, the leutnant was obviously in two minds as to whether he should stay with the prisoners or take shelter in the half-track. In the end he compromised, slipping through the open turret hatch of the Grant.

The bombs continued to fall in a ragged carpet of exploding dirt and dust, singly and in clumps, prefaced by their low, keening, rising whistle that shrieked into Midgeley's eardrums.

The four prisoners tried desperately to scrabble into the loose sandbank, as the bombs fell nearer. If they were aiming at the airfield, Midgeley thought, they were a long way off target.

With a deafening roar, a stick of bombs fell beyond the half-track in a drum-beat ripple, lifting it off the ridge and smashing the rear suspension. Dazed, shaken and deaf, Midgeley glimpsed the long-angled body of the recovery vehicle, in its drab orange-sand camouflage adorned with the white Wehrmacht cross, as it distintegrated. A one-thousand-pound bomb had plunged straight through its steel floor to one side of the crane mounting and exploded, scattering fragments in an unholy rain of blood and fractured metal. Midgeley saw a human arm roll down the slope six feet away. The next bomb landed astride the ridge immediately above their heads, scooping out a great saucer of sand and rock that almost buried them.

Starski got to his feet in the middle of it all and began to shake his fist at the sky;

'Bloody Breetish; Bloody Breetish.'

'Get down, Starski.'

But Starski seemed oblivious. Midgeley guessed that the bombing had triggered off some well-suppressed subconscious response. Midgeley half-wondered, as he pulled the Pole down in a cloud of sand and gritty dust, if Starski's reaction went back to the Warsaw bombing.

Now, a second bomber wave appeared to the north, then the formation broke and Midgeley saw three parachutes open. He tugged urgently at Thomson.

'Come on.'

'Are you mad, Corp?'

'For Christ's sake, it'll be our only chance.'

Midgeley got to his feet and stumbled to the left and round to the rear of the Grant, now circled by artificial dust devils. There, it would be almost impossible for the leutnant to use the pistol ports, without revolving the turret, even if he had seen what was happening. Fleming hobbled along beside them whimpering, his right arm swinging loosely. He was too numb with shock to know that his arm had been neatly fractured by a granite boulder, half the size of football, thrown up by the bomb that had landed at the top of the ridge.

They crowded behind the tank, under the shelter of the rear mudguards.

Fleming said uneasily:

'Now what, you bastard Corporal? D'you want all of us killed?'

'The Jerry leutnant'll have to come out some time to see what's going on. When he does, we climb aboard.'

'Fucking stroll on, some bloody hope.'

'It's worth a try,' said Thomson.

'I don't agree, I don't agree,' Fleming said excitedly. 'I'd rather be on my tod.'

By now the bomb carpet had shifted north. As the sound of the bombs grew more remote, the leutnant peered questioningly out from the Grant's turret through the fog of sand and haze.

'Reuter,' he shouted, 'Reuter?'

His expression changed to one of disbelief, as he clambered out, his white scarf wound across the bottom of his face, and looked in the direction of where the recovery vehicle had once stood.

'Now,' said Midgeley.

He tapped Starski on the shoulder. Starski scurried up the back of the tank and down through the open turret hatch like a frightened rabbit. He was followed by Thomson.

Fleming said:

'You're off your head. You'll never get away with it.'

'There's no time to argue.'

Midgeley darted on to the back of the tank.

Then Fleming tried to use his right arm.

'Oh, God. I can't get up.'

'You should have done it when I told you. Move, damn you.'

Midgeley grabbed Fleming's left shoulder and pulled him up, – and then stepped forward to where Thomson was disappearing into the tank. As he did so the leutnant turned by the half-track, and seeing what was happening, shouted an order. A panzer grenadier bobbed up from the half-track and began to take aim with the 34 machine-gun, firing at Midgeley just as he dodged into the turret.

Fleming followed moaning. Midgeley saw his legs appear in the fighting compartment. The half-track machine-gunner fired another burst, this time at Fleming, as he desperately tried to ease himself through the turret hatch, crying aloud with pain because of his broken arm. The fire was accurate and concentrated and 37 7·92mm bullets caught Fleming in a lateral sweep at a velocity of 2,500 feet a second, punching through his stomach, so that he died instantly, his body flopping over the side of the turret, with his legs jammed inside against the tank commander's seat.

As Starski started the tank and it moved off, Fleming began to disintegrate, the upper half of his trunk sliding down the tank, held only by the spinal chord and vertebrae, until it dropped away behind the tracks.

This time the engine had started easily from the reserve

fuel tank and the Grant accelerated away from the machine-gun bullets which now ricocheted off the rear armour, while inside Midgeley watched, sickened, as blood oozed out of Fleming's abdomen and began to dribble down his K.D. trousers.

Thomson also saw and moaned on the floor, vomiting in shock, disgust and fear, until Midgeley could bear it no more, pushing up Fleming's legs and flapping intestines like a macabre tailor's dummy, until that too fell away beside the tank.

Midgeley's hands were shaking and blood-stained; there was an overpowering nightmare slaughterhouse stench inside the fighting-compartment.

'Bloody Breetish ... bloody Breetish,' Starski shouted. Midgeley unbolted the loader's hatch and made Thomson sit outside. Thomson clutched the hot metal with grim intensity, his muscles taut, frozen in emotional shock, keeping his face rigidly averted from the long streaking smear Fleming's body had made against the starboard side of the Grant.

Half a mile on, they came to a stretch of broken perimeter wire, where Midgeley ordered Starski to stop. At once a cloud of flies found the blood smeared outside and inside the tank, and Thomson slowly climbed down the side, shivering, his teeth chattering. Once on the ground, his head to one side, he desperately began to pelt the tank with handfuls of sand, in an attempt to drive away the flies and obliterate the blood. At the same time he shouted:

'No more killing; no more blood; no more killing. Don't do it any more.'

The ground still occasionally shook from the last salvos of bombs falling on the northern perimeter of the airfield. The last wave of RAF bombers was beginning to turn and go home.

Starski called up from the driving compartment:

'Shit, I only just remember; they take my gold rings.'

Midgeley called back, trying to wrench his mind away from Fleming's death:

'Forget it. They were only brass anyway.'

Gulf of Bomba

KRAUSE watched the circling aircraft from Stormo 6 with satisfaction. The *Brescia* under weigh once more, with the main steam pipe patched up, was now moving south at minimum boiler pressure with a circus of Caproni two-seater fighters and a solitary Cant flying boat as escort. Bertini, who was now more sober than at any time during the voyage, stood, nevertheless, outside the wheel-house on the bridge, gripping the rail with a nervous, fixed rigidity, gazing at the faint rim of purple on the horizon, that marked the North African coastline.

Although repairs had been effected on the turbine steam inlet pipe system, Lampone, the chief engineer, was reluctant to risk a second breakdown, with pressures of up to 2,000 lbs the cubic centimetre, and had refused to press the engines to more than five knots. Krause had been forced to agree, unless he chose to risk the ship and his panzer battalion. However, he felt comparatively reassured in the presence of the fighter escort above, even though they came from the Regia Aeronautica.

Nonetheless, by this time, a distinct feeling of unease had spread throughout the ship, as the *Brescia* followed its change of course. Krause had had a radio report that the Afrika Korps had invested Tobruk, so that the port might fall to Rommel at any time. In case of that event he preferred to change course across the Gulf of Bomba, so that he could hug the coast of Cyrenaica and even make Tobruk itself should that prove practicable.

Alternatively he could stand off Derna or any other available anchorage to the west. In any case the Tiger panzers were equipped with schnorkels so that they could operate submerged in up to thirteen feet of water, he reminded himself; a plan half-formulating in his mind.

The tank crews now preferred to be on deck after the last attack; they crowded round the Tigers, watching the sky.

Bertini said:

'It's the sea they should be worrying about.'

Krause raised an eyebrow.

'What do you mean, the sea?'

'British submarines patrol the coast routes used to bring up Afrika Korps supplies, it's a favourite hunting-ground. At five knots the *Brescia*'s not likely to be a difficult target.'

'Don't worry, Captain Bertini, after all we have Italian fighters to help us.'

Bertini hunched up his shoulders even more and spat over the ship's side before commenting:

'I'd stop chewing my finger-nails if we had a flotilla of destroyers.'

'Can't your people upstairs deal with submarines?'

The coast was almost a definite line now, a long, thin segment of land floating on the edge of the world.

Bertini shut his eyes, he didn't want to talk to the German any more, but there was little alternative.

'God help us all if we're torpedoed; with the weight of your tanks on deck, the *Brescia* will founder like a stone.'

Krause said without a smile:

'You are a pessimist, that's out of character for an Italian.'

Bertini sighed;

'No, Colonel, I'm just a realist; one only acquires that attitude through long and bitter experience.'

The ship slid on through the oily water.

* * *

Five miles to the south-west, Lieutenant-Commander William Reddin of H.M. Submarine *Sharpshooter*, swept the high-power periscope across the northern horizon and altered the image of the distant cargo vessel to 6 magnifications with the twist grip.

It was cold inside the submarine and Lieutenant-Commander Reddin sucked in his cheeks, feeling his beard rub against his white seaman's sweater, which he had not taken off day or night since the beginning of the patrol ten days ago.

'I have a target, Number One. Make bearing green 50 full ahead.'

The *Sharpshooter* turned imperceptibly on the new course, the power from one hundred and thirty tons of battery producing ten knots submerged.

Reddin had calculated that the ship was on a course of due south at a speed of five knots. He had been patrolling the Gulf of Bomba for the last twelve hours and had seen nothing except a couple of E-Boats in a hurry. The target was unescorted but he switched the h.p. periscope to sky-scrape, and as a breaking wave momentarily exposed vision he saw the circling Capronis.

In the Mediterranean it was assumed that a submarine could be observed by aircraft at any depth above forty-five feet, if, that is, the aircraft was looking hard. Lieutenant-Commander Reddin was experienced in weighing one risk against another; when he came up to his attack position, that is to say within a mile of the target, he would creep along at three or four knots, almost elminating the wake of the attack periscope.

'Coxswain, hold her at periscope depth.'

The two coxswains controlled the forward and rear hydroplanes and they were responsible for ensuring a steady platform from which the torpedo could be launched; they were equally responsible for ensuring a smooth and rapid dive away from the depth charge attack that would inevitably follow.

Reddin guessed that the target was probably a valuable cripple crawling towards the safety of Cyrenaica.

He had one torpedo left in the upper starboard forward tube. This was a 21 inch mark IV that was suspected of being faulty. It was all that he had left after his patrol off Cape Bon and Tripoli. Now they were about to return to 10th Flotilla at Valetta he had the chance to be rid of it.

Reddin now changed to the attack periscope as the courses of the hunter and the hunted began to converge. He would bring the *Sharpshooter* to within range of a thousand yards, which would give him enough time to bring the forward tube to bear on the slowly-moving merchantman. He noted, as he looked once more through the graticule, how high the dazzle-painted freighter stood out of the water. She was ballasted, but he sucked through his teeth again as he saw the tanks on her deck.

* * *

After the death of Grunen, Krause had promoted Dieter second-in-command, and the young captain had now joined him on the bridge. Fratelli had gone below; he was now as obsessed as Bertini with the urge to get away. However, in his case, his nervousness expressed itself in a flurry of activity, most of it unnecessary, which involved checking the Breda positions, and seeing that all the available rafts and floats were unlashed and ready should the worst happen.

For Fratelli considered it inevitable that they would be attacked again. He noted sourly how subdued the panzer crew were now, after the attack of the solitary British bomber, and felt they had seen nothing of what could happen. In a matter of minutes the sky could become dotted with planes and the attacks could continue remorselessly, hour after hour, until night fell or the ship made harbour. Even then it would not necessarily stop.

It took half an hour for the *Brescia* to reach the northern edge of the shipping lane that followed the desert coast. By that time the *Sharpshooter* had made its wary approach. Reddin took the submarine in and halted, waiting for the ship to cross his sight. He would aim slightly off the bow, so that unless she zig-zagged, the twenty-one-inch torpedo, carrying fifty-six pounds of explosive at forty knots, would strike her midships.

Reddin said:

'Fire one.'

There was a 'woomp', as the torpedo left the tube with a cushion of compressed air behind it, at the same time throwing a lever which started the torpedo's engine; the air needed for the fuel to burn was provided in the twelve-foot steel cylinder behind the warhead.

'Torpedo running.'

The torpedo went unnoticed by the *Brescia*, but the stream of bubbles drew a thin white path across the sea and was spotted by the observer of the Cant flying boat.

It immediately banked and followed the fading torpedo track backwards as the *Sharpshooter* dived to two hundred feet. It released its depth charge pattern set to explode at fifty, one hundred and one hundred and fifty feet. The resultant explosions caused little damage to the *Sharpshooter*, except to flake off paint, since the Cant had overshot its target.

The crew of the *Sharpshooter* were glad to hear the rumble of the exploding torpedo.

Reddin had in fact miscalculated, although he could hardly be blamed. The mark IV torpedo, having reduced its speed to thirty-eight knots during the latter half of its course, struck the *Brescia* slightly forward of the rudder, blowing a single six-foot hole just above the bilges. The ship reacted immediately, as the sea flooded in, contained by the lower rear hold bulkhead.

Krause and the others on the bridge were thrown to the deck by the force of the explosion. Since the rear hold was divided off by a bulkhead, the immediate damage flooded this compartment to the waterline, at the same time raising the *Brescia*'s bows an additional three feet, so that she was ploughing along with her rear deck almost awash.

The consequential strain on the ship became apparent as rivets and bolts started in the rear of the hull from these newly-imposed pressures. Nobody, however, had been hurt. The Tiger tanks on the aft deck rose and sank uncertainly, their tracks awash.

The *Sharpshooter* surfaced, as soon as Reddin calculated that the pursuit had been called off, and sent a signal to Captain (Submarines) Malta, giving the *Brescia*'s position and suggesting an air strike.

Bertini looked back gloomily at the after-deck. He could feel the ship was heavy when he took the wheel for a moment; what else could he expect but a slow response from the rudder. He turned abruptly to Krause; the water was creeping up the after-deck.

'You must get rid of them.'

'Get rid of what?'

'Your tanks. If they go we have some chance. If not, it is the finish. You can see the trim is going.'

'Could we beach her?'

'You could, if the bombers let us get that far, but, even so, we might not have enough speed.'

Krause's face was strangely set as he called Dieter, as though it hurt him physically to give the order.

'Do as he says.'

'But how?'

'It is better to sacrifice half the tanks than lose them all.' He answered Dieter's unasked question first.

'Listen, start the engines and engage in first gear. The drivers will have at least thirty seconds to get out, once each panzer starts to move.'

Dieter relayed the instructions to the puzzled tank crews and they immediately began to unshackle the holding chains on the rear deck.

Dieter said;

'I would prefer you to give the order, Colonel.'

Krause looked at him contemptuously and shrugged. The drivers were white-faced and tense now they had guessed at what was supposed to happen.

'Better still, I'll show you.'

He went to the nearest tank and climbed down past the breech block until he was at the steering-wheel. Inside the fighting compartment the walls were damp and clammy with condensation, like the ship.

Krause switched on the engine and engaged bottom gear, gradually moving out the clutch, as he heard the tracks beginning to inch across the steel plates of the deck. Then he moved quickly back from the driver's seat, pulling himself up as the tank crushed the rail stanchions and juddered; then out through the turret hatch and onto the engine compartment, as the tracks began to churn onwards into the sea. He stood watching as the Tiger hung poised for a moment and then suddenly dived forwards, its tracks still grinding on, as the *Brescia* wallowed fitfully.

The panzer crews stood silent, mesmerized by what they had just seen. Krause turned to them and shouted:

'Now it's your turn.'

The drivers in the second file of tanks were less concerned, for they had greater margins of safety. Besides, after it had been done half a dozen times it all seemed so easy. When there were only five left on the after-deck, Dieter pointed to the nearest:

'You next.'

The driver, who was only a boy, climbed in hesitantly. The tank crawled forward, its engine purring. As the front track crossed the shattered rail he did not appear through the turret hatch as the others had done. Dieter started to shout at the tank, giving a high-pitched nervous order for him to get out. One of the crew men even ran forward, as if to try and hold it back, but it travelled on remorselessly and steadily into the sea. It crossed the broken rail, already torn away by the Tigers that had preceded it, and as it stood poised for a moment on the point of balance, the boy's head appeared for a moment, looking fearfully round. Then the Tiger slid gently down, sucking him under.

Now that the deck was cleared, the *Brescia* had risen a metre. Krause asked:

'Will we be alright?'

Bertini said:

'That depends. If it was up to me, I would abandon ship.'

The captain pointed to the south-east where a scattered pattern of moving dots had appeared.

'Look, more bombers.'

The Capronis had seen it too and three of them climbed to gain height.

Krause said:

'I want you to signal full speed.'

The land was looming ahead; how far was it, Krause wondered. Five miles? Ten?

Bertini shrugged.

'It can make little difference now, but I shall recall the men from the engine-room.'

Krause did not seem to hear what he was saying.

With the jettisoning of the heavy tanks from the after-deck, the trim of the *Brescia* noticeably improved. That is to say, the counterbalance of the remaining tanks on the forward deck now helped to raise the stern. But even at full steam, under such a load and with the rear hold flooding, she could barely make three knots.

Krause said:

'The fighters will keep them off.'

'Will they, Colonel?'

There was a splash and Krause turned sharply to see a white wooden float drifting back from the *Brescia* with two seamen clinging to it. Krause drew his Walther and fired; but at that range and with a moving target, a revolver was an ineffective weapon. Pale with rage he turned on Bertini;

'Tell your men that if anyone else tries that I'll tell my panzer grenadiers to get rid of them all.'

When Fratelli relayed the message half-heartedly over the tannoy system, the Italian crew members only responded with groans and cat-calls.

The Airfield

MIDGELEY now hated the strange passivity of the desert where nothing ever changed. It was a constant backdrop to the pitiful events that men played out against it. It was impossible to personalize Fleming's death in these surroundings, for it could have happened in half a dozen places; they all looked much the same.

He would have liked to be able to personalize Fleming's death, if only to give some reason for his life. As it was, Fleming's value to the human race had obviously been minimal; in fact he probably only had a nuisance value.

The desert reflected back to him the insignificance and fatuity of Fleming's short life; he had not even survived long enough to apply once more for WOSB, let alone join the ranks of the academically qualified.

None of them spoke for half an hour as Starski took the Grant north, because all of them were thinking about what had happened to Fleming. Thomson was secretly grateful that his number hadn't come up, and it confirmed his view that in a malevolent universe it is better to take orders from those who have a highly-developed instinct for survival; which clearly had not been Fleming's strong point.

Starski was irritated because Fleming had got himself killed so inefficiently, like two dead boys he had seen on the outskirts of Malbork, when they were retreating to Warsaw, who had found an abandoned satchel of hand-grenades and begun to play soldiers with them.

It took them a long time to reach the perimeter of the airfield, because Starski was tired and was forced to zig-zag to the right and left on an irregular course to avoid bomb craters.

Thomson continued to loll against the turret, in what seemed a state of shock. Midgeley didn't care much about anything any more once he had stopped thinking about how much he hated the desert. Life then became reduced to an awful simplicity where he rolled around with the motion of the tank, which made him feel queasy, looking out of the turret hatch where Fleming had stood, or confined himself in the coffin-like space of the fighting compartment.

The only thing that kept him from falling asleep was the knowledge that all too soon they would be out of fuel and water. After the escape he could not even think of the possibility of recapture, particularly since, following the RAF bombing raid, both Germans and Italians would be trigger-happy and anxious to level the score at their expense.

This led him to consider his own attitude towards the enemy. Some of the Germans he had met seemed decent enough, clearly concerned with their own problem of survival. At a distance they became the instruments of terror, mutilation and sudden death. In that respect he wanted to have nothing to do with them, other than to eliminate their menace.

The airfield now lay half a mile ahead. It was difficult without his glasses, but he judged that the bombing had done very little to reduce the effectiveness of the airfield. A line of Italian Capronis and Cigogna medium bombers stood in a broken line in the middle distance and two of them were burning. Beyond these lay a block of buildings and a water tower. The tank of the water tower was marked 'Sidi El Hamra'. There was little movement on the field.

What continued to nag at the back of Midgeley's mind was the fact that they now had only two canteens of water between the three of them, since the Germans had made them take off their webbing and removed the spare jerricans of water from off the Grant. Thomson suddenly said: 'You killed Fleming, Midgeley you bastard. We should have stayed behind the wire.'

'That's not true, he wanted to argue the toss; he didn't move when I told him to. He almost dropped me in it as well.'

'He gave you the needle, didn't he?'

'It's not my fault he was keen to go on the NCO's junior leadership course.'

'Well I think the whole issue is bloody insane.'

Midgeley said:

'You know as well as I do that if we had stayed we would be dead. I wouldn't have fancied our chances once that Jerry lieutenant found out what Bomber Command had done to his mates.'

The thought stopped Thomson in full flow and suddenly he gave way to a spell of panting and sobbing.

'I knew it wasn't your fault really Corp. But screw the fucking war, screw the whole issue.'

'Well, just don't try and shove it my way, that's all,' said Midgeley. 'Those Jerries were all very gentlemanly and lovable before the siren went, they didn't even feel inclined to knock us about. It'll be different now, I'm telling you.'

Thomson stopped crying and then shouted as loud as he could:

'Fuck the god-damned war, that's all.'

'I couldn't agree more,' Midgeley said. 'Personally I'm all for jacking it in, as of now, or once this little lot's over. Wangle a postings clerk job at GHQ. See the other buggers sweat and send them up the sharp end. But to do that, I'd really need a stainless steel conscience.'

Thomson wiped his face with his shirt sleeve and then said rather more calmly:

'It's just the more this jamboree keeps rolling, the less I rate my chances of survival.'

Starski was singing something in Polish as the tank lurched on. Midgeley noticed that the wind had got up and that there were little spirals of dust running across the desert. Sometimes these joined together in a hanging cloud that whirled away and suddenly dispersed. Fleming's death seemed to have induced a curiously desperate effect in all of them. Midgeley had even dropped his usual caution and no longer ordered Starski to halt at every ridge, hull down, to check the way ahead. He became submerged in an ocean of tiredness, that was not so much physical, but a draining of the will.

He had had to take too many decisions, too often. Thomson had quietened down but his hands were shaking.

When they passed a derelict Italian Autoblinda armoured car, Starski pulled up.

'Benzine?'

'No chance,' said Midgeley, 'that thing's been there since the declaration of war.'

'All the same, I take a look; have a pee.'

Midgeley decided against raising any objections, realizing that this was the nearest thing to an emotional release Starski could find in answer to Fleming's death.

'It must be possible to win something in this war,' Starski said as he climbed out of the Grant and began to walk towards the armoured car, that had been ripped open like a tin can on the near side.

Thomson said, with something like his old spirit:

'Where the fuck's he swanning off to?'

Midgeley said:

'He won't find anything, Starski's always looking for things, it seems to give him a reason; otherwise, what's the bloody point?'

'Too bloody true. Corp. What is the point?'

Starski was busy poking about inside the rusting Autoblinda. He discovered that all the tyres had been removed. The doors and hatches were all open, and sand had heaped up on the floor through a six-foot gash in the side.

Midgeley and Thomson walked over to the armoured car and little wisps of sand scudded across their boots.

'He'll be lucky,' Thomson said.

'After the war,' Midgeley said, 'I'm going into the scrap business; there's more old iron littered across the mardam, than in the whole of Tyneside. Somebody's going to make a packet.'

Starski was searching the stowage bins inside the Autoblinda, but all he could find were some oily rags, a rusting spanner and a corroded shell case.

Now his mood had changed, Thomson seemed to get an emotional release from taking it out on Starski.

'No chance, comrade, nothing, not even a sixpenny Woolworth's wedding ring.'

Starski shrugged and took no notice.

'You and your loot. Anyway, if you start collecting badges

and paybooks and the other side catch them on you, they'll want to know what you did with the owners.'

The last of the rear stowage bins had its lid jammed, when the starboard armour had been ripped open by an armour-piercing shot. Starski started to work away at it, using the spanner he had found as a lever.

Thomson said:

'You're bloody balmy, Starski, you'll never find fuck all; you never do.'

This comment encouraged Starski to put all his weight on the spanner so that the lid sprang. He gently raised it, lowering it as he caught sight of a piece of wire dangling on the back of the lid.

'Christ,' said Midgeley, 'that was a booby trap.'

'Sometime, maybe, it was mined. The wire is loose; corroded.'

Starski cautiously raised the lid again and was proved right. Midgeley could see that the pull wire had parted; the armoured car must have been out in the open for years. Starski raised the lid of the stowage compartment and rested it against the wall of the armoured car. He plunged his hand in and took out a little wooden box and a jumble of wire.

'Schüh mine. Made in Italy.'

He threw it over to the far side of the Autoblinda, where there was a 'phut' and a bang that threw up a cloud of sand.

'Ha, fucking, ha,' said Thomson.

Starski ignored him again, now totally absorbed by the contents of the stowage bin.

'Not bad, not bad,' he kept on saying.

'Why did they bother to leave anything?' Thomson asked.

'In the war you never ask questions, just take what's good and what's bad, otherwise what's the point. Every time I have bad trouble, I want something for it. I want to balance the books.'

Starski began to throw out Italian kit bags, one of which contained a wicker-covered flask of chianti, now reduced, through time, to a dry powder.

Midgeley said:

'I'll have those.' He picked up a pair of field glasses

marked Carl Zeiss-Jena from the bottom of the stowage bin. Starski did not seem to object. He was searching each uniform methodically, and turning out the pockets, to find one or two corroding lira and letters in faded ink. There was even a postcard dripping with Latin romanticism, a boy and girl looking into each others eyes with tenderness, a dove perched on their clasped hands. Starski removed the badges he found, putting a pair of cracked leather cross straps and a belt on one side.

'What d'you do with the gear?' Thomson asked.

'Flog it down the bazaar.'

Having disposed of the metal, Starski now proceeded to remove the cloth insignia. Finally all that was left was a German corrugated metal gas mask container which he discarded.

Starski squatted down and examined the fistful of insignia.

'I've never seen these before.'

Midgeley said:

'That stuff's off one of the Blackshirt Divisions from way back. Like I told you, it's a bonus from the phoney war three years ago. That stuff's been gathering dust since General 'Electric Whiskers' marched on Egypt in 1940.'

Starski got up without saying anything, and started to walk back to the Grant, rattling the badges up and down in his hand, but Midgeley could tell that he felt better.

The corporal realized that a dangerous casino-like atmosphere had infected them. They had taken the most appalling risks. Yet, although the Grant was now inside the perimeter wire and could be easily seen, none of the airfield ground crew had taken any notice of them, maybe because of the German markings. Half a mile away, Midgeley could now see groups of Arabs, supervised by Italian pioneers filling in the bomb craters.

In the distance, obscured for a few seconds by a passing dust devil and then re-appearing to shimmer like a mirage in the heat haze, stood the water tower. When he focused his new glasses he found that one of the lenses was cracked, however he could make out a long low silhouette beside it – rows of fifty-gallon aviation fuel drums, roofed over with rocks and sand, which had survived the bombing unscathed.

An Italian truck, loaded with fuel drums, crept out to a Savoia Marchetti 79 medium bomber.

Starski and Thomson were standing aimlessly, watching the scene, as though it was Hendon Air Show before the war, when Midgeley told them to get into the tank.

'For Christ's sake, you think you're invisible, Thomson?'

Midgeley, himself, however, lingered for a moment after the others had climbed into the tank, listlessly watching the Italian activity. The lorry had now stopped by the wing tanks of the bomber and already fuel was being hand-pumped aboard. Midgeley could quite clearly make out the three parallel fascis of the Regia Aeronautica, in their white circle, gleaming against the stone and blobbed green Italian camouflage.

'They don't seem to worry,' said Thomson; 'they've forgotten the blitz.'

The wind had continued to rise and the scurries of sand, moving across the desert had increased. From time to time dustclouds obscured the northern airfield perimeter by the fuel store, like smoke.

'We need petrol,'said Midgeley.

Thomson said:

'Then we've come to the right place, haven't we? What with all those barrels of aviation fuel and all.'

Starski said:

'I wish I was back at Cairo Souk; or Sally Anne Canteen would come out of the bluey.'

Thomson said:

'You got your souvenirs, what more do you want?'

Midgeley pushed away the unending feeling of tiredness yet again and tried to clear his mind. He had locked away the memory of Fleming's death, so that could have nothing to do with it. It was a question of yet another decision. All he knew was that, if they were jumped again, he would be quite happy to put his hands up.

At last he said:

'Well what do you two want? Jack it in? Eat spaghetti for the next five years? Or are you still willing to contribute to the war effort?'

Thomson shook his head and Starski remained silent.

'I'm asking you, you jammy bastards. What happens next?'

Thomson said:

'You're the one with the stripes up.'

'By Christ, and don't you make me feel it? OK, we can't swan about here forever. Drive on!'

Starski started the engine.

Midgeley started to think aloud:

'Maybe we can get behind the bastards. Lie up till it's dark; liberate some of that petrol. Anything's better than sitting on one's arse admiring the view.'

The others still didn't say anything, but suddenly Midgeley felt relieved of the responsibility as much as any of them; after all he had planned nothing from the moment they'd become separated. All that had happened had been that situations had been pushed at him to which he had responded seemingly correctly, as he might on some insane obstacle course.

'OK, OK Corp, don't take it out on us, but after this, start driving east so's we can tag on to some friendly unit. I'm sick of being out on a limb.'

'Christ, aren't we all.'

* * *

Six miles to the north, Krause was also getting tired of being out on a limb. Even at the paralytic three knots the *Brescia*'s engine-room was able to muster, the African coast beckoned invitingly now. The German colonel had got out the chart and pushed it in front of Bertini.

'Now be good enough to show me where we are.'

Bertini wearily drew his wrist across his damp forehead.

'We are here, four kilometres from the sandbanks.'

'What is the draught at high tide?'

Bertini checked the tide table and glanced curiously at Krause, wondering what proposal he was going to be faced with next.

'It is very little, maybe six metres. That is, on top of the bank.'

The chart showed the outline of the humps of the sandbanks that moved in and out, moulded by the currents and linked to each other and the land by broad or narrow invisible highways.

'What is the bottom, Bertini?'

'It will be sand, hard sand.'

Krause glanced at Dieter, curious to know whether he would have guessed what he had in mind.

Dieter sensed that he was going to give an order;

'Sir?'

Krause said:

'Check the schnorkel and seals on the remaining Tigers. See each panzer has a full petrol tank and load on the maximum reserve.'

Dieter's weary eyes widened slightly in surprise.

'Well? What are you waiting for? Get on with it.'

Krause turned and saw through a splinter rip at the back of the chartroom that the rear deck was now awash and level once more with the sea. He realized that the flooded section at the back of the ship was acting as an enormous sea anchor.

Bertini followed his glance and said:

'You are right, Colonel; it is just a matter of time.'

'If we don't beach first.'

The open link between the Caproni escort and the *Brescia* crackled as the leader pilot spat out something in Italian.

'What's he saying now?'

Bertini answered non-committally:

'He says the escort has fuel for two more minutes with us and then he must return to Sicily.'

Krause was thunderstruck by this information; as much because it was outside his calculations as anything.

'Why don't they try another field? God knows, there are plenty of landing strips along the coast to Benghazi.'

Bertini talked to the pilot.

'He says there is heavy fighting south of El Adem, but there is a possibility at Sidi El Hamra. The situation is very fluid and it is hard to tell which fields are in our hands. El Hamra is only a possibility, the runways are being repaired; it was attacked two hours back.'

Krause drummed his fingers on the chart.

'Then tell him he must refuel there. I have every authority up to Field Marshal Kesselring and beyond. No, wait ...' He saw the look of hostility beginning to build up in Bertini's eyes.

'No, tell him it is for the honour of Italy.'

Krause knew that the sentiment was clumsy, but he was also aware that nothing would appeal more to Italian vanity than to know he was doing the German a favour. Put in that form it would be difficult for the escort to refuse.

'How long will they be?' Krause asked Bertini, as the Capronis left the Cant seaplane and made for the North African coast.

'He said, if the situation is good maybe no longer than fifteen minutes.'

Krause now began to notice the debris of sunken shipping that surrounded them as they approached the sandbanks. These lay like an imprecise barrier reef, two miles off Cyrenaica, which was now clearly visible. Behind them, the escarpment beyond the shore line rose like a buttressed wall from sea level. When Krause used his glasses, he could see the Italian fighters dropping down behind the hills, on to the plateau beyond.

Bertini said:

'You are lucky, Colonel, the tide is falling. We can follow this channel,' he pointed ahead, 'and put the *Brescia* aground here.' He again pointed to a crescent-like sandbank a mile offshore.

'The more the tide ebbs, the easier it will be to do what you have in mind.'

Although Bertini still kept the grappa bottle at his elbow, he was, for the time being, fascinated by Krause's apparent refusal to admit defeat, even in the face of what, to any normal man, would appear to be impossible odds. Bertini was also favourably influenced by Krause's intention to run the *Brescia* aground, which meant that, provided they were left alone by Allied bombers, there was an increasing chance that he and the rest of the crew would survive. It was certainly a much better prospect than painfully following the coast west to Derna.

Krause said:

'One problem remains.'

'What is that, Colonel?'

'Our Tiger tanks are designed to travel submerged up to a depth of four and a half metres. This means it is possible to swing them out on to the sandbank where they can make their way underwater to the shore in perfect safety. However 62 tons is a heavy load for your derricks to handle.'

Bertini grasped the point at once; it was one thing to unload such deadweight with the gantry of a dockyard crane, and quite another using a ship's derrick. The *Brescia* mounted two on each deck but it would not be easy. Bertini pondered a suitable answer;

'That's yet another risk you'll have to take, Colonel.'

Krause turned to Dieter;

'Then you will also have to position the recovery half-tracks to control the descent. There will have to be a cable for each pair of shackles at either end of the Tigers; the weight will have to be shared equally between them and the *Brescia*'s derricks. The important thing will be to control the descent until the Tigers reach the sandbank.'

Bertini now lost interest in the conversation, concentrating on the course of the channel they were following, so that they would not run aground too early. This was a matter of luck as much as anything else, since the stern was drawing something like twenty metres. For Krause's plan to succeed, the boilers would have to build up maximum steam pressure, to ensure that the *Brescia* was launched as far into the sandbanks as possible. That was something else. Bertini said to Fratelli:

'I want everything off the ship.'

'Everything?'

'Not the tanks but the soft-skinned vehicles and half-tracks.'

Krause nodded his approval. Forward stood a row of trucks and lorries, which in any case would only be in the way, when the time came to manoeuvre the Tigers over the side. It would be comparatively simple to unshackle the rest, release the handbrakes and manhandle them into the sea.

The panzer crew's spirits had risen the nearer they came to land. They appreciated the significance of the preparations Krause had ordered, but this was not an immediate source of concern. Soon the Tigers were being slowly and painstakingly marshalled in the confined space of the forward deck, to let the half-track recovery vehicles move into position, beside the derricks swung out from their gantries.

Bertini meanwhile stood at the helmsman's shoulder, taking a mouthful of grappa from time to time, as he pressed the chief engineer to extract the maximum power from his overworked turbines, which turned the propeller at a bare thirty revolutions. It was with difficulty that he managed to bring the speed up to a maximum of six knots.

The captain of the *Brescia* was concentrating so hard in keeping to the centre of the channel, that he never noticed the second squadron of British heavy bombers approaching from the east.

* * *

Halfway across the airfield, although it had been obvious for some time, Midgeley suddenly realized that they had very little chance of remaining undetected. Although the dustclouds thrown up by the sand-storm acted as a horizontal screen and hid them from the far side of the Sidi El Hamra complex, it would be quite a different matter from the air.

As the Grant moved in a semi-circle to the east, Midgeley watched a number of aircraft come and go. So far as he was concerned, this was no moment to attack; all that he wanted was to be left alone. The first intimation that they had been sighted came when a Caproni fighter bomber circuited to take a closer look.

Almost before he knew it, the aircraft vanished and Midgeley became aware of stripes of tracer cutting through the dust clouds to their left. He turned to Thomson and said:

'You'll have to load the 75mm.'

Thomson grimaced.

Midgeley began to fire high explosive at the source of the tracer that seemed to be situated in the north west corner of the airfield.

Normally, he would have stopped the tank and gone through the elaborate ranging and fire control sequence which was laid down in the manual, and which would undoubtedly produce greater accuracy of fire. On the other hand, to come to a halt would put him in a totally vulnerable position.

Feeling as he did, he welcomed a Light Brigade charge, firing on the move.

The tracer flipped above and around them in beautiful incandescent curves, as the Grant's fighting compartment filled with smoke and cordite fumes each time Midgeley kicked the firing pedal and the flash flared, out of the muzzle and forward of the barbette, brilliantly illuminating the interior for a split second.

Since he was firing on the move, he could only guess at the range of the gun emplacements firing back at them. But in the distance, and through the dust clouds, the Italians must have thought that the airfield was about to be overrun, for the tracer became wilder and more intense. Fire ricocheted off the ground in front of the tank, and Midgeley heard the clatter of medium calibre shot against the armour.

Starski halted the tank at the edge of the runway, where the repair crews had already bulldozed in the bomb craters and filled any gaps in the runway wire. Midgeley shouted: 'Who told you to stop?' before he became aware of the roar of an aircraft overhead as another Caproni put down its flaps, at the last minute, to plummet on to the landing strip. The pilot must have either spotted the Grant or had second thoughts on viewing the turmoil that filled the field below, for he roared up and out again at full throttle just before touchdown.

Thomson shouted over the intercom:

'Please Corp, if he starts strafing us, we've had it this time, let's bail out.'

But the fighter did not return and so Midgeley ignored the remark, pressing his forehead to the sight as the dust storm subsided momentarily to reveal the water tower and buildings only four hundred yards away. Midgeley took careful aim to the left of this complex, where the guns should be.

'Shut up and feed the bastard gun, Thomson.'

The first burst of aimed HE went wide of the Italian gun pits and exploded on the edge of the fuel store. The disintegrating red-hot splinters punctured half a dozen drums of aviation spirit, so that high octane fuel began to dribble out on to the sand. The next burst ignited a small pool of petrol, so that flames began to lick along in a rush, beside the row of emptying drums, escalating the temperature to something in excess of 1000 degrees centigrade. The resulting explosions detonated each steel drum like a five-hundred-pound bomb, scattering flaming petrol and burning metal over a two-hundred-yard area.

The flames devoured the complex of buildings and the water tower so that they too began to burn, and the fire now spread to an underground ammunition store, where burning petrol began to flare down the concrete steps and under the steel entrance door.

Midgeley, of course, knew nothing of this, since he could only see a curtain of fire, flaming up to a height of ninety feet, before changing into a hovering, sky-high column of thick, black smoke.

'Fucking hell,' said Thomson, 'you hit the jackpot that time.'

The firing from the gun pits decreased in proportion to the intensity of the blaze. No attempt was made to put it out, presumably because this was an impossibility. However, silhouetted to the left was another Italian Caproni and two Junkers 87. Some ground crew had driven out a tractor and were desperately trying to hook on the nearest plane and remove it from the blazing fuel store.

Starski said:

'That looks like goodbye to fuel replenishment. We now have fifteen gallons in the reserve tank.'

* * *

Captain Bertini tried not to notice the English bombers, hoping against hope that they were seeking some other target, maybe even the airfield which the escort had planned to make for. He clung instead to the solution of the immediate problem; so that once on the sandbank, there would be some chance of survival. At one level of his mind, he was aware that this was wishful thinking. However, with another attack imminent, he had become supremely indifferent to Krause's dangerous and far-fetched plans for salvaging his tank battalion. Bertini could now only regard Colonel

Krause as a man who enjoyed throwing live grenades to his friends, with the safety-pin removed, to test the speed of their reactions. Bertini was, in any case, no friend of Colonel Krause, and his own reactions non-existent. Unless a miracle took place they would very soon all be dead. He started to pray in spite of himself while he poured out another glass of grappa.

Colonel Krause scanned the eastward sky with some anxiety. To the south a pillar of smoke was rising high above the escarpment, indicating that a supply dump was on fire. He realized how much he had been in the hands of the Italian escort, who now seemed to have thought better of their mission.

He shouted to Dieter:

'Get the Bredas manned.'

He had only just realized that there were no Italian gun crew and he would prefer to have his panzer grenadiers on the gun platforms, learning as they went, rather than a windy bunch of Italians, who were likely to disappear over the ship's side at any moment.

Meanwhile the bombers kept on their course at two thousand feet. The Wellingtons had an ominous, inevitable quality about them, in contrast to the nervous, jinking approach of the solitary Blenheim.

Captain Bertini glanced at the sky and crossed himself.

'Wellingtons.'

There was nothing else to say; all they could do was wait and hope for inaccurately set fuses and bad bomb aiming. Bertini swallowed another mouthful of grappa and spat over the side, calling out to no-one in particular:

'Watch out, I'm going to run her aground.'

By this time the *Brescia* was well up the cul de sac that ate into the lateral sandbanks at a point closest to the shore. According to Bertini's calculations, it could only be a matter of seconds before the cargo ship ploughed on to the sand.

Krause moved to his side.

'After they've dropped the first salvo, Captain, start burning oil.'

'Burn oil?'

'Make smoke as though we've been hit.'

Fratelli said sarcastically:

'D'you think that'll make them go away?'

Krause ignored him.

At that moment the *Brescia*, moving at five and a half knots, slid on to the sandbank, with the momentum of eight thousand tons dead weight, driving the hull forward for a hundred and fifty yards, until the drag of the flooded stern and the suction of the sand against the keel brought her to an abrupt halt, and the sandbank gripped her firmly in twelve feet of water. Although they were expecting it, the impact flung the gun crews off balance.

Bertini said drunkenly:

'There, Colonel; I have brought you to Africa.'

The rest of his remarks were brought abruptly to a halt by the first salvo of bombs delivered from George King Sugar, the first of the three Wellingtons to attack. The main body of aircraft had been briefed to bomb Benghazi to the west, although they had been given a certain latitude to attack coastal shipping. Unknown to Krause, the *Brescia* was not a priority target, since the Wellingtons had been ordered to concentrate on the Kriegsmarine barges pushing forward supplies for the Afrika Korps from Tripoli, Benghazi and Derna.

Three five-hundred-pound bombs straddled the *Brescia*, throwing up black columns of sand, sea, shrapnel and ammonal fifty feet high on each side of the ship.

Bertini hurriedly relayed Krause's instruction to make smoke to the engine-room, as the German gunners trained their Bredas on the next wave of attackers, scattering flak puffs across the sky.

The next trio of Wellingtons had better aim. On this pass, one five-hundred-pound bomb fell through the forward decking and exploded against the keel. Since, however, the *Brescia* was now aground, it did nothing more than settle her on the sandbank; but it did ignite the diesel oil in the forward fuel tank. The fire was partially contained by the inrush of sea water, but the burning oil was on its surface, beginning to gnaw away at the *Brescia*'s vitals. What was more serious was that the fire began to spread dangerously close to the tanks of gasoline aft, that had been pumped ashore as a fuel reserve for the Tigers by Colonel Krause at the Piraeus.

The forward deck and the structure below gradually increased in temperature; the lines of Tiger tanks on the foredeck became obscured in a pall of black diesel smoke.

However, this proved to be the last attack, the Wellingtons proceeded westwards in search of other targets as the burning diesel fuel cracked the glass of the forward portholes and began to seep out down the side of the ship.

Bertini looked at the growing shambles around him with indifference. The *Brescia* was now close to being a total wreck, but the Tiger tanks remained stubbornly intact, not looking very much different from when they had been loaded at the Piraeus.

He raised his glass:

'It's the end of the line; we've arrived. Anyone killed?'

Krause was simply not interested in Bertini. It was clear to him that he must implement his plan right away and in order to do this he must ensure control of the small fire which seemed to have gained a hold below. He called out to Dieter:

'Get a fire party organized.'

Captain Bertini said:

'Goodbye Colonel, it's been an experience knowing you.'

Krause answered:

'Where do you think you're going?'

'We're abandoning ship.'

'You're not abandoning my panzers.'

'Colonel, I am not a supercargo. At any moment the whole ship may go up.'

Krause fingered his Walther.

'There must be a party to control the derricks.'

Bertini was too tired to argue. His ship was lost, the whole world had gone mad and it was impossible to ignore the Colonel's explicit threat.

He shouted down to the engine-room that they must still make steam for the derrick engines.

* * *

Midgeley knew that beyond the screen of fire they would

come to the escarpment and beyond that to the coast road linking Derna with Tobruk. On the road they would travel faster and the Grant would eat up less fuel.

What Midgeley did not know was that the arrival of his Grant at Sidi El Hamra had prevented the Caproni fighters from re-fuelling, forcing them back to an airfield near Mechili, a hundred miles to the west. The escort did not return to the *Brescia* since they were then despatched to intercept a formation of Wellington bombers, plotted on course for Benghazi, where Italian cargo boats were unloading.

Neither could Midgeley and the tank crew survivors be aware that the *Brescia* was now lying, a burning wreck, on a sandbank three miles to the north, as Krause made desperate efforts to disembark his badly needed tanks.

Midgeley said:

'Press on, Starski.'

'Bloody hell.'

Midgeley shouted:

'Don't you think I haven't had enough? All I want to see is British armour if there is still any.'

Thomson said:

'Sometimes you aren't half the fucking optimist, Corp.'

Midgeley's mouth was dry and bitter with the taste of cordite; he swallowed a mouthful of water from one of the canteens and passed it on to the others. All he wanted to do was sleep, not argue, not make decisions. He shouted again:

'For fuck's sake, press on, Starski.'

Starski put the tank into low gear and lurched down the desert track; he kept in low gear as they came to the gradient that meant they had reached the edge of the scarp; below them, the track snaked away half a mile down to the plain that bordered the sea.

Somehow, the sea looked very peaceful out there in the afternoon light. Maybe, Midgeley thought, he should have joined the navy. The sea was empty, except for a stationary ship that seemed to have run aground.

But the ship, with its striped dazzle camouflage, had an air of mirage about it; perhaps it wasn't really there at all. The camouflage made it difficult to tell which was stern and which was bow.

He looked away as the faint roar of an explosion reached across to them, and even at that distance, Midgeley felt grit from the shock wave lash his face. The stem of the ship lifted as the internal fire finally penetrated the bulkhead compartment in which petrol had been stored. The explosion blew the stern off the *Brescia*, at the same time flinging the ship on to its side, so that in the confusion of movement and smoke Midgeley could still see the outline of vehicles on the foredeck slide into the sea like Dinky toys. Clouds of steam rose from the ship's side as with a thud the boiler exploded.

Thomson began to sing:

'Irene, goodnight Irene, goodnight Irene;
Goodnight Irene, goodnight Irene,
I'll see you in my dream.'

Thomson watched the boat and the turbulence surrounding it, and repeated the chorus.

The track joined the coast road at a point close to the seashore. Midgeley thought he could hear the sound of an artillery barrage further east, but his senses were so deadened by this time, he might have confused it with the irregular murmur of the engine. Starski also began to sing as they turned along the macadam road, happy in the knowledge that it would lower their fuel consumption.

The Grant passed several burned-out vehicles that had been pushed over on to the verge, but this must have happened some time before since there were no bodies. Then the road turned into a re-entrant at the corner of which stood a shell-shattered mosque.

Midgeley shouted to Starski to stop. The driver pulled off the road and parked the tank behind a section of broken wall. They all climbed out.

'Pushing it aren't you, Corp? There could be eighty-eights along this road.'

'I don't give a screw if Big Bertha's round the corner; I've got to get my head down. Besides we're Afrika Korps with these markings, or had you forgotten?'

All their faces were puffy-eyed and white through lack of sleep.

Midgeley lit a cigarette and then put it out impatiently. It tasted vile; his mouth was dry and acid. He took another swallow of water.

'Christ, I could do with a kip.'

'Couldn't we all,' said Thomson.

Then Thomson began to walk nervously up and down on his way to nowhere in particular. Midgeley wondered if, at last he had gone battle-happy with all that singing on the way down.

Starski suddenly pointed, big-eyed, towards the sea. He tried to say something, but couldn't make the words come out. Finally he said:

'Jesus, Corporal, Holy Mother; what the hell is it? A U-boat?'

He pointed beyond the surf to where a tall cylindrical schnorkel was emerging and travelling towards them.

* * *

When the stern of the *Brescia* was torn off, Colonel Krause was already in the water. Not on account of any fear for his own personal safety, far from it, but because he knew that the Tiger crews were reluctant to commit themselves to the schnorkel device.

All they had done with it so far was to ford rivers using it under test. Out here, in what seemed to be the middle of the ocean, it was quite a different matter. In theory nothing could go wrong; but they all knew that the hatches of the Tiger opened outwards, which meant that, in the event of engine failure, the crew would be trapped inside. Krause felt perfectly confident and comfortable as he was slowly swung out from the starboard side of the *Brescia*, for he had ordered his gunner, Meyer, to check the seals on the visor ports, gun mantlet and ventilators, while personally inspecting the pneumatic tube which sealed off the turret ring. He knew that behind them the engine schnorkel rose two metres from the engine compartment to suck in air. It was cool in the fighting compartment in consequence, from this air intake that passed through the tank before being fanned into the engine.

Now they were moving along a compass bearing slightly

west of south, dragging cables that had been secured to the shackles. According to Bertini's chart, the sandbank rose steadily towards the shore from the point at which the *Brescia* had grounded. Krause felt fully confident that the example he had set by leading the way would inspire the remaining half of the battalion to follow. Despite the difficulties they had had to face and the losses they had inevitably sustained, the addition of twenty Tigers could undoubtedly be decisive for the Afrika Korps, in the battles which lay ahead.

The violence of the explosion at the stern of the *Brescia* rocked the tank and made Joachim, the driver, look anxiously round. He could see nothing except a dim green fluorescence through the narrow visor that ran above the three-quarter steering wheel, and it was this unfamiliar isolation from the outside world that upset him. Suddenly they felt a second wave of turbulence and he moved up into the second gear as the tracks continued to gain traction in the hard ridge of the sandbank.

Krause had estimated that it would take at least ten minutes before it would be safe to deflate the pneumatic turret ring and open the hatch. While he was on the bridge, he had examined the coast road with great care and seen movement on it, an apparently captured tank, stencilled with DAK insignia. He glanced at his watch and reached up towards the turret ring.

* * *

Midgeley looked in amazement and alarm, anxiously reminding himself that out of the forty-six rounds they had started with, they now had five smoke, 3 HE and six armour-piercing. Trying to control his exhaustion he confronted this new and extraordinary situation.

They had taken up battle stations in the Grant as Midgeley saw the schnorkel reach up, out of the water, to be followed by a wireless aerial. He watched incredulously as this was followed by a squat, flattened turret with a large-calibre gun, that was part of a tank he had never seen before.

Thomson started to laugh hysterically:

'That's all we needed; a bloody Jerry secret weapon.'

There was no mistaking the colour or markings.

Thomson said:

'It was off that bleeding ship, wasn't it? Christ, there may be a whole squadron, a battalion.'

'No,' said Midgeley decisively. 'That'll be the only one.'

The hatch of the German tank was now open, so that Midgeley could see the commander in camouflage overalls. First, he looked back towards the burning cargo ship, as the frontal armour drew up out of the sea, spilling water. Midgeley could tell that the sight of the grounded and burning ship generated some strong and bitter emotion. Beyond the tank, the ship lay on its side in the shallows, covered in smoke. The German tank abruptly came to a halt at an order from its commander. Midgeley watched its massive armour with foreboding.

Midgeley did not believe it was possible to be as afraid as he was now. This was like no other German tank he had ever seen. Gradually he realized that he was looking down the barrel of an 88mm gun.

The German tank was squat and economic in its lines in contrast to the Grant. He could see a machine gun mounted beside the driver's visor.

Thomson began to sob:

'Make it go away. For Christ's sake don't let it see us.'

The officer in the turret of the Tiger had now turned and was carefully scrutinizing the coast road, lingering on the broken building behind which the Grant was hidden; now they could hear the engine rumble against the wash of the surf.

'Big boy, big boy,' said Starski. 'Like Soviet T.34.'

'What the hell's that,' Midgeley asked sharply.

'Big boy; very big gun, thick armour, our shells would bounce.'

Midgeley felt his stomach knot up inside him; his throat dry with fear.

'Underneath is the only place,' said Starski. 'Where the armour is only to keep out the mud. Where they keep their fanny.'

Midgeley started to calculate whether he could depress the 75mm gun sufficiently to get in a shot as the German tank advanced up to the edge of the coast road. Beyond the road there was a drop of about five feet into the sea, which the German tank would have to climb, and in doing so would be forced to expose its belly armour underneath the hull.

Suddenly the rocks behind and on either side of them echoed to the crack and whine of the German tank's two MG 34 machine-guns, as they methodically sprayed the whole area to their front. Midgeley heard a shot whine off the side armour of the Grant. Then the dish wheels between the tracks began to revolve and the Tiger lumbered forward

The tank could only behave in exactly the way that Midgeley had anticipated; a minute later its tracks were grinding into the pebbles at the edge of the beach and then its hull rose as it climbed the bank on the far side of the road.

Midgeley said:

'Load armour-piercing.'

'For Christ's sake,' said Thomson.

'Do as I say.'

Midgeley heard the shell drop into the breach.

The hull of the German tank had reared to an angle of forty degrees when Midgeley put his foot on the firing pedal.

At that range, the Grant's armour-piercing shot cut through the floor of the German tank's fighting compartment like a needle through butter, since the armour at the point of impact was no more than 26mm; however the angle of incidence increased the effective armour width to 35mm.

As it happened the shot did surprisingly little damage, since it struck the turret cupola at the same angle which again was one of the weakest points on the Tiger. The shot passed through a similar width of homogenous plate, but starred and shattered the glass in the turret rear visors. Had the trajectory of Midgeley's shot been less acute, the shell would have rebounded off the 82mm armour of the rear turret wall and probably killed everyone in the fighting compartment.

As it was, the only crewman who died was the loader Wittmann, when the Grant's armour-piercing shot passed directly through his chest and spine, before making its exit.

The tank faltered. At first Krause could not understand

what had happened to Wittmann, whose body had been thrown back against the rack of 88mm ammunition. His ears were still ringing from the impact of Midgeley's shell. The driver, who thought they had hit a mine or beach obstacle began to reverse.

Krause shouted:

'No, no; go forward, go forward.'

Midgeley, in the Grant, at the same time yelled to Starski:

'Let's get out of here.'

Starski engaged the synchromesh gear in first and ploughed through the corner of the mud wall against which the tank had been standing. Moving the gear into second, third, fourth and fifth as he felt the ground level, he turned right on to the road and raced eastwards along it, in and out of the re-entrant. The retreat of the Grant took three minutes to achieve, by which time the Tiger was on the road, and Krause ordered the gunner to fire in his own time. This allowed twenty-five seconds to get in a shot, as the Grant was forced to slow down to turn the corner fifty yards away.

The gunner, Meyer, had the gunnery badge first class, but he was unable to control his nervousness after the death of Wittmann, besides being one of several panzer crew who had suffered from sea sickness aboard the *Brescia*.

He was therefore unable to load and rotate the turret with sufficient speed to hold the target, in consequence of which the eighty-eight armour-piercing shell skipped harmlessly across the rocks five yards behind the Grant, raising an impressive shower of stones that rattled against the hull and upper armour of the British tank.

Once the Grant had disappeared behind the corner, Krause took stock of the situation. It was quite clear that they had suffered little damage, apart from the loader, and he ordered Schultz, the wireless operator, to take over. What was disquieting to all of them was that they had suffered any damage at all. Krause's earlier battle experience against the British had convinced him that all of them had poor armour and laughable guns.

The sudden ambush, in the context of what had happened when the *Brescia* was sunk and the battalion lost, made

Krause burn with a cold, calculated kind of revenge. The British tank now symbolized the total failure of all his hopes.

The colonel ordered the driver to advance along the road, reducing speed at the corner which had finally hidden the Grant from view. As they slowly rounded it, Krause ordered Meyer to traverse the turret right to confront any possible target. The ground beyond was open as far as the escarpment, although broken by small rises and the lines of watercourses driven through the ground from the higher slopes.

Midgeley stood in the Grant's turret in the wadi, waiting for the German tank. Thomson said:

'You really balled it up this time, Corp, taking on a wonder weapon.'

'So you think they wouldn't have seen us?'

'Too damn right. What with that bloody 88 they're carrying, you'll never get another shot in.'

'Well, maybe this time they won't see us.'

Starski had found a depression behind a boulder fall two hundred yards from the hairpin bend, which gave them temporary cover. Midgeley had positioned the tank so that the heavy armament faced a ridge beyond the road below the escarpment, with the 37mm trained on the coast road. They waited.

Krause did not like the road; it seemed too obvious to him. He therefore decided to move through the open country to the south of it, even though it would mean reducing speed. He ordered Joachim to circle round. Then he said to Meyer:

'I want a kill. I want to get that tank.'

'I know nothing of the armour. It is new.'

'Who cares about that? Just get a couple of shots in and it'll be over.'

Moving steadily along the reverse slope of the ridge, Krause could observe the black ribbon of the coast road and the open ground surrounding it.

Meyer said:

'I have a target.'

As the Tiger moved up the ridge, Krause saw the Grant in the ground below.

'For God's sake fire, then.'

The huge turret traversed round, then Meyer took his forehead off the sight and wiped his face.

'I'm sorry, Colonel, we have a depression problem.'

In the relative position of the two tanks, with the Tiger crossing the ridge above the Grant, it was impossible for Meyer to sight his eighty-eight on to the English tank, since the maximum possible angle of depression was only six and a half degrees.

At the same moment Midgeley heard the menacing rumble of the Maybach engines above. He could tell that Thomson was too frightened to speak.

Midgeley took careful aim at the upper track links, which were only just in sight, and pressed the pedal.

As Krause was shouting to Joachim: 'Get off the ridge, damn you!' The impact of the armour-piercing shot severed the Tiger's port track, so that after twenty yards it began to slew round to face the Grant, immobilized.

Apart from that, there was no further damage to the Tiger, since the 75mm shot, even at a range of a hundred yards, only pitted the 82mm steel of the side hull armour.

Midgeley said:

'He cannot bring his gun to bear on us.'

Thomson said:

'Well, that's just fine. What do we do now?'

Midgeley took the point. So long as they kept in dead ground and out of the sights of the eighty-eight, they would be safe. If they moved to left or right, down the slope and back on to the road, the situation would instantly change in favour of the German tank, which would then be able to lay its gun on them without difficulty.

'That'll keep them quiet,' said Starski.

'Until they mend the track links.'

'They will have to move the tank to do that.'

The Tiger remained stationary, however, since Krause had also realized that if he backed off the ridge he would give the Grant a chance to escape.

'There are only four armour-piercing left,' Midgeley said.

'Try one, you might be lucky,' Starski suggested.

* * *

It said a good deal for the discipline of the German crew, as much as for the authority of Krause, that they all stayed at their posts without question. Now that the Tiger had slewed round, it presented a three-quarter profile through the Grant's gunsight, but the track was no longer exposed and now Midgeley could only range on the turret and the upper hull.

His next shot struck the frontal armour at the corner and to the left of the machine-gun mantlet, scarring the steel, but doing nothing else.

Midgeley said:

'It's not possible.'

'The gun, the gun,' Thomson said excitedly.

However, the shimmer through the sight made a direct hit on such a slender target more than unlikely.

Midgeley got out of the gunner's seat.

'Where you going?' Thomson asked.

'Just going to take a look.'

'For God's sake watch it then. All those Jerry tanks have grenade launchers, to say nothing of the MGs.'

Midgeley said:

'You come with me, Starski, and bring a couple of rounds of HE while you're about it; or we'll never get out of this alive.'

'We're dead anyway,' said Thomson.

'There's a gully up the ridge to the left of us. When we get there give us covering fire with the 75mm for five minutes and then stop. Nothing more after five minutes. Understand?'

Midgeley used the off-side sponson door furthest from the German tank. He took a half-full jerrican of petrol they had used when clearing the fuel leads, and which had been overlooked by the Germans when they had been captured. He wrapped it in his overalls.

When they had got to the gully, they could just see the silhouette of the Tiger at the top of the ridge, squat, hostile but helpless all the same.

Thomson's first HE airburst exploded over the Tiger and rattled shrapnel on its armour as Midgeley and Starski began to clamber up the gulley. The Tiger answered and Midgeley distinguished the faint whistle of dying shrapnel. He took a circular route to the left beyond the lip of the gully, scratching his hands on thorn bushes as he dragged the jerrican behind him. He sensed in some way that this would be the last obtacles he had to overcome.

The duel he was now fighting, although it was a stalemate, seemed to represent the outcome of all the situations they had lived through during the last thirty-six hours. He felt exhilaration, mixed with fear, although on this occasion he was in no way afraid of death. He knew that the steel monster on the ridge crest would be destroyed as inevitably as the eighty-eight millimetre guns had been. The risks had been equally as great then, and the odds against survival just as short.

He continued to work his way round, the loose rock chippings biting into his forearms and knees, while the Tiger and Thomson continued their inconclusive exchange of fire.

Midgeley and Starski came to a knoll which curled up on to the ridge, and was littered with broken rocks. At that moment Thomson stopped firing; after waiting for two minutes Midgeley crawled on until he had an unobstructed view of the tank from the back.

He said to Starski:

'D'you notice something?'

'What's that?'

'There's no machine-gun mounted on the turret hatch.'

'They will see us through the rear turret visors.'

'Not so far they haven't.'

It was not until the Leningrad offensive, when Tiger tanks were first used on the Russian front, that the designers realized their mistake in not mounting a machine-gun at that point: this limiting factor created problems when a Tiger was faced with attacking infantry. The only effective weapon in that situation were the standard, turret grenade launchers and these faced forward on the turret.

'Everything will be wonderful so long as they don't climb out.'

'. . . or look this way.'

Midgeley and Starski worked their way round to the back of the Tiger, aware that at any moment the turret might revolve in their direction to wipe them out with grenades.

Indeed the twenty-five-yard crawl to the back of the tank was the longest ten minutes in Midgeley's life. It was incredible to him that they could not be seen. The overalls round the jerrican were worn ragged, as was his shirt and trousers and his tired and battered body, scraping along the rocky ground surface.

The Tigers parallel air filters loomed up above them, the schnorkel had been disconnected. Starski muttered:

'Let's hope they can't find reverse.'

The Maybach engines occupied a compartment three by two metres square, behind the turret. Midgeley carefully placed the jerrican on its side at the centre of the port engine grille, and struck the cap of a one and a half pound phosphorous grenade. At the same time Starski positioned the two rounds of HE neatly, one on either side of the jerrican, while Midgeley pulled the pin from a Mills grenade with a seven-second fuse, placing it carefully on top of the pile. Then they ran back to the knoll.

Inside the fighting compartment, Schultz shouted too late:

'I hear mice.' He had caught what seemed to be a shadow for a moment against the starred, rear turret hatch visors.

Meyer began to traverse the turret, while Schultz started to pick grenades from the stowage bin and feed them into the multiple chargers. However, as the turret revolved to the rear of the tank, Midgeley's improvised demolition charge exploded. The petrol had already drained through into the engine grille and dripping phosphorus quickly ignited the fuel leads, causing minor explosions in the four solex carburettors. At the same time the HE shells also exploded, jamming the turret and buckling the centre section of the eighty-eight millimetre gun, blocking the driver's exit port forward, and trapping Joachim.

A column of angry flame now spurted from the engine compartment and thick black smoke erupted into the turret as the rear bulkhead began to glow red-hot.

Coughing, the wireless operator and gunner scrambled for the turret hatch, blinded by smoke, since it could only be a matter of time before the rising temperature set off the racked ammunition at the back of the fighting compartment.

They were not interested in the presence of Midgeley and Starski, behind the knoll. However Krause took out his Walther and began to fire in their direction, at the same time that the four main petrol tanks of the Tiger exploded in series, igniting 135 gallons of petrol and bursting open the hatches. Detonating ammunition whined, screeched and exploded inside and outside the tank, in a confusion of multi-coloured smoke trails that criss-crossed haphazardly.

The force of these multiple explosions threw the remaining German crew to the ground as they were starting to run, and in doing so Krause had his wrist fractured by a jumping shell-case that skittered along the ground like an exploding squib. Meyer and Schultz were not so lucky. A hundred and forty-six rounds of machine-gun ammunition had been blown free of the tank and were now igniting, so that the German panzer crew were mown down by a bizarre hail of wicked red-hot tracer.

Now, the heat inside the Tiger reached such a crescendo that the 82mm of armour itself began to glow, and the exploding armoured shot inside began to spray jagged splinteres through the open ports.

Joachim died, pinned down in the red-hot driver's compartment, as Colonel Krause lay dazed in the dust, nursing his broken wrist.

When the fire eventually died down, Midgeley ran over to him, his shoulders instinctively hunched up, and picked up the Walther automatic, gesturing for him to follow.

Colonel Krause drew himself up and tried to regain his dignity, his face black with smoke. Then he said:

'I am a colonel in the Wehrmacht. I wish to give myself up to an officer of field, or equivalent, rank.'

But Starski laughed and said:

'Never mind. Never mind about that. For you Fritz, the war is over. Come.'

* * *

Sergeant Burns, AIF, narrowed his eyes against the onrush of the airstream, as the driver of the four-wheel Canadian Chrysler in which he was riding accelerated.

The two Australians had found themselves in the grand scarper along the coast road, as the Tobruk garrison pulled back its forward posts in the chaos and confusion of the last three weeks fighting. Bringing forward ammo to an imprecise map reference, they had found only empty weapon pits and had their windscreen shattered by machine-gun fire.

'Chuck' Owen, the driver, was still reflecting on this unwelcome experience.

'Christ, Puddin',' he said, 'you'd think they might have bloody let us into the secret.'

Burns rearranged the two Owen guns that slid along the leatherette seat, as Owen took a bend, and pushed back the empty pigeon box with its leather strap.

'Well you know how sloppy they are at Battalion. Percy'd never let us down; would you Perce?'

Burns solemnly released the catch on the carrier-pigeon box and tilted back the lid, positioning the index finger on his right hand beside the opening to allow the invisible pigeon to hop on to it.

'They don't feed them proper at Batt. Scorpions and rubbish like that. Out in the blue his rations are MacRobertson's finest wallaby corn and black woolly caterpillars. If it had been Perce they'd released he'd have got the message through and we'd not have been sprayed with shit from spandaus.'

'Come on Percy,' said Puddin'. 'Time for tea. We got to keep your strength up if you're flying in the Sydney Sweepstake.'

The sergeant elaborately took a pinch of invisible seed out of the air and cupped the hand holding it to the head of the invisible pigeon. Private Owen began to whistle 'We're off to see the wizard.'

The two Australians were 'troppo merchants' for at that time, most AIF Battalions in Nine Divvy had their establishment of invisible carrier pigeons winging their way across the desert and east across the oceans to Australia. The pigeons were tended by officially appointed pigeon handlers, among them Sergeant Burns. Two weeks back he had almost been 252'd for losing Percy, and his company had spent several days searching their perimeter and anxiously scanning the skies to find the invisible champion carrier pigeon that had gone mysteriously absent, in between fighting Italians.

'We're almost out of the MacRobertsons I scrounged in the Delta too. We'll have to get him back on the ration strength now he's back, or the poor little devil won't stand a chance over the Timor Sea with all those sharks, to say nothing of the Jappies and their Zeros. He's grown so skinny he could hardly make the next telegraph post.'

'Yeah, but he's got pluck and stamina, remember the time he took the good news to Canberra, when we nabbed that organ-grinder colonel. There and back before tea-time.'

'Maybe all he needs is a nice sand bath.'

'He's got lots of scope for that.'

'There's not a bird like him in the whole M.E.'

In spite of the elaborate pretence, both men were all too aware of their uncertain predicament; there could be German armour anywhere in this fluid battle. Secretly, both were grateful that the Canadian Chrysler had four-wheel drive which meant that they could take to the desert in the last resort.

'How far the perimeter, Chuck?'

'Four or five miles.'

'Better send Percy with a message for General Klopper. Line up some artillery support.' General Klopper was the South African commander, the garrisoning of Tobruk being largely a South African responsibility.

'Better lend him your Afrikaans dictionary.'

Burns suddenly waved Percy out of the window and, lithe as a cat, picked up his Owen gun as he saw four men at the roadside. They passed a broken-down building on which the slogan; VIVA L'ASSE ROMA-BERLINO had been daubed.

'What's that circus? Eyeties?'

'Don't look like it.'

Owen slowed down to where Midgeley was standing behind Krause, Thomson and Starski.

Burns shouted:

'Are you the relief column they're talking about?'

Midgeley said:

'Am I glad to see you, Sarge.'

'Who's this?'

Burns jerked his thumb in the direction of Colonel Krause, who was standing under the cover of the Walther pistol Midgeley was holding on him.

'Some Jerry colonel; says he wants to give himself up to the top brass.'

'He'll have to walk a long way. The bastard's lucky to have got this far in one piece. Where's your transport, Corporal?'

'Out of gas.'

When they got back to the Grant, Midgeley realized just how lucky they'd been. Two minutes after Starski had pulled the self-starter the engine went dead.

'Out of water, too.'

'We got water and ammo. Anything you want – Horlicks tablets, "K" ration. Three days supply for an invisible company.'

Taking the last canteen, Midgeley had gone back to the coast road, realizing that the positions could be reversed at any moment. Krause also appeared to be aware of this and upset all of them by projecting a certain kind of impatient arrogance in his manner, as much as to say 'Your finger may be on the trigger now, but for how long? It's quite clear your situation is hopeless.'

The realization of what Krause was thinking irritated Midgeley through his tiredness, and it was the German officer's self-assurance that angered him most. At that moment he had taken charge of the Walther, since it was their only weapon. He trusted neither Thomson nor Starski, but for different reasons. Thomson, because he could tell that the cumulative experience of the last three days had brought him to a point of emotional collapse. Starski, because he suspected that at the least provocation, he would shoot the German colonel. So far as that was concerned he was not entirely motivated by reasons of humanity, for while Krause remained with them in one piece, he was a valuable insurance policy should they be picked up by an Afrika Korps patrol.

Now they had met up with these Australians, the situation had changed. Burns said:

'You better nip in the back.'

'What about the Jerry? Shall I tell him to scram back to his friends?'

Burns considered for a moment until Owen said:

'To hell with that, he looks a bloody-minded bastard. I wouldn't miss seeing him behind the wire for quids.'

Starski added:

'He caused us enough trouble.'

Burns said:

'He better come in front with you then Corp. If you want to take him along, you take care of him, O.K.?' He beckoned to Krause. 'Here mate, get in.'

Krause reluctantly pulled himself in with his good arm, disdain written all over his face.

The German colonel shrugged as the Australian sergeant passed Midgeley the second Owen gun.

'Take any pot shots you like but mind you don't down any AIF pigeons.'

Krause was squeezed between Midgeley, who was nearest the door, and Burns, who was now sitting beside Owen. The others slumped down in the back of the truck in the shadow of the canopy. For the first time since the Grants moved to a forward position, Midgeley felt that he could relax. The reason for this was simple: the Australian in the driver's cab had sergeant's stripes, so Midgeley had become once more a cog in the military machine.

* * *

What Midgeley wanted to do more than anything else was to sleep. He knew that it was impossible under the supercilious scrutiny of Krause, but he was grateful for the rush of air through the windscreen that stopped him from drifting into a sea of oblivion. In the war he had seen soldiers sleep anywhere and everywhere, on the pavements in the dust, and he understood the exhaustion that led them to sleep on the march.

Suddenly Owen said to Burns:

'I've got a feeling things aren't so hot. Maybe it would be

better to fork right for the Axis by-pass and head for the wire. I've got a sneaky feeling.'

'Percy'll find us alright, anyway I'm sick of sieges and a trigger-happy patrol might get the wrong idea about us.'

Krause began to smile.

'Watch what you say, that Kraut bastard knows our lingo.'

'What's the joker got to grin about?'

'It's obvious; he thinks he's going to run into the panzers.'

Midgeley said, screwing up his eyes to the distant dust column ahead of them:

'He could be right at that.'

Burns said:

'So what? We're all going the same direction. Step on it, Chuck.'

Krause could hardly restrain himself as they came up to the tail end of the German supply convoy made up from DAK Opel-Blitz lorries, and a battery of Krauss-Maffei tractors towing howitzers, besides a great many British Bedford three-tonners.

Owen said:

'No boast, no brag; what do we do now to get out of this mess?'

Already they could see the rear BMW motorcycle combination that brought up the end of the column.

Midgeley said:

'We'll use the Jerry officer.' He pointed to the circular hatch built in to the roof of the cab. 'Up you get.' Krause looked as though he was going to refuse. Midgeley cocked the Owen gun.

'You want your head blown off? Just do as I say. Stand on the seat and put your head out, look important.'

'Nichts verstehen.'

'You verstehen all right or you'll end up with a torn uniform.' In his impatience to get the German to co-operate, Midgeley began to jab the muzzle of the Owen gun into Krause's stomach.

Krause's face went white with a mixture of rage and fear.

He reluctantly clambered up on to the seat and stood tensely looking out through the hatch, his good arm resting on the cab roof. Midgeley wedged the machine-gun close in to Krause's thigh; if he had to fire, the contents of the magazine would end up in Krause's abdomen. Krause seemed well aware of this for he stood rigidly against the hatch ring, afraid to make any move.

Burns lit a cigarette and handed it to Midgeley, as Owen raced alongside the column, overtaking where he could.

'Christ,' said Burns, 'at this rate we'll be in Cairo before stumps are drawn.'

'It's another flamin' Gazala Stakes,' Owen said. 'I wish we could run as fast the other way.'

He continued to drive on in silence for several minutes as they steadily moved towards the head of the column.

'This mob must be investing Tobruk,' Owen said again.

'Whatever it is, it looks like they're doing something nasty,' Burns replied.

* * *

Some time after, they left the column, or rather the column left them, swinging north and off the macadamed road. Owen pulled the Chrysler away to the south, anticipating correctly that soon they would come to a Feldgendarmerie post set up to direct the convoy seawards to the latest DAK supply depot.

In fact it was two hundred yards to the north when they passed it, but nobody took any notice of them and after that they were on their own, heading towards the wire that Mussolini had put up to mark the frontier between Egypt and Libya.

'You can get down now,' Midgeley said, jabbing Krause's leg with the barrel of his Owen gun. Krause got down slowly and painfully, his face set in an unnatural rigidity which barely concealed his feeling of total defeat. As he sat down he knocked off the wooden box with the leather strap that lay on the bench seat alongside Burns.

Burns said:

'Don't fool around with my pigeon box; there's no telling when Percy will be back.'

Krause shrugged and looked away as Owen began to whistle 'We're off to see the wizard.'

To the east Midgeley began to make out the squat hulls of Valentines, half-concealed by a fold in the desert. Then he leaned back and shut his eyes.

THE END

THEY CAME FROM THE SKY BY E. H. COOKRIDGE

The Special Operations Executive was created by Churchill in the summer of 1940 to 'set Europe ablaze'. Working secretly behind enemy lines to 'sabotage and subvert', they operated all over Europe, and some of the most active agents were in the French Section. It was dangerous work, and many agents did not return: a few, like Christine Granville, became famous names, but for the most part their exploits remain unsung. Here now are the stories of three members of the French Section – true stories that make more exciting reading than any novel . . . They had little training, and their unconventional methods were frowned on by the top brass of the Army, but what they lacked in style, they more than made up for in courage and initiative . . .

0 552 10136 2 75p

THE SAVAGE CANARY BY DAVID LAMPE

The Danish resistance movement was described by Montgomery as 'second to none'.

The Savage Canary is a fantastic but true account of the Danish efforts to help the Allies and cripple Germany in the Second World War. By May 1945, illegal newspapers had published a total of about 26 million issues; illegal broadcasts were transmitted regularly; boats were running a timetable service between Britain, Sweden and Denmark and 7,000 Jews had been shipped to safety. German ships were unable to move from Danish harbours; a vast number of German troops were kept from the main fighting points by Danish sabotage of the railways and aerodromes. This book, the story of an impudent, almost foolhardy heroism, is a salute to the people of Denmark.

0 552 10101 X 65p

HORNED PIGEON BY GEORGE MILLAR, D.S.O., M.C.

George Millar was an army lieutenant fighting in North Africa when he was captured by German soldiers. Handed over to the Italians, he was taken to Italy and imprisoned in a concentration camp at Padula. Despite dysentery and hardship, George's courage and determination kept him from despair. His first planned escape failed by a hair's breadth and he was transferred to a punishment camp. After the Italian armistice he and some fellow-prisoners attempted a second break-out, but were foiled by the Germans. Next Millar was moved to a German camp near Munich. He made his third daring bid for freedom at night, from a fast-moving and closely-guarded train. As he jumped, he was shuddering with cold and fear of failing once again.

0 552 09901 5 60p

SUBALTERN'S CHOICE BY DUNCAN MACNEIL

In the Queen's service, in the service of the British Raj, men had to die. It was inevitable. Over the years of the Empire, many thousands perished in mutiny, in open action, in riot and pillage and fire, and in drowning during crossings of swollen river fords. The North-West Frontier was soaked in British blood, its lonely, terrible mountains salted by whitened British bones when there had been no time to bury the dead, salted by the mouldering corpses in the shallow rocky graves along the passes into Afghanistan, corpses that had come from almost every regiment and corps of the British Army. The 114th were simply following on in the tradition, and that, really, was all...

0 552 10013 7 50p